Pocketbook Diaries

The Escape From Aphrodan

TO: Kim

Best wishes!

I hope you get lost in the pages like I did writing it!

L.C. ROGERS

L.C. Rogers

First Edition

PAGE PUBLISHING, INC.
New York, NY

First originally published by Page Publishing, Inc. 2017

ISBN 978-1-68348-096-9 (Paperback)
ISBN 978-1-68348-140-9 (Hard Cover)
ISBN 978-1-68348-097-6 (Digital)

Printed in the United States of America

Chapter 1

Lillian Grace Varella

(ZYAIRE)

It is funny how we teenagers go through life thinking we know everything, thinking we have the whole world figured out; then something incredible happens, something out of this world, and we realize we actually never knew anything at all.

The year was 1993 when my dear great-grandmother died, and her most shocking secret almost died with her. She was only sixty-eight years old at the time of her death. I would never know her, and she would never know me. Just one month shy of my birth, she succumbed to a short but brutal fight against lung cancer, and died in Boston, Massachusetts.

My mother told me that she believed my great-grandmother knew her death was near. In fact, she called a meeting with her loved ones the evening before she would depart from this life. That night was bitter cold. "One of the coldest nights I had ever known," my mother once declared. This was a phenomenal feat for a place like Boston, which was no stranger to chilly days and ice-cold evenings. She said she could almost feel death in the air as she headed to Boston

Memorial Hospital with my grandparents. "Each breath we exhaled hovered in the air like a thick fog."

I had seen a photo from that final meeting: my great-grandmother was lying in a hospital bed with a breathing tube in her nostrils, and several parts of her body hooked up to various machines all around her. In the photo, my grandmother ("Vovó," as I liked to call her), grandfather, and mother were crowded around my great-grandmother's hospital bed awkwardly smiling, as if there was anything cheerful in such a devastating situation. Even my great-grandmother was smiling. I could see the weariness in her eyes, and yet, even under those circumstances, one could still look beyond her frail body, narrow face, and gray thinning hair, and know she was the beautiful willowy woman that had once adorned many magazine covers for decades. When I looked closely at that picture, I was touched to see my great-grandmother's delicate hand placed in the center of my mother's enormous belly that housed me inside. I felt an immediate connection to her although I never got the opportunity to meet her.

As I got older, I found myself wanting to know everything about her. Yet my mother did not speak much of that final evening they spent with my great-grandmother. In fact, she did not speak much about my great-grandmother at all, which was quite odd since I was often told of how close they were. My grandfather, who I call "Papa," told me I was to be named after her, Lillian Grace Varella. I always thought that was a lovely and timeless name, and Lilly would have been the perfect nickname. Yet after my great-grandmother's death, my mother changed her mind and named me Zyaire Renae after my father's step-grandmother who had passed away just the year before. Zyaire Renae is not as elegant a name as Lillian Grace, but it is my name, so I put up with it. My Vovó said she was heartbroken when my mother did not name me Lillian Grace, after her own mother. I feel even from the belly, I was probably heartbroken as well. From then on, my mother and Vovó's relationship was never the same again. My Vovó took it as great disrespect that my mother would tell my great-grandmother in the days before her life ended that she would name the baby growing inside her belly after her, then instead name me after a woman she barely knew.

These days my mother and Vovó barely say more than two words to each other. I am the only thing that continues to keep them connected. Otherwise, I doubt they would have anything to do with one another.

My mother's tight lips did not prevent me from pursuing all things Lillian Varella. Over the years, I grasped for anything I could that would help me get to know the woman who obviously loved me before I even saw the light of day. I have become so enthralled by the world my great-grandmother lived in that I am convinced I was meant to be born in her time. My friends even sometimes say I speak as if I was from another era. I guess that constantly reading old novels, and watching old movies as I do, could possibly begin to change a person's dialect.

I wanted to know everything there was to know about Lillian Varella, but oddly enough, there were very few things to discover that would explain Lillian the person beyond Lillian the celebrity. I sensed over the years that they were two different people. Despite the fact that my great-grandmother was a famous model by the age of sixteen, and her noted career appearing in comedic roles in some of the most popular films of that time, there was not much about her personal life that was made public.

A few things I did find out was that at the age of fifteen my great-grandmother became the face of her family's clothing store, Varella's Dresses and Suits.

I also found out that my great-grandmother was a true socialite and threw lavish parties almost every weekend. On the weekends she was not throwing a party, she was attending one. She was without doubt a known celebrity. I often wondered if that was all just a front to cover up a possible loneliness she was feeling. After all, her husband, my grandmother's father, had died in a ski accident before they could return from their honeymoon. She didn't find out she was pregnant with my grandmother until a few weeks after he died. She never married again. My papa told me he thought it was because she never got over her husband's death.

My Vovó only spoke of her mother on rare occasions. Even all these years later, my great-grandmother's death was still like a dagger to her heart.

Yet one day on one of my many visits to my Vovó's home, she recalled my great-grandmother's looks, calling her a breathless beauty, with emphasis on *breathless*. She said when my great-grandmother walked into a room, people stopped whatever they were doing and just stared, because they were in awe of her beauty.

She pointed to the portrait of my great-grandmother that hung above the fireplace in her study, and then told me that I looked just like her. I was beyond flattered, but when I looked at that portrait, I could not imagine that I, who was more often than not insulted by my mother for my lack of fashion sense and all out dullness, could truly possess such beauty. Whenever I visited my grandparents' home, I would stare at that portrait, and would be in awe of my great-grandmother's striking features just as my Vovó said others always were. Her skin was not pale like her father's; it was bronze like her mother's who was Cape Verdean. I had also inherited my great-great-grandmother's darker skin tone. Her hair, like mine, was dark like the night, and flowed past her long neck. Her eyes were as blue and bright as the morning skies. She looked more like twenty-one than seventeen, the age she actually was at the time the portrait was painted. The gown she was wearing was long and graceful, cascading down to the floor like a beautiful flowing waterfall. The color was almost as blue as her eyes. Her lips were full and painted plum red. They looked nothing like the pale, thin lips in the photo taken one day before she died. Each time I visited my grandparents' house I would stare at that portrait for hours, and could feel the connection that formed between her and me, even though she had never gotten the chance to look upon my face. I wasn't sure If I could be anyone's fantasy as my great-grandmother had been, or if I would ever be called the greatest beauty in New England as she had, but one thing was for sure, through me my great-grandmother's history would repeat itself, and it would send me on the most miraculous adventure of my life.

Chapter 2
The Discovery
(ZYAIRE)

I first happened upon the inexplicable thing that would alter my life forever in the fall of 2009. I never thought I would find something so life changing and so amazingly profound right in the walls of my own home. A home I had begun to hate because of the things it now represented for me. Fighting parents, a disappointed mother, prying media, and oh, the awful money-green wooden French doors that closed my father into his office on the seldom days he was home. There were many days I wished I could rip those doors from its now squeaky hinges, an act of rebellion against everything its purpose had taken from me. At the least, if only for just a moment, it would get my father to pay attention to me as he used to before he was "Mr. CEO."

Despite my growing hatred for my home, it was also the one thing that was constant in my life. I had lived there since I was born. It was a place I could find refuge from everything that had sent my life in a never-ending spiral of disaster. The only thing it could not shield me from was my parents.

My parents, John and Geraldine Ryan, owned our home on Prairie Lane in Plymouth, Massachusetts, for over a decade and a half, yet my father probably only spent half that amount of time in it. Busy with his life, he spent his days and nights running his family's multibillion-dollar fishing company that he was now CEO of after his father's death.

My mother, after fourteen years of being a homemaker, one day announced during one of my parents' infamous arguments that she was over the school bake sales, the PTA meetings, and the carpooling of unmannerly teens. "I'm going back to work, you're not the only one around here that can earn a buck," she yelled at the top of her lungs before fiercely storming out of the room. The next day she took a position as senior marketing director of her family's famous clothing stores, Varella's, and the rest is history.

Despite their long marriage together, my parents could not have been from two worlds that were more separate. My father is Irish. His family settled in the great town of New Bedford, Massachusetts, back in the late 1800s. They were successful anglers and had their big break in the mid-1900s when they started a frozen food company named Ryan's. You can now find Ryan's shrimp, fish, and whatever else has a place in the sea in the frozen food section of any major supermarket chain in the country. My father also recently opened three upscale seafood restaurants, their names, Ryan's Seafood house. One of the restaurants is perfectly situated in downtown Boston, and another in the fast-paced Manhattan, New York. The final location opened its doors just last week in Los Angeles, California. The guest list for the opening night was overflowing with famous actors, singers, and the not so famous other rich patrons of California, leaving the "mere mortals" wanting to attend to be chosen by a lottery. The lucky twenty graciously sat at the back of the restaurant. I managed to find myself mingling with them for most of the night. The Los Angeles location honored Hollywood with pictures of legendary actors from the past adorned on the silky almond-colored walls. A beautiful picture of my great-grandmother in a cherry red dress was one of the first seen when you entered the restaurants' lavish doors. It was the one suggestion I made that my father actual honored. If it were up to me, instead of opening three restaurants, I would have much preferred animal shelters.

My mother, on the other hand, also comes from a prominent family. She, however, was of Cape Verdean and Italian descent. It was from one of these cultures where the name Vovó became the pet name for my grandmother. It was Cape Verdean tradition to call one's grandmother by that name. My mother's family first made their name famous in Boston, Massachusetts, two generations ago when they opened Varella's Dresses and Suits. The company has since built a reputation amongst the rich and famous for employing some of the greatest designers in the world. My mother's posh and glamorous life was a huge contrast of my father's life on the sea. I was a mixture of both their lives. I love the water, and going out with my father as a child on fishing expeditions is still some of my most treasured memories. I have known how to bait a fishing line since the age of three, a feat my father proudly boasted about to all his friends and family. On the other hand, my mother was determined to make me a sophisticated young woman. I took ballet from the age of five until I was twelve. Also at the persistence of my mother, I became nearly fluent in Latin, and a gifted pianist.

My mother would have had it no other way but for me to attend Einstein Prep, a private school that educates some of the most prestigious children in Plymouth. There, I am top of my class, and top of many scandals due to my father's company's misdealing that had gone public several years ago, along with some other scandals that had recently befallen him.

The day I discovered my first true connection to my great-grandmother started out like any other. I was sprawled across my bed, belly down, my feet wiggling aimlessly in the air, and my nose buried deep in a book, a usual pastime of mine. I was just about to find out if James was the secret admirer that had been leaving love notes for Sarah when my mother stood at the bottom of the spiraling staircase and called out to me.

"Zyaire, please come downstairs. I'm heading to the office and Mary Josie needs your help."

"Yes, Mommy, I am coming now." I came trampling down the steps. It was Saturday morning, but it was not odd for my mother to be working on the weekends.

"I really wish you would not call me that," she said as I hit the bottom of the staircase.

"Call you what, Mommy?" I asked with a look of defiance in my eyes.

"Yes. I think Mother is more suitable, don't you?"

"I have been calling you Mommy forever. I don't see why it should change now."

My mother walked closer to the daughter she could never figure out and stared me straight in the eyes. "You're fifteen years old now, soon to be sixteen in a couple of days. You are a young woman, not a child. Children have mommies, young ladies have mothers." Then she stepped back and finished tying the belt on her silk coat. "Besides, I don't want any of the community mothers hearing you speak like an infant. You are just as sophisticated, mature, and certainly more intelligent than their daughters are, and I will not have rumors circulating to the contrary. Despite your father's positive intent to ruin our good name, you and I will remain respectable in our community."

She leaned over and kissed me on the cheek, and our eyes met as she pulled away. I could see the disappointment in them as I always had. She didn't understand anything about me. My refusal to embrace the rich girl attitude that most of my peers had, my simple approach to fashion, my lack of interest in anything that required me to be the center of attention, my dedication to charity beyond just writing a check, and my love for animals that in her opinion exceeded my actual love for humans. The truth was I was an introvert, a loner of sorts. I am not sure if it was by choice, or by default. There is something about your family's name being drug through the mud that would make anyone want to run and hide; but not my mother, she was a social butterfly. She loved attention and thrived off her family's status and money.

"I may be home late. I'm having dinner with some new clients," she said, interrupting the daydream I was having. I did that a lot.

"Okay, Mother," I said with a forced smile. "I'll see you later."

She grabbed her handmade leather briefcase from Varella's business accessory line and walked out the door. My mother's unrealistic need to be sophisticated at all times was like a dog collar around my neck. It allowed me to walk a few feet away from her expectations but yanked at my neck once I drifted too far from my owner. However, I wanted to be free to wear what I wanted, to call her Mommy if I pleased, to thrillingly slide down the rails of the staircase instead of boringly walking down the steps, to play on the girls' baseball team instead of flaunting around in a tutu on my tiptoes in ballet, or at least do both. I did not feel there had to be only one side to me. I am a free spirit, yet still a mixture of my mother's sophistication and my father's outdoor nature. There was a time my mother accepted that, but now her need to be an absolute snob, in my opinion, has overwhelmed my life.

I went to the living room window and pulled back the heavy custom drapes so that I could watch my mother pull off in her brand-new Porsche. I had developed a habit at a very young age of watching my father pull off from our driveway when he first took over as CEO of Ryan's after his father's death. I was always so sad to see him go, and was never sure how long it would be until I would see him again. I would stare out the window, watching as he put his briefcase in the trunk and hung his suit jacket on the backseat before finally climbing into the car and pulling off. I would savor every ounce of him, watching intently until his car's tail lights were completely out of view. Nowadays my dad is usually gone long before I even wake up, so when my mother started working, I continued the tradition with her.

Once my mother's car was completely out of sight, I called out to Mary Josie, and she came from around the corner with a large cardboard box in her hand.

"Yes, Ms. Zyaire," Mary Josie said, tiredly plopping the big box down onto the floor.

"Mary Josie, I told you that you don't have to call me Ms. Zyaire. Just Zyaire is fine."

"Yes, but Mrs. Ryan insists," Mary Josie said, smiling.

I took a deep breath then let it out slowly. "Okay, well, Mrs. Ryan is not here right now, so how about for the afternoon you just call me Zyaire?"

"Okay, but only for the afternoon," Mary Josie reluctantly agreed.

"So what did you need my help with, Ms. Mary Josie?" I teased.

"Mrs. Ryan wants to get rid of some of your great-grandmother's old things that have been stored in the attic. She wants you to help me sort through them to see what is suitable to go to charity."

"Oh, my mother and her oh-so-charitable heart," I said sarcastically. "My mother never even told me that there were things of my great-grandmother's in the attic," I said to Mary Josie.

I got excited, hoping that maybe there would be something there that would let me learn more about Lillian the person and not just Lillian the celebrity. "What does she want to do with the things that are not suitable?" I asked.

"She wants me to arrange for them to be taken to the county dump," Mary Josie said plainly.

"What!" I said in disbelief. "How could she just throw my great-grandmother's things away like they don't even matter, like she didn't even matter? Maybe they do not matter to her, but they sure as heck matter to me. They're the only things left of my great-grandmother's, and the fact that she would just throw them away with not so much as a thought makes me…" I paused and grunted furiously. "Let's go and get these things that my mother is so eager to part with." I stormed out of the room toward the attic, and Mary Josie followed quickly behind me.

Against Mary Josie's resistance, I helped her bring the rest of the things out of the attic. "Thank God you did not get a scrape, or your mother would have had my head," Mary Josie said as we put the last box in the middle of the family room floor.

"Mary Josie, don't let my mother scare you. Her bark is much bigger than her bite. Just ask my father. He has humiliated her more times than you have waxed our kitchen floor, yet despite the many threats to leave and all the arguments that I was never supposed to hear, she is still by his side playing the part of the ever-so-faithful wife.

"Ms. Zyaire, you shouldn't..."

"What? Speak the truth," I interrupted. An awkward silence ensued between us until it was broken by a knock on the door.

"I'll get it," Mary Josie said, but I jumped to my feet.

"No. I'll get it. You start unloading the boxes."

I ran down the hall and opened the door expecting to see the mail carrier. Instead, Netasha, the executive assistant at Varella's headquarters, met me.

"Hello, Zy," Netasha said when I opened the door.

"Hi, Netasha, what are you doing here?"

"I am dropping off this dress for your mother to look over before it is shipped to Miranda Cosgrove," she said.

"Miranda Cosgrove?" I screeched.

"Don't get your panties in a ruffle. We dress the stars all the time. You know that, girl."

"Yes, I do, but Miranda is a teen idol. She is beautiful, and all the guys love her in my school," I explained.

"You're not so shabby yourself, beautiful, so I'm sure they love you too." Netasha lovingly pinched my cheek.

"I doubt they see me as beautiful," I said.

"Are you kidding me? Just because you hide behind those plain clothes and that hung head, nothing can hide that beautiful face you have, and those gorgeous blue eyes." Netasha pulled at the white cotton pants I was wearing. "And don't think they don't notice that hot body you have hiding under there."

I smiled and giggled, embarrassed.

"Even if they do see me as beautiful—" I paused at the thought of even putting myself in the same sentence as that word. "Their parents' opinion of my father will keep them from ever dating me," I continued.

"Don't be so hard on your father. His ruthless determination has made him a huge success."

"It's not only his ruthlessness in the workplace that bothers me, Netasha."

"Well, that may be true, but he is still your father, and you should have nothing but kind things to say about him."

"I barely know him anymore. It's not like when I was a little girl. He spends most of his time at the office, and when he is home, he locks himself in there." I pointed to the French doors that enclosed my father's home office. "So tell me, Netasha, how do I defend my father against the opinions of others when nowadays I barely know him myself?"

Netasha cleared her throat and not so subtly changed the subject. "Don't you have a fabulous party this weekend? Sweet sixteen!" she shrieked. "Your mother asked me to help with the planning and believe me, miss…it's going to be fabulous!"

"Oh, you mean the party where my mother hopes to prove that I'm just as sophisticated as all the other stuck-up daughters in her circle?" I asked.

"Yes, that party," Netasha pointedly confirmed. "And it's too bad you're being such a sourpuss. Come on, what happened to the little girl I used to know, who was always smiling and telling me about all her great adventures out on the ocean with her father? Who loved to dress up and pretend she was a princess lost at sea?"

"She grew up and realized happiness doesn't last forever," I explained.

"Listen, gorgeous," Netasha said and gently grabbed my face, "you're a teenager, so everything is going to seem like it is the end of the world to you right now, but believe me, it's not. No one is thinking about your father's issues. He is not going through anything that thousands of others have not gone through. It is just that his life is public, so his mistakes are always going to be highlighted. As for your mother, she loves you very much and is very proud of you. I know some days it may not seem like it, but when you are not around, she brags about you."

"Does she really? What does she say?" I asked, surprised.

Before Netasha could reply, Mary Josie came into the foyer and interrupted us. "Hello, Ms. Netasha," Mary Josie chirped.

"Hello, Mary Josie. I would tell you there is no need to call me Ms. Netasha, but what would be the point?" We all laughed.

"Mary Josie, can you take this dress and put it in a safe place for Mrs. Ryan to see when she gets home?" Netasha asked.

"Yes, ma'am, right away." Mary Josie took the dress and headed out of the foyer.

Netasha turned to face me. "I have to get back to the office, but remember what I said, and smile, kiddo. You are amazingly beautiful when you smile."

I smiled lovingly at her. Netasha could always make me beam.

When Netasha left, I went back into the room once again to help Mary Josie. I was excited to see what things I would find of my great-grandmother's.

"Ms. Zyaire, look at this box. It has a note in it," Mary Josie exclaimed when I walked through the door.

I took the box from Mary Josie's hands. Besides the light dust covering that had settled on it, the appearance of it looked like it did not belong in an attic. It was not a plain box; in fact, it was embroidered with beautiful rhinestones and lace. It looked as if someone took a lot of time to decorate it and had done a beautiful job.

"It's lovely, isn't it?" Mary Josie asked.

I rubbed my fingers across the lace fabric that was perfectly bonded to the box.

"Yes, it is very beautiful. I wonder who made it." I opened the lid of the box and saw the note that Mary Josie spoke of situated right at the top. There was also a small rectangular one-sided card that was tucked off into the side of it. I picked it up first and read it. "Happy sweet sixteen, Lillian. Remember, true beauty is not determined by the outside appearance but is often found within." It was signed simply Z. "Oh, my gosh! This gift was given to my great-grandmother when she turned sixteen. Wow, that was…" I ran numbers quickly in my head. "That was sixty-eight years ago," I said to Mary Josie, amazed.

"That is so weird that you find it now when you are about to turn sixteen."

"I guess it's fate," I said and reached for the note that Mary Josie spoke of. It was inside a gold envelope with black raised floral border all around it. I was surprised to see that the envelope was still tightly sealed. Directly in the middle of it, written in fine handwriting were the words "To my dearest granddaughter, Geri." I knew right away that Geri was short for Geraldine, my mother's first name. "Do you think I should open it?" I turned and asked Mary Josie.

Mary Josie shrugged her shoulders, not wanting to get involved in my mischief.

"Okay. I am going to open it then," I declared. I broke the seal on the letter that was clearly meant for my mother. It had obviously been in the attic for almost sixteen years, the day when a young couple first walked into the perfectly decorated house with their brand-new daughter.

"Read it aloud," Mary Josie uttered.

"Look at you, Mary Josie, you are just a curious as I am." I giggled.

I pulled the lavender-colored paper out of the envelope and read its words loud enough for Mary Josie to hear:

> *My dear Geri, in this box I am leaving you the best part of me. The day I came upon this precious gift, I discovered who I am, and the knowledge that true wealth sometimes lies beyond our imagination. Many things you may have longed to know about me will be answered. It is because of the "Seal of Secrecy" that I am only sharing this with you now, after my death. When the leaves are at their best, and the moon first lights the way, then shall you come, but you cannot stay. Please tell Aimilios I love him dearly, and not even the grave could break that love.*

The end of the letter was signed, *"Your dear Vovó Lilly."*

"Wow, it's from my great-grandmother Lillian," I said, looking up from the letter, stunned. I lifted what appeared to be an inside lid of the box and dug through the colorful shredded paper in search of what was inside. I finally felt a bulge of some sort, and I grabbed ahold of it and pulled it out. "It's a purse," I told Mary Josie and held it up in the air for her to see it.

"Oh my, it looks really..." Mary Josie paused, trying to choose the right word to describe it. She finally settled on the obvious. "It looks really...hideous!" she said and broke out into a contagious laugh. "I'm sorry, but it does," she said, apologizing. "Maybe you should put it back," Mary Josie added.

I could not help but laugh with Mary Josie, and she was right. It did look hideous. It was made of leather, and the color was a dull mustard green. It was a large purse with thick tattered straps. The threading was atrocious. It looked as if it was sewn together by a two-year-old child. The leather had a wrinkled, bubbly look to it. So much so that it had an appearance of something that needed a good ironing. It was awkward to look at, yet the more I glanced over it, the more I loved it. I didn't know if it was because I had always seemed to take a liking to the things that others wouldn't be caught dead in, or if it was because I could not help but love anything that belonged to the woman I had never met but admired and idolized for so many years now.

"Is the leather at least real?" Mary Josie asked.

"I think so. I have never seen anything like this before," I said, rubbing my hands across the purse's coarse leather.

"Me either," Mary Josie said, unimpressed.

"You better be careful rubbing your hands across it like that, Ms. Zyaire. It looks like it could cut you."

I laughed, amused at her concern.

"It's fine," I assured her. "It's actually very soft, and it's definitely vintage," I declared. I had gone shopping for clothes with my mother on many occasions, and she had taught me the huge fashion statement one could make wearing vintage-inspired clothing. That was, of course, if you couldn't get your hands on the real thing, which would be even better. My mother even headed the project of some vintage designs at Varella's. Despite all this, I somehow knew her weak spot for vintage, and her owning of more than a few original pieces from the most famous designers of the sixties would not make the likes of this purse a welcomed piece in her wardrobe. Because of this, I felt completely justified in keeping it for myself.

"Look, there is a label at the bottom," Mary Josie said, pointing to the purse as I held it up.

I looked closely at the writing on the bottom. "It's the words from the letter," I exclaimed. "When the leaves are at their best, and the moon first lights the way, then shall you come, but you cannot stay.

"Now things are getting fun," I said to Mary Josie, quickly realizing this was a riddle to be solved.

Just then, I heard the voice of my mother yelling from the foyer.

"Mary Josie, come help me with these bags. Could you not hear me knocking at the door?" my mother called out angrily.

"Coming, Mrs. Ryan," Mary Josie answered and ran to the foyer. "I'm sorry, Mrs. Ryan, Ms. Zyaire and I were sorting through the things to go to charity."

"Good, how is that going?" she asked.

"It is going great, Mother," I rushed into the room and interrupted.

"Is there anything worth keeping?" my mother asked.

"Not so far," I responded quickly before Mary Josie could. I was still in disbelief and angry about what little concern my mother had for her grandmother's things, but I knew well enough not to challenge her. Instead, I kept my thoughts to myself.

My mother walked into the family room where everything from the attic was spread across the floor. Mary Josie and I followed behind her. Mary Josie looked around and immediately noticed there was a certain box missing.

"It does not look like you two have gotten much done," my mother complained. "Mary Josie, make me a cup of coffee to go please. I have to leave out again for another meeting, and where is the dress Netasha dropped off?" she asked, annoyed.

"In your bedroom closet, Mrs. Ryan," Mary Josie replied.

"When I get back this evening, Mary Josie, I expect to find my home decent and in order, and looking nothing like the pigsty it does right now. Do you understand me?"

"Yes, ma'am," Mary Josie replied.

"Get me that coffee," my mother demanded before walking off to look at the dress Netasha had left for her to see.

"I'm sorry, Mary Josie. My mother should not talk to you like that," I said once she was gone from the room.

"It's okay, Ms. Zyaire. I am tougher than I look. Where did you put the box?" Mary Josie whispered.

I leaned in closely to Mary Josie and spoke in a hushed voice, "I hid it in my bedroom closet. Please don't tell my mother about me opening the letter. It is the only thing I have of my great-grandmother's that might help me finally know the real her. My mother obviously did not care much about it, or she would not have left it in the attic all these years, and so willingly be parting with it now."

"I don't like keeping things from your mother, but I will do this for you," Mary Josie promised me.

"Thank you, Mary Josie!" I happily gave her a hug then stepped back and took a seat on the couch. I leaned over, placing one elbow on my thigh, and then I placed my slightly closed fist just under my chin as my father always did whenever he was deep in thought. I looked up at Mary Josie as she squinted her eyes, curiously gazing at me and wondering what I was thinking. After a long pause I finally spoke. "Now I just have to figure out what my great-grandmother was talking about in that letter and who this Aimilios is that she is confessing her undying love to?"

Chapter 3

The Return of the Pocketbook

(ZYAIRE)

The summer was ending, and the nights had already begun to grow cold. I tossed back and forth in bed before finally awaking and pulling my covers tightly around my neck. It was not long before I heard the voices of my mother and father. I grabbed my cell phone from my nightstand to see what time it was. "Three a.m.?" I questioned aloud. What could they be arguing about at this hour? I thought to myself.

I walked over to the door and slowly cracked it open, attempting to eavesdrop on their conversation. I could hear my mother's raised voice. That wasn't unusual. Her voice was always the loudest during her and my father's arguments.

"Do you think I am a fool, John? No man works this many hours. You are determined to make me the laughingstock of this town, but I will not let you. I will leave you first," my mother threatened.

I slowly closed the door. I had heard enough, and besides I had heard my mother make that threat many times. Sometimes I wished it were not an empty one so the fighting would just stop already. I plopped down on the bed and pulled the covers over my head. I tried not to hear the screaming that continued between my parents, but the covers gave little relief from their loud voices, and it certainly could not stop the pain that was in my heart.

I hated to hear my parents argue. Maybe I should just run away and escape from it all; I contemplated silently as I lay there. When I was eleven, I attempted to do just that. I waited until my parents were asleep before sneaking into the kitchen. I made myself two peanut butter and jelly sandwiches, and grabbed two juices from the pantry, before dropping them into a paper bag. I slowly headed for the door, my sleeping bag in one hand and my lunch bag in the other. When I got to the door, I began to swing it ajar. It made a slow squeaky sound as it opened. I pushed at the door very slowly, so not to wake my parents. I had gotten the door open just wide enough to slip out when I heard my mother's voice behind me.

"Where are you going?" she asked in a raised voice. I was so frightened by the unexpectedness of her presence that I dropped everything I was holding in my hand and quickly turned to face her. I took one look at her before feeling light-headed and fainting to the floor. When I came to, both my parents were standing over me with concerned looks on their faces, and I was lying on the family room's couch with a cold compress on my forehead. I was honest with my parents that night, and told them how their constant arguing was making me feel. I even told my dad how much it hurt that he was never around.

At my mother's insistence, they took me to the doctor the next morning because she was so concerned that I had fainted. The doctor diagnosed me with something called neurally mediated syncope, or common faint. Turns out it can occur in many situations—emotional distress, severe pain, and fear. My mother told me she was also diagnosed with NMS as a teenager, and it was why she wanted to take me to the doctor. The doctor's medical instructions for me were simple. He ordered me to avoid stress.

For a few months, my parents made an effort to cease all the arguing, and my father even came home earlier several nights a week to have dinner with us. However, as time passed, that soon wore away, and things were back to this.

My mother's constant accusations of my father, and my father's many scandals that according to my mother had brought shame on her family's good name, was taking a toll on me. I could still hear them arguing, so I closed my eyes tightly and imagined I was away in a far-off world—a world where I actually mattered, a world where my parents were not.

When I awoke to a knock on my door, I hadn't realized that I'd fallen back asleep. The light peered in from my bedroom window, and the house was silent again. The knock came again before I got up to answer. "Just a minute," I yelled out as I threw on my purple robe. When I opened the door, Mary Josie was standing there with a big smile and a hand full of balloons.

"Happy sixteenth birthday, Miss Zyaire, I prepared a special breakfast for you downstairs. It's your favorite." She winked.

"My favorite?" I probed.

"Come and see it for yourself," Mary Josie demanded.

"Okay, I will be down in a minute." I told her. I looked at myself in the mirror as I was brushing my teeth. I rinsed my mouth and then stared at myself for a moment longer. I didn't know what it was, but I felt pretty, and more mature. Not that sixteen made me a woman. I mean, just one day ago I was fifteen, but for some reason when I was looking in that mirror, I felt a sense of confidence. I felt comfortable in my own skin, and that was something I had never felt so strongly before.

When I walked out of my bathroom, I grabbed a pair of gray cotton pants from my walk-in closet and put them on, and then I grabbed a white T-shirt off one of the shelves. I pressed the T-shirt to my nose and took a deep breath, smelling the fresh scent of the Summer Breeze fabric softener that Mary Josie used to wash my clothes. I pulled the shirt over my head then looked up at the top shelf. I eyed the box holding my great-grandmother's purse in it. I thought about the cryptic riddle in the letter and the fact that the riddle was also written at the bottom of the purse. What could it mean? I wondered again. I would have to spend more time trying to figure it out later. I closed the closet door, then slipped on my flip-flops, grabbed a hair tie from off my dresser, and put my hair into a ponytail. I headed downstairs excited to see what special breakfast Mary Josie would surprise me with this year.

When I entered the kitchen, I was shocked to see both my parents sitting at the table, especially after the fight I had overheard between them only hours before.

"Happy birthday, sweetheart," my father said, looking up from his laptop and smiling.

"Yes, happy birthday, Zy," my mother chimed.

"Thank you. I almost forgot," I said before taking a seat across from my parents. Waiting for me was a perfect stack of three chocolate chip pancakes, some cut strawberries, melon, and a glass of orange juice. Sitting next to my plate was a thin crystal vase with a white rose in it.

"Thank you, Mary Josie," I exclaimed, looking back at her as she busily cleaned the dishes from the meal she had just prepared.

"You're welcome, Ms. Zyaire," she replied.

"Well, don't forget about the big party we are throwing for you on Friday," my mother reminded me. "We only have four days to spare until then. I am going to pick you up from school today and take you down to Varella's. You can pick out a dress from one of Claudia's new designs." Claudia Rains was one of the head designers for Varella's.

I gave the best smile I could muster up. "Sounds like fun. I can't wait," I replied cheerfully. I knew what that really meant. My mother was going to criticize all my choices, and in fact pick the dress herself. At least I could see my parents were putting forth an effort to make my birthday special. My dad never stuck around to have breakfast with us anymore. In fact, he usually left the house before I even woke up, and returned most nights long after I went to bed. The last time we all had breakfast together, I was still in elementary school, and my dad was still an employee, instead of the CEO.

"It's good to see you home, Dad," I said genuinely.

"I would spend all my time with my girls if I could, honey, but it's not easy being the CEO of a multibillion-dollar company." He picked up his cup of coffee and sipped from it with one hand, while still busily punching the keys on his laptop with the other. "Besides, no beautiful sixteen-year-old wants her old man hanging around and keeping her away from all the boys."

"There are no boys, Dad, only you," I assured him.

"Well, not now maybe, but there will be someday," he insisted. To that, we both exchanged smiles.

My father stood up and wiped his mouth with the cloth napkin that had been sprawled across his lap. I stood up as well, knowing that this meant breakfast was over and it was time for him to rush off to work. He hadn't kept his eyes off his laptop since I'd entered the room. I gave him a kiss on the cheek, and he placed a hand gently on each of my shoulders. "Happy birthday, Zy. You can buy whatever dress you want today, on me." He gave me a kiss on my forehead just as he always had since I was a little girl; then he kissed my mother softly on the lips before heading out the room. He could not cross the door's threshold before my mother yelled out to him, "Will it be a long night again, John?" She asked with a dull hint of hostility in her voice.

"I will call you if I'm going to be unusually late, Geri," he sneered. He walked out of the room and rustled at the front door for a moment before I could hear it slam shut. I could feel the tension between my parents, and figured they had not resolved whatever they were arguing about in the wee hours of the morning.

I silently finished my breakfast. No matter how many times my father had embarrassed me, or how often he missed the most important events in my life, whenever I was around him, he was able to charm me, and I became Daddy's little girl again just as I had been once before.

Things were great between him and me until my father began training to take over *Ryan's* as his father grew deathly ill. The truth was he was never good enough for his father, so in the last years of his life, my father worked tirelessly trying to win his father's respect and the right to carry on his father's legacy in the company he'd built. He sacrificed everything to make his father happy, even my mother and I. His nights at the office grew later. There were no more family vacations, or even family dinners. His father thought he was too accommodating and kind to run his company. Therefore, my father felt the only way to earn his rightful place was to show how ruthless he could be.

When he found out his father had been employing illegal immigrants in the factory so he could pay them far below minimum wage, he was disgusted, but he closed his eyes and pretended he had no idea it was happening. What made it even worse was he had also employed the minor children of some of these employees, and was not providing these employees with the required breaks for shifts. Some workers even complained that they would work an entire eight-hour shift with no break at all, because no one was scheduled to relieve them from their duties. It was not until a legal worker was seriously injured on the job, due to one of the minors' neglect, that the story went public.

Against my father's advice, my grandfather tried to wiggle his way out of paying the female employee's medical expenses and time off from work. Well, she took her story to the press and told of the working conditions at the Ryan's food factory. The public was stunned and outraged. However, they could not blame my grandfather; he was incapacitated by the time the story broke, and died during legal proceedings. This left my father to bear all the scrutiny, the worst being the offenses concerning the minors.

My father successfully denied any knowledge of the conditions of the factory in court; however, the company did not go unscathed just because my grandfather had died. The US Department of Labor fined them an astounding amount. It could have crippled the company, but my father worked tirelessly over the years to rebuild the public's trust in Ryan's. He cracked down on the employment conditions, and he opened the doors of the factory to the press so that they could report on his efforts; also, he let go of all employees who were illegal immigrants. Yet, he hired a lawyer to work with them to see if anyone was eligible to apply for citizenship. He gave the remaining legal employees of the factory a significant raise and adequate medical coverage for themselves and their families. He made sure there were breaks and time off allotted. The public's faith in the company and my father was slowly restored. However, it was during this time when my father began to distance himself from us that I had begun to distance myself from everyone and everything I had come to know and love.

I was so lost in the thoughts of my father that I did not hear my mother when she told me it was time to get ready for school for the second time. "Do you hear me? It's 7:15. You have to wake up from that daydream if you want to be on time for school," she warned.

"I'm sorry, Mommy, I mean Mother," I stammered. I stood up to head upstairs and get dressed, but turned to her before I left the kitchen.

"Mother, I think Daddy does love us, and he is still a good person. I think he just had a lot of difficult decisions to make, and in some cases he made the wrong ones."

My mother did not reply, so I headed up the steps without another word.

When I was finished getting dressed, I stood at the mirror and admired myself. I was wearing an early birthday gift from my mother—a new pair of fitted black designer jeans with a vintage, cream-colored, satin top, complete with pleated-shoulders. For my shoes, I threw on a pair of low-cut leather boots, black in color with cream accents. Then I reached up to the top of the closet and took down my great-grandmother's box. I took out the purse, and again read the inscription at the bottom. "When the leaves are at their best, and the moon first lights the way, then shall you come, but you cannot stay."

I stood at the mirror wondering again what the meaning behind the wording on the purse was. Finally, I draped its straps across one shoulder. "I like it," I said to myself, and decided right then and there that I would be wearing it to school.

When I got downstairs, my mother looked at me as if she had seen a ghost. "Where did you find that?" she asked.

"In the attic. You've seen this before?" I asked, stunned. I thought for sure she would not even recognize it. Otherwise, I would have kept it hidden.

"Yes, often, unfortunately," she replied. "It was your great-grandmother's. She treated it as if it was some buried treasure. She had that ratty thing for as long as I could remember. It was always around, but she did not want anyone touching it, which was fine with me. I always hated that purse, but she left it to me in her will. Go figure." My mother chuckled briefly.

I purposely did not mention anything about the sealed letter and the card I had found. I figured since she did not bring it up, it was a possibility she did not know about it. My mother walked over and lifted the purse from my side, staring disgustingly at it.

"You know this was the only thing your great-grandmother left for me in her will? So much for being her favorite." My mother shrugged.

It was then that I think I might have gotten a glimpse into why my mother seemed angry at my great-grandmother for all these years, and why my name was Zyaire, instead of Lillian. After all, she was worth millions, and all she left my mother was an old purse. I could see how that would infuriate a person like my mother.

"You're not going to wear that God-awful thing to school, are you?" my mother asked, interrupting my newfound daydream.

"Yes, I am. I like it," I declared.

"Only you would," was all that my mother said, smiling and shaking her head. Then she gave me a kiss on the cheek. "That ugly purse aside, you actually look very lovely today. It's like you're glowing," she said kindly.

It was rare that I got that kind of compliment from my mother. "Thank you," I said with surprise in my tone.

"You are welcome, now go! Have a good day. Happy birthday!" she said again before looking down at my purse one last time, sighing deeply and finally walking off.

I put on my black leather backpack that my mother had given me from Varella's "back to school" collection and glanced at myself once more in the full-length mirror that hung on the narrow wall to the right of the front door. I rubbed my hand across the purse that now hung at my side. I got a chill when I thought about the words I had just exchanged with my mother confirming that my great-grandmother had in fact once worn it. If it was a good enough gift for her sixteenth birthday, then it was certainly a good enough gift for mine. I quickly walked out of the door. I was excited to get to school and show my best friend what I had discovered over the weekend.

When the door closed, I looked through the glass of the single sidelight alongside our front door and watched as my mother strutted swiftly into the dim foyer shaking her head. Her dress billowed out about her. She was grumbling something to herself. I could tell by the way her hands wagged from side to side as they always did when she was talking intensely. I wasn't sure what the exact words were, but my guess would be something like, "Of all things in the world to be discovered by that little girl, it just had to be that repellent purse."

Chapter 4

The Musical Pocketbook

(ZYAIRE)

The weekend had gone by far too fast, and the school day dragged on for what seemed like forever to me. When the lunch bell rang, I was anxious to see my best friend, Teresa.

"Hey, I have not seen you all day. Where have you been? Ditching me for some hot guy I hope," Teresa said, walking up to me from behind.

"Do you ever think of anything besides boys, Teresa?"

"No. What else is there to think about? I mean look at them, they are so interesting."

Teresa leaned up against the lockers and watched as the captain of the football team walked by.

"Hi, Tyler," she called out.

"Hey, Teresa. Hey, Teresa's friend," Tyler said, smiling, as he walked by.

"Great, my name is Teresa's Friend now."

"You have no one to blame but yourself for that. You are the one who decided to become a social outcast just because your father got involved in some minor scandals."

"I would hardly say they were minor."

"Get over it already—everyone else has. I want my best friend back. Not this zombie who is currently occupying your body," Teresa said, lightly shaking me back and forth by my shoulders.

I rolled my eyes. "Does my best friend even know what today is?" I asked.

"Not only do I know what today is, birthday girl, but also I got you a gift, but first, I have to ask, what is up with the ugly purse? I love the rest of the outfit, but the purse, what happened?"

"First of all, it is not ugly, it has character, and secondly, it was my great-grandmother's," I replied, only slightly offended.

"Shut up!" Teresa said, shocked. "How do you know it was hers?" she asked, grabbing the purse in her hand.

I gently tugged it from her grasp. "Be careful, it's vintage." Teresa giggled at that statement. "It is vintage!" I declared.

"Yeah, maybe, but it's no Pierre Cardin," Teresa joked. "So spill it, where did you get it? You have been obsessed with finding out information on your great-grandmother for years and now you find that. This is so cool."

"Oh, it gets so much better, you have no idea. Get this, she got this as a gift for her sixteenth birthday."

"Shut up!" Teresa said again, stunned.

"Yes, and apparently, according to my mother, she used to wear it all the time, and she left it in her will for her."

"In her will? How strange. Why would someone as loaded as your great-grandmother leave some beat-up old purse like this in her will for her only grandchild?" Teresa asked.

"I don't know. I guess it is strange," I admitted, having thought the same thing myself.

"Wait, before you say another word." Teresa dug into her backpack and handed me a small wrapped box. "Open it," she demanded.

I unwrapped the box and opened it to find a delicate white gold necklace with a beautiful blue pear-shaped stone dangling from it.

"I got it for you to wear to your party this weekend," Teresa explained. "It matches your amazingly blue eyes."

I rubbed my fingers across the smooth stone. The gift surprised me, because I knew Teresa must have worked hard to be able to afford it.

"I love it, Teresa," I finally said, breaking my wandering thoughts. I gave her a huge hug.

"So are you inviting anyone from school to your party?" Teresa asked.

"Do you think I should?" I carefully put the necklace into the box and put it into my great-grandmother's pocketbook.

"Um, yes," Teresa replied, but not before she threw in a dramatic pause. "It would officially take you out of the misfit category."

"I don't know," I grunted. "What if I invite people and they don't want to come, or even worse their parents forbid them from coming?"

"That's not going to happen." Teresa laughed. "You're unpopular by choice. People want to be in your company, you just won't allow them to be. Look at you, you are ridiculously pretty, yet you don't know it, or act like it. You're smart, funny, and you're like Mother Teresa for God's sake with all the charity you do. Oh, and let's not forget, your family is loaded."

"Money is not everything, Teresa," I pointed out.

"I beg to differ, and only people who have money say that," Teresa declared and began to walk down the hall signaling me to follow. Just then, I saw Mandy Pierce approaching, and wanted to turn and run in the other direction. Teresa had become more than acquainted with Mandy over the past months, and I did not approve of their newfound friendship.

Mandy came bopping toward us. Her long auburn hair was pulled up into a ponytail and swinging from side to side. It was

Monday, so she was wearing one of the varsity football players' jerseys, a long-running tradition for EP.

Every Monday during the football season, the varsity players wore dress slacks, dress shirts, and ties, and the cheerleaders wore their jerseys. Mandy was the head cheerleader, so of course she was wearing Tyler's jersey, because he was the starting quarterback and captain of the football team.

"Hi, Teresa," Mandy said cheerfully. She turned and looked at me coldly. "Zyaire, it's good to see you socializing again," she sneered. She looked down at my purse with a look of repulsion, but surprisingly said nothing.

"Yes, she is back, and ready to have fun. Right, Zyaire?" Teresa nudged me slightly. I just rolled my eyes at her.

"Mandy, you should be happy I stepped out of the social circle for a while. It allowed you to move into my spot," I said, smiling.

"Your spot?" Mandy asked rhetorically. "I hardly need to move into anyone's spot. I'm popular, head cheerleader, and my parents aren't the town's joke."

"Okay, okay, that's enough, you two," Teresa said, stepping in before the insults went any further. "It's time for you two to put your differences aside. You have so much in common, and you used to be great friends. I have the perfect idea," Teresa proclaimed.

"Mandy, Zyaire is having a birthday ball this weekend. You should come, and bring a few friends." I tried to speak up in protest, but Teresa cut me off.

"So, Mandy, you will come, right?"

"I have never been known to miss a good party. I will even bring a gift, a new purse maybe." Mandy devilishly grinned, and then she looked down at my great-grandmother's purse that hung from my shoulder. Teresa smiled, and I practically foamed at the mouth.

"Great! We will see you this weekend," Teresa said and pulled me down the hall by my hand before I could object.

As soon as I knew we were out of earshot from Mandy, I let Teresa have it. "I can't believe you just did that."

"Did what?" Teresa asked innocently.

"You invited that nightmare to my party. You know our history, you know she only wants to see me fail. Who knows what that psycho has planned to ruin my whole night?"

Teresa rolled her eyes. "Come on, Zyaire, you are being overly dramatic. Besides, she and I are friends now. She won't do anything to hurt you because she respects me."

"You can't be this delusional," I said, dumbfounded.

Teresa continued in her campaign. "You two were friends before I even knew you. That must count for something?"

I shrugged my shoulders. "You would think so."

"You know what, despite your horrible attitude right now, and in spite of that offensive pocketbook you are wearing, you somehow look extra pretty today. Are you wearing makeup?" Teresa asked me.

"No, but I do actually feel quite pretty today."

"Well, that's a first," Teresa stated honestly.

"Don't think your compliments have made me forget that you just invited my worst enemy to my party," I complained.

I could not stand the fact that Mandy had taken time to cozy up to Teresa. I knew it was not genuine but did not want to hurt Teresa's feeling by telling her so. Unlike most of the kids at Einstein Prep, Teresa did not live a lavish life with rich parents. In fact, it was just the opposite. Her mother was a secretary at a public elementary school and would never be able to afford the tuition at EP. Her father was not in any better of a position to afford the high cost of EP either. He was a substitute teacher, barely making enough money to pay their everyday bills while he was still paying off his college loans.

Teresa's parents had met in college, but Teresa's wealthy grandmother did not approve of the match. When Teresa's mother came home one weekend to say she was pregnant and was going to marry the man her mother disapproved of, she was pressured by her mother to have an abortion and stop seeing him, but she refused.

When Teresa's parents got married, Teresa's grandmother disowned her mother. She removed her from her will and refused to continue paying for her education.

Her one redeeming action was that she agreed to pay for Teresa's schooling. Every day a driver that her grandmother pays for picks Teresa up from her modest neighborhood in New Bedford, Massachusetts, drops her off at school, and picks her back up in the afternoon. Because of Teresa's parents' lack of wealth, Mandy always saw her as beneath us. She used to call her the most horrible names.

"They would let anyone attend this school," she used to say, rolling her eyes in disgust every time she saw Teresa walk down the halls. When I ended up in a class with Teresa in eighth grade, we hit it off and became friends. Mandy was totally against it. "How could you hang with that poor white trash?" she had said to me one day. "It's either her or me," she threatened.

I looked at her pointedly. "It's her," I said, ending our friendship not just for the sake of Teresa but also for the sake of decency.

The truth was I never approved of the way Mandy acted, but because her mother and mine were best friends, it forced us together from a young age.

I never told Teresa the true reason Mandy and I stopped being friends. I blamed it on the scandals from my dad. Even after I saw Mandy using Teresa just to get under my skin, as much as it made me boil inside, I still did not have the heart to tell her. The truth was Mandy was just jealous of Teresa because Teresa was beautiful, likable, and adventurous. She was not afraid to take risks. We were all shocked last year when she strutted into school sporting her once long blonde hair in a stylish short cut like the model Twiggy from the sixties. Teresa was nothing like Mandy, which was probably why I loved her so much. She was funny, bubbly, and always flashing her beautiful smile. More importantly, she was a genuinely good person, something I could never say about Mandy.

Teresa and I strolled into the lunchroom. It was not the typical scene that one would expect to encounter in a high school lunchroom. There were no loud voices and laughter, or kids wandering from group to group gossiping. At Einstein Prep, such behavior would not be tolerated. The school's motto was, "In all things, there shall be order." The food was not what you would expect either— no burgers, french fries, or greasy pizza. Cottage cheese, salads, fruits, and other healthy food items are what filled most kids' lunch bags. There were no cooks, a decision voted on by the PTA, who felt it was more sanitary to have kids bring their own lunch. When Teresa and I sat down, we both pulled lunch bags from our backpacks.

I had not eaten in the lunchroom for quite some time. I usually stayed in the library and hid—yes, hid. Although, I was beginning to wonder if there was really something to hide from, or Teresa was right and the kids had moved on from my father's issues. After we sat down, I hung my purse on the back of my chair and pulled out a half turkey sandwich and a small Caesar salad to eat that Mary Josie had packed for me. Teresa, always different from the rest, pulled out a full peanut butter and jelly sandwich, a pack of Oreo cookies, a bag of potato chips, and a canned Dr. Pepper.

"I don't know how you eat like that and stay so thin," I said jealously.

"I don't know how you eat like that and stay so sane," Teresa fired back with a smile. A faint whisper broke our conversation. It was a kid named Andrew, who was sitting two seats down from Teresa.

"Pass this to Zyaire," he mouthed. He passed a note to the girl next to him, she handed it to Teresa, who then gave it to me.

"What is this?" I said, looking at the letter as if it was a foreign object.

"I don't know, open it and read it," Teresa urged. I opened the letter, and Teresa leaned in to get a look.

I cleared my throat. "Excuse me. It says for your eyes only," I said, and pointed to those words written in large script across the top part of the letter.

"I hope I am invited to your party, beautiful," the letter read. Both mine and Teresa's mouth dropped to the ground when we read the name that was signed at the bottom, "Tyler."

"Tyler?" I whispered to Teresa. "This must be a fake," I insisted.

"Why? I see him looking at you all the time," Teresa claimed.

"What are you talking about? He doesn't even know my name, apparently. He called me 'Teresa's friend' this morning, remember?"

"Oh, he knows your name all right, and he wants to know a lot more about you," Teresa teased. I looked over at Tyler, and he was smiling at me, so I smiled back.

"I will be right back. I have to use the ladies' room," I told Teresa, before getting up to head to the bathroom.

"Wait, you forgot something," she said and handed me my purse from off the back of my chair. "We wouldn't want someone to think that this thing was with me, would we?" she said, smiling.

"Very funny, it's not that bad," I whispered and took the purse from her hands.

"Yes, it is," Teresa said back in her version of a hushed voice.

I headed to the bathroom that was just outside the lunchroom's doors. Just knowing Tyler was looking at me made me nervous, and getting nervous always made me have to urinate.

I opened door after door, looking for the cleanest stall. After finally choosing the least of all evils, I went inside and hung the purse on the door hanger. I pulled my clothes down and squatted over the commode. The sound of my urine was loud as it hit the water inside the toilet bowl, but I swore I could hear a slight drumming sound. I halted in my attempt to relieve myself, but it was completely quiet around me, so I began urinating again. Once more, I heard the faint sound of a drum beating rapidly, and it sounded close. It was as if it was coming from my purse, but again when I stopped to listen, the sound was gone.

I finished up, grabbed my purse, and then went to the sink to wash my hands. When I was done, I set the purse on the countertop and searched throughout the pockets, seeing if something was inside that could have been making a noise. There was nothing, and since I could no longer hear the noise, I figured it must have been coming from somewhere else.

When I got back into the lunchroom, I quickly ate my food and finished it just moments before the bell rang. Teresa and I both got up quickly and dropped our trash in the large waste buckets.

"Call me after school?" Teresa said. "I want to hear the rest of the details about that purse."

"I am going to pick out my dress for the party after school, so I will call you when I get home," I promised.

Teresa and I passed a quick peck from cheek to cheek before turning to walk down the hall in opposite directions. The space between us widened until finally we disappeared around our respective corners.

After a stop at my locker, I quickly walked down the long corridor that led to my fifth period advanced chemistry class. I was moments from being late, so the hall that led only to this particular classroom was empty, besides me. Just as I got within steps of my classroom's door, I heard the drumming sound again. This time it was louder and quicker. I lifted my great-grandmother's purse and put it right up to my ear, trying to isolate where that sound was coming from. This time there was no denying it; it was coming from the pocketbook.

Chapter 5

Memories Unwanted

(GERALDINE)

It was Friday, the day of my daughter Zyaire's sweet sixteen birthday party. There was so much to do, but I could not stop thinking about my grandmother Lillian. Until now, I had successfully wiped her from my thoughts. Yet ever since Zyaire came strutting down the steps with that God-awful purse, she has all but consumed me.

Now here I was, sitting out in the foyer like a child, twisted over, and rocking back and forth as I guided my fingers gently through my hair. The thoughts of my grandmother had caused me to become overwrought by painful memories. I cried out to myself inwardly as my gentle strokes through my hair became closer to tugs. "Lillian Varella, I will not let you do this to me. Not even in thoughts. I will not let you suck me into your orbit, only to disappoint me again."

I stood up with purpose and headed to the Great Room. There was much to be done, and I was not going to let the ghost from my past stop me.

"Mary Josie, did you check with the caterer to see what time they would arrive?" I asked when I entered the room.

"Yes, Mrs. Ryan, they will be here at four o'clock," Mary Josie answered while busily doing the other task I had assigned to her.

Mary Josie had been good to me over the last nine years. She came well recommended by my neighbor Mrs. Vector. She had been their house attendant for five years before they relocated to Napa, California. She did not come cheap but was worth every penny. A wonderful neat freak, she revamped my kitchen, and every other area of the house that needed organizing. That was all in her very first week. She was a skilled cook and a great nanny to my daughter.

Unlike others, I had managed to keep the lines drawn between work and family with her, and I made sure not to cross that line as many other families had when it came to their house attendants.

My grandmother had left two million dollars to her house attendant Lucy and her daughter Olivia when she passed away. That was something I could never understand, especially since she had left me no money at all. When it came down to Mary Josie, no matter how great of a person she was, I was determined to remember that she was an employee, and not family.

For this reason, I had made certain that she called none of us by our first name, because that was too personal. She respectfully called me Mrs. Ryan, and my husband Mr. Ryan. I even insisted on her calling my daughter Ms. Zyaire, despite the fact that Zyaire hated it. Mary Josie was never invited to family functions, except as an employee, and I never asked about, or got involved with her personal life. Some of my friends with house attendants thought this was cold, but I told them without apology that it was professional.

"Can you believe this day is already here?" Mary Josie asked.

"No, I can hardly believe it," I said, smiling and keeping our conversation pleasant but short, as I always did. Mary Josie was right, this week had flown by, and I was determined to have Zyaire's party go off without a hitch. My assistant Netasha and I went over every detail repeatedly to make sure nothing was left undone. I was not going to leave anything to chance, especially since I had invited the media. After so many years of scandal, our family could use some good publicity.

"Mary Josie, when you finish up there, you can go and check the decorations out front. Make sure no lights have blown please."

"Yes, Mrs. Ryan. No problem. I am almost done here."

Mary Josie was always ready and willing to do whatever I asked of her.

Netasha, my assistant, entered the Great Room. The heels of her red stylish pumps tapped against the marble floor. "They look beautiful, Mary Josie," she complimented as she admired Mary Josie's works of art.

"They do, don't they," I agreed.

"Absolutely, we made a good choice going with Mary Josie's magic hands," Netasha announced.

I detected a hint of victory in her voice since it was she, and not I, who had the confidence in Mary Josie to make the decorations in the first place.

Except for the rectangular tables that lined the walls, the room was wide-open space. The party was set up to be a mix and mingle, so no chairs were in place either. There was a sitting room just outside the Great Room's doors if anyone wanted to grab a seat for a while, but other than that, the room was perfectly arranged for dancing.

Being a jack-of-all-trades apparently, Mary Josie had created beautiful pillars made of white and gold balloons for each corner of the room. Remarkably, she had also made a gorgeous seven-foot golden archway out of metallic white and gold balloons. We set the archway directly in front of the Great Room's doors so that each person would walk under the archway before crossing onto the red carpet that stretched from the doorway and straight across the wide-open space.

The tables were covered with white linen, and each would eventually bare an elegant floral centerpiece of white and pink lilies with white-waxed flower stems, and baby breaths exquisitely arranged in gold antique vases.

"This night is going to be dazzling," Netasha giddily declared.

"Of course it is, I would spare nothing to impress my daughter on her special day, and the media, of course," I said flippantly.

I pulled out my cell phone to look at the time. It was three o'clock. Everything was in place except the food and centerpieces. I, as always, insisted on real flowers, so only a same-day delivery would be acceptable.

Mary Josie announced her task was complete, and so she left Netasha and me to check on the decorations out front. Just like inside we kept the outside decorations simple yet elegant, lining the walkway with miniature pathway lights and decorating the trees surrounding the front yard with clear lights. When lit, they looked magical, beautifully mixed with the colorful leaves that had just turned with the start of autumn. No other decorations were needed. We tested the look on the previous evening, and it was breathtaking. Netasha called the florist and caterer to make sure they were on their way.

"The florist is almost here, and the caterer will arrive in about an hour," Netasha said, hanging up from her call.

"Great, that means that they are on schedule."

"So can you believe it?" Netasha asked as she walked around checking that all the tablecloths were perfectly straight.

"Can I believe what?" I asked.

"Can you believe your little girl is sixteen and practically a woman now?"

"I know. I can hardly believe it." I gave a smile of reminiscence. "My little Zyaire…I remember when she was just a mystery in my belly." I rubbed a hand across my stomach envisioning a time when it was much bigger. "Did you know she was supposed to be named Lillian, after my grandmother?" I asked, thinking about the lilies that would soon be placed on every table. Lilies were my grandmother's favorite flower, and ironically, Zyaire's too.

"No, you never told me that," Netasha said, intrigued.

I had never spoken of the woman that made Varella's famous. Now here I was ready to tell all.

"So what happened?" Netasha asked.

I smirked and slightly giggled through my next sentence. "I probably would not be thinking about her right now if it weren't for that stupid pocketbook."

"What pocketbook?" Netasha asked, confused.

I sighed at just the thought of the pocketbook.

"Zyaire found an old pocketbook of my grandmother's last weekend that was in our attic. She was wearing it when she left for school on Monday. I almost had a heart attack when I saw it. I always hated that ugly purse."

"Lillian Varella with an ugly purse?" Netasha asked, surprised.

"I know. I could never understand why a woman as stylish as her would be caught dead with a purse like that. She said it was a gift for her sixteenth birthday."

"Wow! Sixteenth birthday. That is so funny that Zyaire would find it now. It can't be that bad, right?" Netasha asked.

"Oh no, it's that bad," I assured her.

"So what's the deal with it? Give me the 411."

"Well, the story goes like this. My grandmother had just played a flawless Snow White in the opening night of *Snow White and the Seven Dwarfs*, and a woman, who was a frequent customer at our family's store, requested to come backstage and give her a gift. She and my grandmother had become friends from their conversations when the woman would visit the boutique. Apparently, she fascinated my grandmother. She would sit in the waiting area with this woman for hours and listen to the fantastic stories that she would tell. The infamous purse was a gift from her to my grandmother for her sixteenth birthday. Apparently, my grandmother never saw the woman again after that. My mother called it the 'magic money pocketbook'; she claimed money would just appear in it out of thin air."

"Oh, wow!" Netasha said, now more intrigued than ever.

"My grandmother Lillian was a fascinating woman herself—beautiful, gorgeous even. She and I were closer than close. She would pick me up almost every weekend and take me on these lavish shopping sprees, then at night we would put on silk pajamas, eat popcorn, and watch old black-and-white movies. My favorites were the ones she was in."

I smiled at the thought of my grandmother.

"She was nothing like the images that now adorn Varella's walls. In them, she seems untouchable, perfect, and famous; but she was down to earth, vulnerable, and like a best friend to me. I told her everything. Truth be told, I think she hated her celebrity status. She would even disappear from the world and her family at least once every year, telling no one where she would go. I think it was her time to just escape it all."

I shrugged and let out an awkward laugh. I had not spoken of my grandmother in years. It was odd now, allowing myself to go back to that time.

"So anyway," I said, getting back to my original point, "like I said, Zyaire discovered the hideous purse in the attic." I exhaled deeply. "I always hated that thing. It always gave me the creeps as a kid. My grandmother did tell me it was very special to her, but never told me why. That was all she ever said about it. All that I know about the purse and how my grandmother first happened upon it was from the stories my mother told me as a child.

"My grandmother always kept that purse in her sight. She said it reminded her that neither true beauty nor happiness was measured by someone's outward appearance, but that in order to find it you have to be brave enough to look inside and see what was deep within."

"Well, that's true," Netasha said, agreeing with my grandmother's wisdom.

"Yes, but it's ironic coming from a woman who was drop-dead gorgeous, don't you think? But I guess it was her way of remembering to stay humble. She was a mysterious woman, and I loved her very much, and I thought she loved me too."

"Do you think otherwise now?" Netasha asked.

"I don't know, maybe I am measuring the proof of that love the wrong way." Before Netasha could ask what I meant, Mary Josie led in the florist and her staff carrying the centerpieces.

When Adela walked through the double doors of the ballroom, she made her presence known. "Geri, my love," she said in her slight East London accent.

"Adela," I replied with equal enthusiasm.

We met in the middle of the room and shared a faint kiss on both cheeks. She and I had been friends for years. Adela was the owner of *Perfect Petals*, a flower shop she first opened on the corner of Massachusetts Avenue in Dorchester. It now was the largest floral shop in the nation.

"Where is the birthday girl? I have a gift for her," Adela asked.

"She is out on a spa day with her best friend Teresa. I wanted her to be surprised at the decorating we have done. She will be arriving in a limo to the party already dressed and ready to make a grand entrance."

"Your idea, of course, and not hers," Adela said.

"How did you know?" I laughed. Adela knew Zyaire detested being the center of attention.

"Well, I regret I cannot stay, my dear. Please make sure Zyaire gets this for me." Adela reached down into her purse, and pulled out a little black box and handed it to me.

"I have another prominent family to deliver to, a bar mitzvah, and the misses will surely go off in a tantrum if we're late," Adela declared. Adela was known to ride along on deliveries to her most prominent clients, even traveling out of state to make sure the most prestigious events and guests were taken care of properly. She and I walked around together to check that all the centerpieces were in "Perfect Petals" condition, and they were. I waved goodbye to her at the front door, just as the caterers arrived fifteen minutes early.

Everything was in place for the party, and the guests had already begun to arrive. Zyaire phoned me on her way in and asked that I grab her new earrings from atop the nightstand in her bedroom. I purchased them specifically for her to wear tonight, but she had forgotten them. *Typical Zyaire*, I thought. That girl would lose her perfect God-given nose if it was not attached to her face.

I decided I would grab them from her room now and give them to the host, Trish. She would lead Zyaire in when she arrived. This way Zyaire could have them to put on before she made her grand entrance.

I entered the room and stopped just beyond the door. Aside from the light coming from the full moon, Zyaire's room was dark. The moon supplied a steady stream of light over the window seat. There sitting on top of the window seat was my grandmother's pocketbook or mine if you wanted to be technical about it.

My skin crawled, and I began to feel nervous. Something about that pocketbook sitting there illuminated amongst the darkness sent a shiver up my spine. I quickly walked over to the nightstand, grabbed Zyaire's earrings, and scurried away like a small child running from the boogeyman. Just as I went to close the door, I heard what I thought was the sound of a beating drum. I looked back at the pocketbook, and the light from the moon seemed to have brightened, because the area where the pocketbook sat was more glaring than before. I could no longer hear the drum, only the beating of my own heart. "You got to get a grip, Geri," I said to myself, realizing how silly I was being.

I walked back into the room with purpose, and violently sent my hand swinging backward, hitting the pocketbook with full force and sending it flying off the window seat and onto the bedroom floor. "Thanks but no thanks, Grandmother," I said, once again voicing my disdain of the gift she had given me sixteen years ago.

I glanced back as I closed the door of Zyaire's room, and even still, the light from the full moon stretched beyond the window seat and illuminated the pocketbook and all its ugliness.

Chapter 6

A Party to Forget

(ZYAIRE)

As the limo entered the gates of my house, Teresa and I watched in amazement at all the cars that lined the long driveway. There were valets taking each person's car as they entered the roundabout at the front entrance of the house. I saw one valet signaling to the arrival of our Limo. My palms began to sweat. I did not like all the attention I was about to be thrown into, but my mother insisted on a grand entrance.

"This is so cool," Teresa said, rolling down her window and sticking her head out.

"Who are all these people? I only invited a few guests," I said in a panic.

"I may have invited some people for you," Teresa said.

"Teresa, by some people, how many do you exactly mean?"

"Fifty or so, maybe less, maybe more," she admitted.

"I am going to kill you," I yelped only half jokingly.

"No, you're not, because I took the liberty of inviting Tyler." Proud of herself, Teresa did a little dance in her seat.

"You didn't?" I asked and gently pulled Teresa's arm, forcing her dance to a stop.

"Yes, I did. What is the matter with you? You had a crush on him all last year," she reminded me.

"And he ignored me as if I didn't exist."

"That's because of Mandy. She would not let anyone get near him. But as you can see, he obviously was not interested in her, but you all of this time."

I shook my head and paused. "I just don't understand his sudden interest in me, that's all."

The limo came to a stop and the door slowly opened at the hand of one valet. A very thin, handsome, caramel brown, young man popped his head into the door's opening. "Good evening, Zyaire, and happy birthday. You look beautiful," he said with a broad smile.

"Was it in your job description to say that, or do I really look beautiful?" I asked suspiciously.

The valet nervously laughed. "Both," he finally said.

"And what about me, do I look beautiful too?" Teresa asked.

"Of course, you both look beautiful," he said, holding out his hand to help me out from the limo, and then Teresa.

Teresa was led inside first. My mother had already planned for me to walk in alone.

I walked the hall that led to the Great Room accompanied by the host my mother hired, a very stern woman with a pleasant face. She was tall and thin with short brown hair. She wore glasses, but that still did not conceal her bright green eyes. She was probably in her mid-forties. I had never seen her before, which was unusual. My mother was very meticulous and seldom used new people outside her team of workers she had staffed herself with over the years. I figured it must have been someone Netasha recruited. She was charming and greeted me with a smile.

"Don't forget these," she said and handed me the earrings I had left on the nightstand. I thanked her and quickly put them on. "Are you ready to make your grand entrance?" the woman who had introduced herself as simply Trish asked.

"As ready as I'll ever be," I said, my legs practically shaking.

The double doors to the Great Room were closed, but I could still hear the start of the newly released Black-Eyed Peas song "I Gotta Feeling" escaping through it. I loved the song selection, but I was sure Netasha was the orchestrator of it because I knew my mother detested music with words.

The doors opened on each side, and I walked into a crowd of people lined on both sides of the red carpet staring at me. I felt like Hilary Duff in that movie *A Cinderella Story* where she made her grand entrance into a Halloween party dressed as a princess and everyone stared at her enchanted, as she stood at the top of a staircase in her beautiful gown.

Cameras began to flash, and I realized then that my mother had invited the "paps." She would do anything to prove our family was normal, or at least make sure we appeared to be. I smiled as the camera flashes went off one after the other, just as I was taught to do from a young age. At least I was dressed for the part. I was wearing a beautiful dress inspired by one my great-grandmother had made famous: a sequined, shimmery, multicolor, strapless cocktail dress that stopped a few inches above my knee, fit me to perfection. Not even I, with all my insecurities, could look in the mirror and deny how beautiful I looked in it. The black sheer tulle that opened from the waist and cascaded down the back into a short train gave my look a touch of elegance. I could definitely see my great-grandmother in something just like it, dazzling the crowd at one of the many parties she gave.

My jet-black hair hung loosely into spirals, and the blue-stoned necklace that Teresa gave me brought out the blue in my eyes as she intended. The diamond-studded earrings my mother picked out thankfully were simple yet beautiful.

As I stood on the red carpet posing for pictures, I could hear the conversation of my mother and Vovó in the near distance.

"She looks just like your grandmother," Diane Mitchell, my Vovó, said as I smiled and repositioned for each photo.

"Yes, she does, Mother, and I guess the next thing you will say is her name should have been Lillian, right?" my mom replied in a hushed yet hostile voice.

"Not here, not now. Today is about my beautiful granddaughter and not your bitterness."

I looked back to try to get their attention, and maybe signal that their conversation was being overheard, but my Vovó was already approaching me with a smile. She linked her arm with mine and walked me to the end of the red carpet. My mother followed behind her.

"Zy, you look so beautiful," my grandmother said and gave me a peck on the lips.

"Yes, sweetheart, you look fabulous," my mother agreed and gave me a huge hug.

I could feel the genuineness of it and knew it was not just for the cameras. Maurice Mitchell, my Papa, came from behind to hug and kiss me as well.

"You're getting prettier every day, kid," he said in his raspy voice that I loved.

"Thank you, Vovó and Papa." Seeing their smiling faces and proud expressions somehow settled my nerves. We talked briefly before my mother excused herself to go and check on something.

"You go too, sweetie," my grandmother insisted. "Have fun. All your friends are waiting to talk to you."

"Do not let us two old geezers hold you up all night," my papa said.

My grandmother looked at me and smiled before I could walk away to greet my guests. Tears filled her eyes and my grandfather noticed.

"Oh honey, don't get all mushy," he said.

"Looking at her is like looking into the face of my mother. I wish she could have met her great-granddaughter," my grandmother said and gently patted my cheek with her hand.

My grandfather put his arm around his wife. Her once long brown hair was surprisingly still naturally brown, but cut short. His hair was long since gray. Her eyes were still bright and perfectly round as they had always been, but now showed the weariness that being the president of Varella's had marked them with. Diane Mitchell was fifty-eight years old but was just as beautiful as she was the day my grandfather first met her, and he was just as in love. She laid her head against his chest, and they swayed back and forth to the blaring music. I walked off into the crowd.

"Zyaire, over here," Teresa called out.

I looked and several other kids from our school surrounded her. So far, I did not see Mandy or Tyler, and I was relieved. I also noticed another face was missing from the crowd—my father.

One of my friends from school, Philip, walked up and gave me a hug. "Happy birthday, Zyaire, this party is amazing."

"Thanks. I am glad you came, Philip, and everyone else too," I said, acknowledging the others that stood in the group.

"Thanks for inviting me, Zyaire," they all chimed one by one. I wanted to tell them that their gratitude was due to Teresa, but I decided against it.

"It's time for the birthday girl's first dance," the DJ announced over the speakers.

I looked around terrified. With whom would I dance? I had no date unless you counted Teresa, and I certainly would not dance with her.

"Hey, Zyaire, would you mind dancing with me?" a voice said from behind. I slowly turned around to see who was asking, and was surprised to see Tyler. My mouth practically dropped to the floor.

"Sure," I said without hesitation.

I could hardly believe what was happening. I decided to go with the flow of things. We both walked to the middle of the dance floor, and I quickly realized my favorite love song "Falling for You" by Colbie Caillat was playing. Tyler wasn't the best dancer, but for me that did not matter. My nerves quickly melted away as he clumsily whisked me across the floor. I closed my eyes, rested my head on his shoulder, and pretended I was dancing with him in some far-off land. I pictured us dancing in the middle of a beautiful field full of daisies, the sun setting just off the field, and he and I dancing cheek to cheek, as we gazed at the sunset's beautiful burnt auburn and yellow colors. He whispered into my ear and told me how dazzling I was tonight. Well, he didn't actually, but I imagined he did, and it was beautiful.

I didn't know why but in that moment I thought about my great-grandmother. I wondered if she danced with the person of her dreams at her sweet sixteenth party as I was doing now. Then I thought about her pocketbook. My guess was it had not been a likely accessory to whatever gown she had chosen to wear on her special night. I still couldn't figure out where the musical contraption that was making the drumming noise had been sewn in. When I told Teresa about it, she suggested that maybe it was haunted. However, I was far too much of a realist to believe something like that. If I hadn't felt the warmth of Tyler's body close to mine, I might not believe what was happening just then. After a while, others joined in, and the floor filled with graceful bodies. Yet in my daydream, it was still only Tyler and I.

When the music stopped, it took a moment for me to realize I was still at my party. The room had briefly gone silent. I stayed there for just a second, my head still on his shoulder, smelling the cedarwood scent of his cologne. Finally, Tyler stroked my hair, and I snapped out of my daze. When I opened my eyes, there were more than a few people gazing at us.

Feeling nervous, I excused myself from Tyler for a trip to the ladies' room just as the DJ began to blare the next hit song through the speakers. Teresa offered to tag along, but I declined. I had not seen my mother for quite some time and wanted to look around for her. I didn't have to look far. When I walked out of the Great Room and into the quiet hallway leading to the guest bathroom, I saw her from behind with her cell phone to her ear.

"Where in the hell are you?" I heard her yell into the phone. "You better not hang up on me, you prick. John, John!" my mother yelled frantically into the phone. Apparently, my father had hung up, because my mother's hand dropped to her side, and her head collapsed toward her chest.

I had never witnessed my mother use foul language before, not even during the many arguments I had overheard between my parents. She said lowlives and people who lacked sophistication used curse words. My mother rubbed her forehead and slowly turned around. She was startled to see me standing behind her.

"Zyaire, you almost gave me a heart attack. How long have you been standing there?" she asked.

Tears weld up in my eyes. "He's not coming, is he, Mommy?"

Heartbroken for herself and me, my mother did not mind hearing me call her Mommy in that moment. Maybe it reminded her of better times in our lives.

"Of course he's coming," she assured me. "He said he had a crisis with one of his clients and that he would be here soon."

My mother reached into her pocket and took out a tissue to wipe my eyes. "Don't cry, it will ruin your makeup, and we have not sent the press home yet," my mother said shamelessly. I could not help but laugh at her relentlessness.

"What am I going to do with you, Mother?" I said.

We both smiled and shared a warm look of affection. If there was one thing we had in common, if not anything else, it was the heartbreak brought on by my father's unwavering dedication to his job over his family.

When I walked back into my party, my mother was already dry-eyed and mingling with her snob friends and their daughters. She desperately wanted me to form a bond with them, but I much preferred the company of people like Teresa.

I searched the room for Teresa and found her standing next to Mandy and Tyler. My heart began to pound. I figured there was no point in putting it off, so I reluctantly walked over to the corner where they were.

"Birthday girl," Mandy said and gave me what seemed to be a real hug. "Your party is so cute. My mom sends her love, she is very sorry she could not make it, something tied her up, but I put her name on my gift."

Mandy's mother and mine used to be great friends. They did everything together. That was how Mandy and I had become so close. Lately, they had been estranged from each other. I figured my mom's busy schedule was the reason for that.

I looked over at Tyler, who now seemed to be avoiding eye contact with me. One thing Teresa was right about, I did have a huge crush on him all last year. What girl wouldn't? He was so handsome and popular, yet down to earth, although he did have his "rich boy" moments. I managed to overlook that because he was just so cute. He had dark hair that he wore in a curly, low cut. I used to sit behind him in English class in ninth grade. I would sometimes get the urge to just reach out and run my fingers through his curls, but of course, I never did. His eyes were dark brown, and his cappuccino-colored skin was smooth and very lightly freckled just on his noise. His smile was broad and gorgeous, and to top it all off, he had the best sense of humor, but not in a class clown type of way, but a clever type of way.

He was one year older than I was but moved in the same circles as I once had. Being the quarterback of the varsity football team almost licensed him to date a cheerleader, and I watched as he dated Kristin, and then Samantha, before he finally was single again. Mandy had long since claimed him as her best friend and was the reason for his breakup from both Kristin and Samantha.

"Thanks for the dance, Tyler," I said, deciding to break the unexplained awkwardness that had now risen between us.

"You're welcome, you look very pretty," he said, smiling at me. "Oh, and happy birthday. I didn't get to tell you that."

Tyler and I both smiled adoringly at each other.

"So you two danced together?" Mandy asked, reminding us that she was still there.

"Yes, you weren't here yet," Tyler explained.

"How cute," Mandy said sarcastically before quickly moving on to a new subject. "Well, is it time for the presents yet?" she asked.

"Don't worry, you weren't so late that you missed it," I grunted. Besides, I didn't understand why Tyler felt like he had to explain himself to her.

Before Mandy could fire back an insult at me, the familiar song of every great party began to play. The "Electric Slide" thumped in the speakers, and the dance floor filled with both adults and teens. I was amused to see my grandparents join in on the popular line dance. I went out onto the dance floor to join them. For once, I allowed myself to be caught up in all the fun—so much so that I forgot my father was still missing.

The night grew later and my party was nearing its end. My mother took the microphone to thank the guests with me by her side.

"I want to thank everyone for coming out tonight, and making this party so special for my not-so-little girl. She looks gorgeous tonight, doesn't she?"

Everyone clapped and cheered. "Happy birthday, Zyaire, happy birthday!" they yelled.

The wait staff rolled in a large cake with sixteen candles placed around the outside edges in equal distance of each other. Everyone began to sing—everyone but Tyler and Mandy. They were off alone in a corner toward the back of the room. Tyler whispered into Mandy's ear. Whatever he said must have upset her because Mandy violently pulled away from him, mouthed a few words, and then stormed off.

Mandy walked closer to the front, and Tyler followed quickly behind her. The crowd roared with cheers after I blew out the candles that adorned my cake. My mother took to the microphone again.

"Thank you so much everyone. My husband, who unfortunately could not be here with us tonight because of an unexpected emergency, and myself, have one more surprise for our daughter, and I would like everyone to follow me outside to give it to her."

I could not imagine what else my mother could have up her sleeve. I also could not imagine what emergency was important enough to keep a father from his only child's big night.

Whispers suddenly fell all across the room in anticipation of the surprise to come. However, the whispers were suddenly overtaken by a loud voice. Mandy made her way through the crowd.

"Wait, Mrs. Ryan, before you give Zyaire your gift, is it okay that I give her mine?" Mandy asked. She approached my mother and me at the front of the room. Mandy smiled broadly and batted her fake eyelashes.

"Well, I was about to lead everyone outside, but I don't see a problem with a brief interruption," my mother complied.

My mother gave Mandy the microphone, and I wondered what she was up to now. Mandy spoke loud and clear to the audience of people staring directly at her.

"Zyaire and I have known each other since we were in diapers. I use to call her my BFF. We have spent a miniseries as friends slash enemies, but she still holds a special place in my heart." Mandy paused and cleared her throat before continuing.

"Anyway, despite our recent separation, her family and mine continue to share a bond. Therefore, today to thank Zyaire and her family for the impact they have made on my life, I have brought her a very special gift. Tyler, can you bring the gift over please."

"Mandy," Tyler protested.

"It's okay, her mother said this is fine, right Mrs. Ryan?" Mandy confirmed.

"Yes, dear, but hurry up, I would like to get on with things, the press is waiting," my mother reminded her.

"Come on, Tyler." Mandy motioned with her hand. "We don't want to leave the press waiting."

Tyler reluctantly walked over with an oversized square object covered neatly in shiny black wrapping paper.

"Has everyone met my boyfriend Tyler? Isn't he cute?" Mandy planted a kiss on Tyler's lips.

My heart sank, and the rest of the group from our school were stunned. Since when were Tyler and Mandy dating? That was the the question I'm sure was going through all of their minds. Mandy took the gift from Tyler's hands and turned it toward the crowd.

"Happy sweet sixteen, Zyaire, you deserve a night like this." She grinned cheerfully.

I just stared at her. "Well, come on, silly, get up here and tear it open," Mandy demanded.

I could not imagine feeling more devastated and humiliated as I did in that moment, but I put on a smile for the paps just as my mother had taught me to do. Composed, I stood up to open my gift. As I tore away the paper, I saw my father's tall frame walk through the double doors.

"Zyaire, don't," he yelled out from the back of the room, but it was too late. I had pulled away the last of the wrapping paper, and the audience gasped in disbelief. I stared at the gift and quickly realized my aforementioned thought was incorrect. I had just managed to be more devastated and humiliated.

The flashes from the paps' cameras went off like lightning bolts. There in an oversized image was my dad and Mandy's mother locked in a passionate kiss, her shirt hanging off from her shoulders and my father, shirtless. My dad ran from the back of the room and slammed the photo to the floor, shattering the glass at impact. My mother looked at her husband completely bewildered.

"How could you?" she yelled out, before running from the room. Her hands covered her face as she ran crunched over and trying to conceal herself from the cameras that she had welcomed into our home. The place was in chaos.

"Dad, is this real?" I asked in disbelief. "She made this up, right? That picture was photoshopped to ruin my birthday, right, Dad?"

He stood there and said nothing, so I searched his face for an answer. When I found it, I burst into tears and ran from the room. The paps tried to chase after me, but the security guard closed and blocked the double doors behind me.

When I entered the hallway I found Mandy standing there with her mother. I quickly assumed that she must have followed my father there.

"Are you out of your mind?" I overheard Mandy's mother yelling as I ran frantically down the hall. I tried to whisk past them but was stopped by Mandy with a grab of my arm.

"You needed to know, Zyaire. You and your mother needed to know."

"Not like this we didn't. You are so evil. You did it like this because you hate me," I scolded.

"It's not about you," Mandy yelled. "It's about your horrible, selfish father, who ruins lives. I found out on my birthday, you know. I took that picture of them together in our home on my birthday," she said wildly, pointing at herself. "I thought it was only fair his daughter found out the same way."

I could see the hurt in Mandy's eyes as the tears dropped down her cheeks, and so my reply was pleasant in comparison to the fury I actually wanted to release on her.

"Fair? Does any of this seem fair?" I asked calmly. I turned and looked at Mandy's mother in disgust before walking off and leaving both her and Mandy standing there in silence.

When I got back to the main house, I found my mother in the living room. The lights were out, and she was sitting in a fetal position on the couch, sobbing. I put my arms around her, and she rested her head on my shoulder. There was so much to say, but we both said nothing. We just lay there and let our tears do all the talking that night.

Chapter 7
Riddle Me This
(ZYAIRE)

It was after 1:00 a.m. when I slowly slipped my mother's sleeping head from off my shoulder. We were suddenly covered by a blanket, which I assumed was the doing of Mary Josie. I took the blanket off and then covered my mother back up before tiptoeing out of the room. I walked the long halls down to the Great Room. The place was completely empty and clean. There was no evidence that a party even took place there or the disaster that ensued at the end of the night.

I was sure Netasha had taken care of getting the guests out and the place cleaned. That was what made her so irreplaceable—her ability to handle a crisis. I walked to the other end of the house and opened the interior door to the garage. My father's car was gone, and in its place was a silver colored BMW with a gigantic red bow tied to the front. I had totally forgotten about the surprise that was waiting for me out front before Mandy interrupted with what she called "a gift" for my birthday. I was sure that this was my mother's surprise.

I was far too depressed to be excited about my new car. I didn't even bother going over to look at it. Instead, I headed up to my room. When I got inside and closed the door, I thought to take off my dress, get into my pajamas, and bury myself under the covers. Instead, I looked and saw my great-grandmother's purse thrown onto the floor by the window seat. I went over and picked it up then sat on the seat and peered out of the window. I quickly stood back up and pulled out a picture of my great-grandmother that my Vovó had given to me. At the window, I stared at the photo of my great-grandmother Lillian. I rubbed my fingers across the worn picture. I had looked at it many times. It was not a professional picture as so many others were; instead, it was slightly out of focus, and off center, but Lillian Varella could not have looked more beautiful.

She smiled brightly from underneath the wide brim of her white hat. Her eyes beamed as if she adored the person on the other side of the lens. When I had asked my Vovó if I could have the photo, she happily agreed, but she did not know where the photo was taken, or who took it.

I reached underneath the window seat and grabbed the box that my great-grandmother's purse was in, and then I carefully pulled my great-grandmother's handwritten letter from its envelope. The room was still dark, so I leaned in toward the window and used the light coming from the full moon to see its contents:

> *My dear Geri, in this box I am leaving you the best part of me. The day I came upon this precious gift, I discovered who I am, and the knowledge that true wealth sometimes lies beyond our imagination. Many things you may have longed to know about me will be answered. It is because of the "Seal of Secrecy" that I am only sharing this with you now, after my death. When the leaves are at their best, and the moon first lights the way, then shall you come, but you cannot stay. I love you, my*

> *dearest. Please tell Aimilios I love him dearly, and not even the grave could break that love.*

"What is the Seal of Secrecy?" I wondered to myself. "And who is Aimilios?" My Vovó told me that my great-grandmother was never serious about anyone again after her husband died tragically in that skiing accident. She obviously was wrong.

I stared at the picture. My great-grandmother didn't appear to be a day over twenty-five or twenty-six in the photo. I looked back down at the letter. *Maybe my great-grandmother was losing her mind toward the end. Maybe this all means nothing, I shamefully thought.*

I stared at the letter again, frustrated. "When the leaves are at their best," I repeated. I glared out into the night and could see the colorful leaves on the trees just outside my bedroom window. Mary Josie's decorative clear lights illuminated the darkness.

"When the leaves are at their best," I said aloud again, thinking deeply. "Autumn, the leaves are at their best in autumn. They are beautiful—they are bright and colorful. That's it," I said, having convinced myself that I had figured out the first part of the letter's riddle. I stared back at the letter to figure out the rest.

"And the moon lights the way," I read, and continued to read over and over again. "And the moon lights the way..." I leaned closer into the window so the light from the full moon would shine down on the letter as I reread the handwritten words. "That's it," I proclaimed again. "A full moon lights the way."

I read the letter's contents again, and again. "I got it!" I finally declared, to no one, as I was still the only one present in the room. "It has to be talking about the first full moon in autumn." I always did love riddles, and was always good at figuring them out, a gift I inherited from my mother.

I sat up straight as my excitement increased, and read the rest of the coded passage. "Then shall you come, but you cannot stay." I paused deep in thought. "Maybe my great-grandmother wanted my mother to go somewhere, but not stay."

Just then, I remembered the same words were inscribed at the bottom of the purse. I once again reached inside it to see if I had missed something. It was completely empty. I held the pocketbook in the air and directly up to the window to get the light from the full moon. "This is silly," I thought and jumped up to turn on the lamp nearby.

Holding the pocketbook in the air, I read its inscription aloud, "When the leaves are at their best, and the moon first lights the way, then shall you come, but you cannot stay."

"Where can I come?" I wondered. "I would rather be anywhere than here right now," I said honestly. Suddenly my hands began to tremble. At first I thought it was my nerves from the stressful night I had just had, but I soon realized that it was not me shaking but the pocketbook. I quickly dropped it to the floor, but it still shook ferociously. A great light, blue in color, burst from its opening. I backed fearfully into a corner as the pocketbook grew in size. I began to hear what sounded like a train racing down its tracks, and ever so slightly, the beating drum as I heard before. I closed my eyes tightly, covered my ears, and sunk down to the floor. "What's happening?" I screamed to no one. I buried my head between my knees. I was afraid to open my eyes again, for fear of what I might see. The raucous went on for a few minutes until I could no longer hear anything but the pounding of my own heart. I lifted my head and slowly opened one eye, and then the other.

On the other side of the room I could see that the pocketbook was no longer shaking, but the great blue light continued to glare from the inside. I stood to my feet and slowly approached it. My good sense commanded me to run, but my curiosity wanted to know what would happen next. I cautiously got closer and closer until I was standing directly over the pocketbook and the great blue light.

I nervously reached down, daring to make another attempt to put my hand inside. As I got closer, the light seemed to brighten, and when I reached the mouth of the pocketbook with my hand, a great gravity pulled at my arm. I tried to resist the force, but the more I pulled back, the stronger the force became. I squealed, squirmed, and leaned backward with the force of all my weight like I was in a match of tug of war. I tried all I could to free myself, but it was all in vain. My arm went down into the pocketbook, and as it went deeper, there seemed to be no bottom. I wiggled my fingers around for any sign of fabric, but all I felt was a cold breeze. The force continued to pull me, and my body went deeper and deeper into it, but still there was no end. It sucked me in past my left shoulder, and then my head began to go in. I screamed out to my mother, "Help! Help!" My voice oddly echoed off the wall and came screaming back at me. Finally, half my body was in the once small but now large opening of the pocket-book. My legs dangled aimlessly in the air. When I finally grew weak from resisting the force's grip, my body went limp, and immediately the rest of me was pulled inside the pocketbook.

Chapter 8
The Capture
(ZYAIRE)

I opened my mouth and tried to scream, but my voice was silent. As I fell endlessly, I became painfully aware that I was suspended somewhere between infinity and nothingness. I reached out desperately hoping to grab something that would cease my falling, but there was nothing there except empty space. The darkness was frightening. I could not tell if my eyes were open or shut. I reached out again, to what should have been the front of my face, but I could not see my own hand before me. I panicked at the thought that I would just continue to fall forever. My body dropped at an accelerated rate. Anxiety was a play date compared to the fear I was now feeling, yet I strangely remembered something my mother always told me: "Zyaire, whatever you do, do it gracefully."

However, there was no grace in my fall. My body jerked violently from side to side, and my hair whimsically swept in the wind. I continued to scream until I became light-headed and a feeling of faint came upon me. I resisted and regained strength when a dim light attempted in the darkness. I was not sure if it was just delirium, but my fall seemed to be more graceful, like I was soaring on the wings of eagles. It was then I became aware that I was actually in control of my flight. I could fly! I soared toward the dim light, and although I was still terrified, the heaviness had lifted away. I felt somehow carefree.

As I flew closer to the light, I could see a large arched opening with what appeared to be daylight peeping through. I angled my body toward it, and for the first time in what seemed like forever the ground came into sight. Despite my inexperience with my newfound gift, I landed effortlessly. As I thumped to the ground firmly on my two feet, I heard something else fall with me. I looked down, and just behind me, there it was, the pocketbook! A heel on my shoe sank into the dirt as I reached down to grab the pocketbook. I pulled off my shoes and held them and the pocketbook in my hands. I walked toward the peering light. It was coming from a large dark wooden door that was slightly cracked. The door stood at least nine feet in height and was about 4 or 5 feet wide. It was much larger than the average door. It looked like something out of the Middle Ages. I was inside what appeared to be a cave or dungeon. Hearing a rustling sound, I quickly turned around to look over my surroundings.

"Hello, is anyone there?" I asked, my voice shaking.

No one answered. I suddenly thought to fly back to where I came from but would soon discover I no longer possessed the ability. I Jumped up and down in the air, but nothing happened. I tried to focus on happy thoughts like those that I had once read about in the *Peter Pan* books when I was a kid, but still nothing.

"Where is pixie dust when someone really needs it?" I mumbled, referring to the magical dust that helped give Peter Pan and his band of misfits flight. No longer feeling carefree, I trembled as a cold breeze swept across my face. I was terrified of what could be on the other side of that door, but I decided to take my chances. I slowly approached the door until I was standing right in front of it. I peeked out from where the light streamed in but could see nothing.

I slowly reached out for the large half-moon-shaped metal handle and gripped the inside of it. I began to pull the door open, slow and steady. It was heavy, and I grunted as I pulled with all my might. When it was ajar, just enough for my slender frame to fit through, I slowly began to squeeze my way out.

Before I could get through the small opening I had made, I heard the same rustling noise as I had earlier, but this time I was not going to stick around to see if someone was there. I quickly stepped one foot forward; it was all I was able to get out before I was grabbed from behind. The hand of someone covered my mouth before I could scream. I was struggling, kicking, and then trying to bite at the hand covering my lips. My heart was fiercely pounding. I felt what was beyond fear and equal to dread. The same feeling of faint that had come on as I was falling in the darkness returned. This time there was no relief. My body grew still before my eyes rolled into the back of my head, and I collapsed into my captor's arms.

Chapter 9

Trust Me

(ZYAIRE)

"Her eyes are opening. Go and get Acaeus," I heard as I sluggishly came to. Still a bit dazed I moaned and tried to open my eyes wide. When I did, all I could see were clear bright lights beaming in from several hanging lanterns above me. I slowly turned my head and saw a blurry vision standing beside me. I blinked my eyes several times until it came into focus.

A man, small in stature and frail in frame stood before me. His face was kind and gentle. He was smiling at me with one side of his lips turned up slightly more than the other was. His lightly shaded mustache looked odd on his boyishly thin face. His thick brown eyebrows hung over his perfectly curled eyelashes. His eyes were brown and weary looking, as if he had not slept the night before. His long, dark, brown, shiny hair was pulled back into a neat ponytail. I skimmed over the rest of him. He was wearing black terry cloth balloon pants that fit tightly at his ankles and up to his knees. His black boots were newly polished, and a bright yellow vest buttoned neatly over a long-sleeve black silk shirt. In the right hand corner of the vest were the letters *NA* inscribed in red. I wondered what that meant.

"Who are you?" I asked in a feeble tone.

"I am Marco, servant to Acaeus, a great and wonderful master," he said, sounding strangely rehearsed as he nervously wrenched his yellow vest with his tiny hands.

"Does your great and wonderful master teach you that it's okay to kidnap people?" I asked.

"We did not kidnap you, we saved you," a voice said from behind me.

Marco quickly bowed in recognition of the voice. I turned my head but could not make out a clear image of the tall male figure standing at the door. The area around him was dim, except for the shadow of lights cast across his face. He looked like a glowing angelic figure, and I wondered if he was God, and I had died and gone to heaven.

"God?" I asked in a still weakened voice.

"You can just call me Acaeus," he said, stepping forward out of the light and into the dim lit room.

"And what can we call you?" he asked.

"I'm Zyaire," I said nervously and attempted to sit up. Acaeus rushed to my side to help me. He grabbed me by the hand. His hands were strong but soft. We met face-to-face as he pulled me to a sitting position. Our gaze locked briefly, and I stared into his olive green eyes. I looked away, breaking our gaze, and then anxiously pushed one of my loosened curls behind my ear. "Where am I?" I asked.

"You are in Aphrodan," Acaeus replied. Suddenly remembering the pocketbook, I became frantic.

"Where is my pocketbook?" I asked.

"We put it somewhere safe where no one could find it," Acaeus assured me.

"I need it back, it's mine, and it's special."

"The pocketbook has been confiscated and locked away. It's up to the king to decide if you will get it back."

"So you people steal and kidnap?" I snapped back.

"You should be thanking me. If it were not for us, you could have been hurt," Acaeus bluntly revealed.

"Well, thank you for grabbing me against my will and taking me to who knows where."

"Did you miss the part where I said we saved your life," Acaeus said, growing frustrated by what he probably viewed as a lack of gratefulness on my part.

"I'm sorry, but I am not feeling very saved right now. I mean, look around. It looks like I am in a prison." I looked around at the white stone walls that surrounded me. Aside from the narrow bed I sat on, and a small wooden chair and desk in the corner, the large room was virtually empty and cold.

"We had to come up with somewhere safe to take you until we could figure out what to do with you," Acaeus said.

"I know what you can do with me. Take me to the nearest airport so I can get a one-way ticket out of here."

"There are no airports here, have you forgotten that you traveled here in a pocketbook?" Acaeus called to mind.

I was surprised he knew how I had gotten here. I buried my head into my hands, "Don't remind me," I murmured.

A knock came at the door, and Marco opened it. "We are ready for her, sir," the woman standing on the outside said.

"Ready for what?" I asked, petrified. "Please, just send me back home," I pleaded. Without thinking I jumped up from the bed to run, but I was so weak I just crumpled to the ground.

Acaeus kneeled down beside me. I hung my head, so not to look at him.

"Look at me please," he said softly.

I lifted my head, but my eyes still looked toward the ground.

"You have nothing to fear from me. Let us start over again," he offered. "I am Acaeus. I am one of the generals here in Aphrodan."

"You look kind of young to be a general," I said, barely gazing up at him.

"The youngest general actually," Acaeus confirmed, "but I am more than able to take care of you, and I won't let anything happen to you. I promise." He stood up and reached out his hand for me to take. "Trust me," he advised, lowering his eyes and once again gazing directly into mine.

ACAEUS

I had just made Zyaire a promise I was not sure that I could keep, but I made it with good intentions on doing just that. I could not help but notice how lovely Zyaire was. Her beautiful bronze skin only accented her hypnotic blue eyes. I spoke to myself inwardly, "Acaeus, don't even think about it. She is off-limits."

Zyaire paused in thought for a moment, and then repeated the conclusion she must have come to in her mind. "I don't think I have a choice but to trust you." She reached out her hand and grabbed mine. I pulled her to her feet, and she stumbled when standing. I hurriedly took her in my arms and wrapped one hand around her waist to support her from falling.

"I got you," I declared. When my arms wrapped around her, I could feel her trustingly leaning against me. She took her arm and swathed it around my lower back. "Okay. I trust you," she affirmed, probably feeling the first sign of safety since Marco and I grabbed her from the cave. I led her out of the cheerless room, and when my expression was free from anyone's eyes, I tenderly smiled down at her.

When I settled Zyaire into her room, she was out of it, and I worried about how weak she was. She had quickly closed her eyes once her head settled on the soft pillows of the bed.

Marco was waiting for me outside the door when I walked out.

"I want you to stand guard outside her room in case she wakes up," I commanded.

"Yes, of course, and what about the king, sir? Should we send someone to let him know what is going on?"

"No, the king is off on his retreat and he will return soon. There is no need to trouble him with this, or anyone else. I will tell him about her when he returns, and I will take care of things until then."

I got closer and looked my faithful friend in the eyes. "Tell no one," I whispered. "It's lucky that it was us who saw the light coming from the cave and discovered her, and no one else," I said.

"I know what you mean, sir. I will tell no one," Marco promised.

I patted Marco on the shoulder. He had been a good friend to me, and I knew I could trust him. I glanced inside the room and looked at Zyaire who was fast asleep. I closed the door and locked it with a key. I sighed heavily and put my hand on Marco's shoulder.

"At least for now she is fast asleep and has no idea how much danger she is actually in."

Chapter 10

Gone Missing

(GERALDINE)

I awoke to a ringing doorbell. I stretched, still lying down, and looked around noticing I had never left the living room. It was morning, and the sun beamed through the sheer white curtains that hung at the window. I squinted my eyes, unwillingly taking in the daylight.

The doorbell rang again. I called out to Mary Josie, "Mary Josie, get the door please," but there was no reply. Zyaire was no longer lying next to me. It was the first time in sixteen years of owning this house that I had ever stayed the night on the couch.

I sat up and felt that oh-so-familiar emptiness one feels after waking from a nightmare. The doorbell rang again, but this time it was accompanied by a loud knock. I thought to lie there until whoever it was went away, but it rang once again. I slid off the couch, and the blanket covering me dropped to the floor. I slowly walked to the front door, and before I could reach there, it rang yet again.

"I am coming," I yelled out, annoyed, and picked up my pace.

When I opened the door, my mother was standing there. I took one look at her sympathetic gaze and painfully realized that there had been no nightmare, that last night had actually happened. We stood staring at each other for a moment, speaking without words. Then I, forgetting all our differences, wrapped my arms around my mother's waist and buried my face into her chest. I wept profusely. My mother hugged me tightly, and slowly walked me into the house, closing the door behind us. We broke our embrace just for a moment, but quickly clung back to each other, taking in the nostalgia from all the years of hugs we had missed. When we finally broke our embrace again, my mother suggested we head into the kitchen for coffee.

A fresh pot of coffee was already waiting, just as it usually was every morning. Mary Josie had obviously brewed it, but she was still nowhere in sight. My mother grabbed two mugs from the cupboard and poured the coffee while I grabbed a bowl of fresh-cut fruit from the refrigerator, which was also the doing of Mary Josie. When we sat at the kitchen table, my mother noticed a note propped against the napkin holder with "Mrs. Ryan" written largely on it. She handed it to me, and I read it aloud.

> *Dear Mrs. Ryan, I am sorry, but I have a family emergency so I have to leave right away. I did not want to wake you. Sorry for any inconvenience this might cause you."*

It was signed "Mary Josie." The truth probably was there was no emergency. Mary Josie was there last night when the scene with my husband had unfolded. I am sure it was heartbreaking for her to watch. Mary Josie never did well around people who were in pain. She always seemed to say the wrong thing, or her awkward silence was uncomfortable for everyone around. Therefore, I was sure there was no emergency, but she had just decided to take a day off to let things settle, and start fresh tomorrow. I was okay with that. She had no place in family affairs. Although I knew how much she loved Zyaire.

"Well, I guess that means no second pot of coffee, huh?" my mother said lightheartedly. We both shared a smile and light giggle, and then she placed her hand on top of mine.

"I am so sorry, Geri. Sorry for you and Zyaire." She paused and looked around. "Where is she by the way?" she asked.

I took a sip of coffee before answering. With each word I spoke, I had to brace myself to keep from crying. "The last time I saw her was when she found me in the living room. We hugged and..." I distressingly paused. "We hugged and cried together," I had continued, a single tear now falling down my cheek. "I guess I've known for quite some time that there was someone else," I admitted. "But I guess I did not want to accept it. Sure, I accused him many times, but I never went looking for evidence of my claims. I only had assumptions, and assuming is no match to the pain of knowing."

My mother pulled her chair close to me. She did not care about anything that had distanced us from the past. All she cared about in that moment was her daughter's pain. I was sure she wished she could somehow take it away, but only time could heal this wound.

I laid my head on my mother's shoulder, just as I used to do as a child. Diane Mitchell, my mother, stroked my honey nut-brown hair, forgetting the heartbreak I had caused her over the last sixteen years.

"What am I going to do, Mom?" I asked, choking back tears.

"I'll tell you what you're going to do," she said, and turned and faced me. "You are going to cry, and cry until you feel like you can't, or shouldn't cry anymore, and then you're going to cry again. I will be here to wipe your tears. Then eventually those tears will fade away, and you will become furiously mad, and I will still be here, and you can take your anger out on me if you like. That anger, too, will one day fade away, and you surely will be depressed. On those days, I will be here to remind you to get out of bed in the mornings, take a shower, brush your teeth, comb your hair, put on makeup, and dress your best. I will emphasize how smart, and beautiful you are, and what a foolish jerk John is to have taken you for granted. The depression will eventually turn to acceptance, and acceptance will eventually turn to better minutes, those better minutes will eventually turn to better hours, those better hours will turn into better days, those better days will turn into better weeks, the better weeks will turn into better months, and better months into better years. I know right now you are feeling like, how can I live without him? But I promise you, amidst all of that, one night you will lay your head down to fall asleep and realize you have gone a whole day without thinking about him at all."

My mother smiled and affectionately patted my cheeks. "And if after all that you find that there is a way you two can still find your way back to each other, I will support that too."

I smiled back at her and then laid my head on her shoulders. I wondered how I had gone all these years without my remarkable mother constantly at my side.

The morning drifted away. My mother had brought over old comedy movies and popcorn. She and I snuggled up on the couch in the family room and watched them together. The last one we watched actually had a few scenes with Lillian Varella in it. My grandmother, Lillian was a wonderful actress, and I'd wondered as I watched her on the screen why she had not taken it more seriously.

"You're right," I said to my mother, "Zyaire does look just like Vovó."

I called my grandmother the same pet name that Zyaire now calls hers. It was Lillian's idea for me to call her "Vovó," never being able to come to grips with being called Grandma. "It is a Cape Verdean tradition to call your grandmother Vovó," she had said to me when I was probably only five or six years old. This was true, and the other truth was she did not look much like a grandma even in her much later years.

As the credits rolled, I looked down at my watch to see the time.

"I can't believe it is already twelve o'clock and Zyaire has not made an appearance," I mentioned.

"Maybe she stayed up late and is sleeping in," my mother replied.

"Probably, but I will be right back. I am going to go and check on her."

I left my mother in the family room and trotted down the hall to the steps leading upstairs. I got to Zyaire's door; it was closed. I knocked softly at first, and then more loudly. There was no answer, so I let myself in. When I opened the door, I looked around the room and noticed the bed was still made. Zyaire had obviously not even slept in it.

"Zyaire," I called out, stepping over the tall lamp that was knocked over when I reached the other side of the room. "That's odd," I said to myself. I walked toward Zyaire's bathroom. The door was slightly cracked and the light was on. I knocked once and gently pushed the door ajar.

"Zyaire," I called out again, but there was still no reply. I ran out of the room and trampled down the stairs in a panic. I went straight to the interior garage door and swung it open. Zyaire's car was still in place.

My anxiety increased as I looked around the house and found no sign of Zyaire. I thought about the time when she was little and tried to run away because of the arguments her father and I were having.

"Mother," I called out desperately, my legs becoming increasingly weak with each step toward the family room. "Mom!" I yelled out again. Feeling lightheaded, I braced myself with a hand on the hallway's wall. "Mom," I yelled out one last time before she finally ran into the hall after hearing my desperate voice.

"Geri, what's wrong?" she asked, looking at her obviously terror-stricken daughter.

The walls were spinning, and the chaos of the party began to play in my mind. I just kept seeing the picture of my best friend with my husband, flashing into my head repeatedly; then as if I was there again, I saw myself staring up at Zyaire, and I could see the devastation on her face.

"Geri, tell me what is wrong," my mom asked again.

The pressure of it all had made me speechless in that moment, but I managed to mutter two words before fainting to the floor: "Zyaire's gone."

Chapter 11

A Diary Revealed

(ZYAIRE)

I awoke suddenly in a state of confusion. I pulled the covers off of me, and sat up in the strange bed I was lying in. I had no idea how I got there, or where I was. A mental image of myself being grabbed from behind flashed into my mind. As the memories of the events that had transpired flooded my thoughts, I broke out into a sweat. Nothing felt real: the pocketbook, being sucked inside, falling endlessly in the darkness, being taken hostage. I began to touch my arms and face to make sure I was still alive. I felt real, and my skin felt warm. I blew out a gust of air into my hand and gripped my wrist to feel for my pulse. My heart was still beating, so I took that as concrete proof that I was still in the land of the living. I peered over at the window and could see that the sun was now shining. I remembered it was dark when my eyes were last open and wondered now how long I had been asleep. I looked around the room. It was lit by gold-colored lanterns hanging decoratively in all four corners. The room was elegant, and inviting, fit for a queen. I scooted over and sat up at the edge of the bed.

First, standing up slowly, I began to walk around the room. I had gained some of my strength back and could walk on my own now. I took in the beauty of my surroundings. The walls were dressed with what looked like thin, delicate shreds of gold. I rubbed my hand across them and could feel its ripples like raised Braille beneath my fingers. I thought to myself, "If the walls did have words, it would say something beautiful." I continued to stroll across the large room until I was standing in front of a blazing fireplace. It was made of a gold-toned marble. It was also beautiful like the rest of the room, but what was most striking were the figures of a male and a female carved on each side of that fireplace. The female statue was sculpted wearing a long dress, and the male, only a drape around his waist. They both gazed toward each other intensely, lovingly, adoringly.

When I walked to the window and looked outside, the view was of a garden filled with colorful lilies. Seeing them made me think of the lilies that sat in the vases at my party. Pain crept through me as a flash of the image of my father and Mandy's mother in an intimate embrace shot through my head. Just like that night, I wanted to run from the room that now seemed to close in around me. I hurried to the closed door and turned its knob, only to find it was locked from the outside.

"Let me out!" I screamed repeatedly, but no one answered.

I headed back to the king-size bed and sat on the edge. The mattress sat high off the ground, so my feet dangled. I looked down and noticed my shoes that I wore at my party lying on the floor. I also realized I was still wearing the dress my mother had picked out for me.

Across the room, I saw a brush sitting on a vanity. When I walked over to it, I found something else sitting there too. It was a cordless CD player. I pressed the Play button and was surprised to find it actually worked. A beautiful instrumental began to fill the room, and I was stunned when I realized that I knew its melody. It was one of my mother's favorites, a famous piece, by Mozart. I decided to keep the music playing. It gave me a comforting feeling of home.

I headed back toward the bed, but not before combing my hair. It was a mess when I looked at myself in the mirror. I could hear my mom's voice telling me, "Zyaire, despite what anyone says, people do and should judge you based on your appearance, so always look nice." I guess that was my mother's way of teaching me good grooming habits. My hair no longer had any trace of the beautiful spiral curls that were present at my party, but its natural waves were still there. My makeup was almost nonexistent, except for the remnants of smeared mascara just underneath my lashes. Before I could sit down onto the bed, a faint knock was at the door. I dashed to it.

"Hello, who's there?" I called out.

"It's Acaeus. Is it okay if I come in?"

I tried to remember if that was the name of the person I met in the prison. "Are you the one who helped me before?" I asked.

"Yes, I am," Acaeus declared.

"Then come in, if you have the key," I said, backing slightly away from the door. I heard Acaeus fumble with the keys on the outside before he finally turned the knob and opened it. I was standing there when he did.

"Good, you're awake," he said, smiling. "I brought you something to change into. Can I come in?" he asked, still smiling.

I melted looking at deep green eyes and his beautiful smile. I stepped to the side and held my hand out as to say, "come right in." Acaeus stepped past the threshold and I closed the door behind him. I wanted to talk to him privately.

"How long have I been asleep?" I asked.

"Almost two days," he replied.

"Two days?" I asked, astonished.

"Yes, I was worried about you for a moment, but the doctor checked on you yesterday and said by all accounts you were fine. You did stir when interrupted, and babbled every now and then, which were all good signs."

I stared at Acaeus, confused by it all.

"I hope you like your accommodations," he said politely.

"You mean my new prison right?" I asked brashly.

"I thought you would like this room. It is the most beautiful in the castle, even more beautiful than the king's."

"Wow, does his come with a locked door too?"

"We had to lock the door. We could not risk you waking up and just walking out. I am trying to protect you." There was a hint of desperation in Acaeus's voice. It didn't go unnoticed by me.

"Protect me from what?" I asked with more than a hint of desperation in mine. "Tell me, am I in danger?"

Acaeus answered carefully, "In danger of getting lost in a place you know nothing about." Then he smiled to lighten the mood, and I felt those butterflies in my stomach once again, the same ones I had felt when he put his arms around me back at the prison.

I unknowingly stared at Acaeus for a moment. His tanned skin and perfectly chiseled features could only be described as godlike. His young bare face was perfectly symmetrical. Each part made to complement the other. He had an attractive nose situated perfectly above his pleasantly plumped lips, his skin looked smooth and radiant, his shining hair was dark brown, and his eyes large and almond shaped.

I finally realized I was staring and broke my gaze. "So, what did you bring me to change into?" I asked.

Acaeus handed me a clothing bag. "I hope it fits. One of the women of the castle went to the clothing store and bought it while you were asleep. They bought you a few more things too. It's in that bag."

"Clothing store?" I said, puzzled once again. "This place has stores?"

"Yes, and we have food too. You must be hungry," Acaeus pointed out.

"I am sorry, but in some ways it seems ancient here, and in other ways I see things that I would see back at home. It just seems odd."

"Aphrodan isn't anything if not odd," Acaeus said.

"That's right, Aphrodan, that's the name of this place," I remembered.

"So are you?" Acaeus asked.

"Am I what?" I replied.

"Are you hungry?"

"I am starving actually," I admitted.

"Okay, well, change into this and you can join me for a late lunch in an hour, unless you'd rather eat here in your room?" Acaeus asked.

I was definitely not looking forward to being trapped in one place for any while longer, so I delightfully accepted his request to join him.

"There is a washroom through that door," Acaeus said, pointing to a door just off from where the vanity sat.

"So I don't have to wash outside in a bucket?" I teased.

Acaeus laughed. "Not unless you want to."

He went to walk out the door, and I called out to him, "Acaeus." He turned and faced me. "When can I go home?" I asked.

"I don't know," he replied honestly.

"Did you mean it when you said you are trying to protect me?"

He nodded his head. "Yes," was all he said, yet that was enough to assure me. I wasn't sure why, but I knew I could believe in him. "So can I leave this door unlocked and trust that you will not leave here until I come back and get you?" he asked.

I paused for a moment and then grinned, "No, you better go ahead and lock it." We both laughed, and then Acaeus walked out and closed the door behind him, leaving it unlocked.

I opened the garment bag he left behind for me. I was surprised to see a very modern-looking dress inside it. I opened the bag that hung from it and found undergarments, and a pair of sandals to match the dress, along with some other clothing, a toothbrush, floss, and toothpaste. I hopped onto the bed, pulled off my diamond earrings, and put them on the nightstand next to it. Then I reached around my neck and took off my necklace. I held it in my hand for a moment and thought about my best friend, Teresa, who had given it to me. I wondered if I would ever see her again. That thought caused my eyes to tear up. I gently placed the necklace on the nightstand next to the diamond earrings; then I jumped off the bed and plopped to the floor, sending one of the earrings rolling beneath it.

I got down on my hands and knees and fully extended my arm beneath the bed to feel around for it, but could not find it. I went deeper, now squeezing my head in addition to my arm under it. I looked around, it was dim, but I finally saw the diamond sparkling next to a single white box that was under the bed. I grabbed the earring, and the box, and carefully slid my head from underneath the box spring mattress. I sat down on the floor and crossed my legs Indian style before opening the box. When I did, inside was a book. I pulled it out and tossed the box to the side. The book cover was shining gold, and the spine was brown leather with raised bands, gold in color, evenly streaked up and down it. I opened it, and once again found myself in an unbelievable moment. The inscription inside the book read *Pocketbook Diaries* by Lillian Grace Varella. My hand sprung to my mouth as I let out a loud gasp.

"Oh my god," I whispered. Unable to contain my excitement, I quickly turned to the first page, and there was a date entered at the top. I read it aloud, "September 22, 1952."

I stood up on my feet, book in hand, and paced in a circle. "This can't be for real," I said. I couldn't believe I was actually reading something written by my great-grandmother. "She must have been here," I thought. I hopped up on the bed to read more. I read its contents carefully, taking in every word and punctuation.

> *It's no wonder this phenomenal world would lie inside a pocketbook. The mystery of a lady's pocketbook and its contents has always been one of intrigue. Indeed, this brings new meaning to sayings like, "You can find anything in a woman's purse."*

I looked up at the door to make sure no one was watching me. There was no one there, so I read on:

> *It is my second year coming to Aphrodan. However, the first time I wasn't aware of it. I now realize the first time I was brought here was the night of my sixteenth birthday party. I had snuck off from all the cameras with a bottle of wine in hand. My mother had just embarrassed me, as she so often did. I was devastated, so I went off into the loft of our house and I drank that whole bottle by myself. I had never had more than a few sips of champagne before then, so I was drunk out my mind. I sat in my room, crying and holding the pocketbook that my dear friend had given me earlier, when I heard a knock at the door. It was her, Z, or at least that was all she would ever tell me her name was. That night is still foggy to me, and I had first attributed some of my memories or lack thereof to the alcohol or a possible drunk girl's dream. I now realize there was no dream, but Z had taken me here and we sat on a high peak and looked down toward a land more beautiful than I had ever seen.*

Now here I was five years later for the third time. He was surprised to see that I actually returned. Given my experience the first time I coherently happened upon this phenomenal yet complicated world, I am just as surprised that I returned too. I guess my love for him outweighs my fear. This entry was far more inviting than the last time, to say the least. When I arrived, his guards were waiting for me. They took me directly to him. When he saw me, he took me in his arms, and kissed me tenderly, and deeply. Our connection was still there, as if I never left, and as if I would not have to leave again. However, I would have to leave again. The first year I came here, my absence from home went unnoticed to even me, and the second time was not much different. Everyone thought I was on a sabbatical or a much-needed break from all the cameras, and my life as a celebrity. However, I never made it to my destination. I was sucked into this world before I could ever leave. This time, being gone for so long will not be easily accepted. I am sure rumors are flying of a nervous breakdown, or that I am off in some rehabilitation clinic. If I could have left without telling a soul, I would have, but now the location of my whereabouts is questioned constantly, not just by the media, but also by my responsibilities. Still, I had to come here again, no matter what other people's opinions might be of me being away for so long. I had to see him. The waiting was not easy. I dreamt of his face every night. I am quickly learning there is nothing more agonizing than wants. Wanting to see him, wanting to hear his voice, wanting to kiss his lips, wanting to touch him, and for him to touch me."

I blushed at the words written in the diary, but continued reading.

It is this same want that I wish to spare him of—this same want, which forces me to keep some things close to only my heart, and in the pages of this diary.

The end of the page was signed just as the letter I had found addressed to my mother, "*Lilly.*"

I quickly skimmed through the thick book, and almost every page had an entry. I wanted to read on but knew I had to get dressed before Acaeus returned. I put the diary in the box and slipped it back underneath the bed. "Later," I whispered, then grabbed my clothes, and headed into the bathroom.

Before I could get to the door of the washroom, I heard a drumming sound, the same sound I had heard coming from the pocketbook when I was still in Plymouth, but this time it was coming from the area near my room's window.

I opened the window and peeked my head out, and there stood a man to the far west in what seemed to be a band uniform, yellow and white in color, strumming a single drum hoisted over his shoulder. The sound started slow, and then it sped up and became louder, as it was when I was in the hall on my way to class. Thinking back, I realized it was as if the sound coming from the pocketbook was compelling me to figure out the meaning of the riddle, and to end up where I was right now, in the place where my great-grandmother had once been. It all seemed predestined now. I shuddered to think what would happen next.

Chapter 12

Déjà Vu

(ZYAIRE)

When I was finished getting dressed, I sat up in the bed with my bare feet propped. I could not believe what I just read in my great-grandmother's diary, or that I even found her diary at all. I could barely contain myself.

I wanted to read more, but I didn't pull it out again for fear of Acaeus walking in and finding me reading it. I wondered if anyone else even knew about it beside me. I wondered if my great-grandmother had been in this room, or maybe even slept on the same bed that I was lying on now. My mind was racing with questions. I got goose bumps at the thought of it all, and gently rubbed my hands up and down my arms. I thought back to the words of the letter my great-grandmother Lillian had left for my mother. I had read the letter so many times that now I easily replayed its words in my mind.

> *Many things you may have longed to know about me will be answered. It is because of the "Seal of Secrecy" that I am only sharing this with you now, after my death.*

I wondered what secrets could be in that diary. My curiosity began to get the best of me, and I jumped down from the bed to sneak another peek at that diary; but just as I was leaning down to reach for it, there was a knock at the door. I quickly jumped up and sat back on the bed.

"Come in," I yelled.

Acaeus walked in. "Good, you're still here," he observed, smiling.

"Yes, but it is probably because I did not know the door was unlocked." Acaeus searched my face to see if I was joking, and I was.

I was grateful to have him there with me. His kindness was keeping me sane. I felt confident that I could trust him, but I would not tell him about the diary, at least not before I have the opportunity to read every page of it.

"You look very pretty," Acaeus said, making me blush.

"Thank you. They made a good choice."

The dress they picked out for me was simple but nice. It was a two-layer wrapped dress that was cream and brown in color. It had a halter neckline and an elastic waistband with a side enclosure.

I stood up at the edge of the bed and slipped on the flat brown sandals. When I leaned over to fasten the straps around my ankle, I could feel Acaeus looking down at me, so I looked up at him and smirked.

"You look nice too," I muttered shyly.

"Thank you, but I can't take the credit. I didn't pick these clothes out myself, my mother did," he said.

"Oh no, do you have a controlling mother too?" I laughed and started working on the left foot's strap.

"No, not controlling according to her. She calls it dedication to my image." We both chuckled in amusement.

"Well, don't ever let her meet my mother," I pleaded. We both fell silent for a moment as I stood up, knowing all too well that would be an easy request to fill.

"Actually, I usually dress myself, but today's a special day, so she bought me something new for the occasion," Acaeus stated for the record.

"You don't mean me, do you?" I asked.

"No, little Ms. Vanity. I mean me, it's my birthday today."

"No way, my birthday was last week, I think. Wait, what is today's date?" I asked.

"It's September 29th, 2009."

"Then, yes, my birthday was last week, September 22nd." I held my head. "Oh, I'm so confused."

"Don't worry about it. You will get your bearings soon," Acaeus assured me.

"How old are you?"

"I'm eighteen, how about you?"

"I'm sixteen, and I can't wait until I'm eighteen so I can be out on my own. That's if I ever make it home," I said somberly.

I walked away and took one more look into the mirror. Acaeus walked up behind me and placed his hands on my shoulders. "You will get home. I promise," he said, again making me a promise that I only hoped he could keep.

"And don't be in such a rush to get older. I'm not," he declared. "I am enjoying my youth. There is an excitement in being young."

He held out his hand to me. I looked at him with curiosity.

"Are you ready?" he asked.

"Ready for what?"

"For some excitement!" he beamed.

I put my hand inside his, once again having to trust him; then he let go of my hand and instead draped my arm around his. We walked out of the room together. As we passed through the door, a feeling of déjà vu swept over me. It was as if I had been here before.

Chapter 13

Where, Oh Where Has Our Little Girl Gone

(GERALDINE)

The police took a statement from John in the living room while everyone else sat at the kitchen table. He had rushed to the house from the hotel he was staying in after he got a call from my mother telling him that our daughter was missing, and I was inconsolable. My mother was trying to hold things together here, but she was devastated as well. Her granddaughter had not been seen since last night. The evening was soon to fall, and I was having all kinds of scary thoughts of Zyaire out on the streets at night alone. Teresa and her mother had arrived a few hours ago. My mother contacted them as well, hoping Zyaire had gone there, but no such luck. The last time Teresa saw her was when she'd ran from her party in tears over her father's betrayal. We held out for as long as we could but no one had seen Zyaire, so we finally called the police.

Detective Chavez showed up at our door within minutes after our call along with two other officers. It did not take him long to sense the tension in the room. He sat down to speak with both myself and John at first and asked us all sorts of questions like, "Was there anywhere else Zyaire could have gone, perhaps a place she used to hang out at as a child, or were there any other friends or relatives that we might have missed?"

John and I both answered those questions with ease. It was the question that followed that sent us, or should I say me, into a frenzy.

Detective Chavez asked us directly, "Is there anything that happened that would have caused her to run away?"

The room suddenly became very quiet when that question was posed. Finally, like a madwoman, I leapt from my seat in fury and hollered out, "ask my husband," before stomping out of the room in tears. Chavez asked the other two officers to leave the room so he could talk to John alone. He sent them to go speak to Teresa and to make sure she really did not know the whereabouts of Zyaire.

Once Detective Chavez and John were alone, he got right back to the point, and I listened from the room next door.

"So tell me, what happened here with your daughter, Mr. Ryan?" He asked.

John remained silent, and Chavez could probably see that whatever it was, he was embarrassed to talk about it, so he dug deeper.

"Listen, I am not here to judge you, Mr. Ryan. I am here to help you find your daughter. I need you to answer all my questions, even the tough ones. It is what it will take to bring your daughter home safely. So please tell me, what happened?"

John grunted and then cleared his throat before speaking. "My daughter and my wife found out last night that I have been unfaithful," he finally admitted. He coughed, but not out of need. It was a nervous cough. That was something he had always done from the time I first met him whenever he was forced to talk about something that made him uncomfortable. He was silent again after that, so I got up and peeked my head around the corner and peered into the room.

He was sitting in the chair across from the detective rocking back and forth. He looked pathetic and sad, and I almost felt sorry for him. Almost. "My daughter was very upset, and I am sure that is the reason she is not home where she belongs right now," he finally continued. John's voice cracked as he spoke, suddenly realizing the possible devastation of his actions. "If anything happens to her, it's my fault," he wailed. "I am a horrible husband, and an even worse father, and now she is gone, and could be..." His voice became hushed and desperate. "Oh God, please don't let anything happen to her," he finally said before burying his face into his hands. Tears began to stream down my face as I looked on.

Detective Chavez got up and sat in the chair next to him. He patted John's back with his hand. "Don't worry, Mr. Ryan, we are going to find your daughter. We have no reason to believe she is in danger. It sounds like she ran away and just does not want to be found yet."

With that, I walked off into the other room. The two officers were questioning Teresa. They asked her if it was okay if they looked at her text messages to Zyaire. Her mother answered for her.

"Of course you can, give them the phone, Teresa," she demanded.

The officer looked at the text messages between Teresa and Zyaire. I had done the same earlier, and the last one came from Teresa at 3:00 a.m. She was telling Zyaire how sorry she was for what happened at her party and that she could call her if she wanted to talk. There was no response from Zyaire. The detectives probed Teresa more, but she swore she had no idea where Zyaire could have gone, and they believed her. Teresa was in tears when they finished talking to her. One of the officers had pointed out to her that, sometimes, bad things happen to kids who run away, and that if she knew where Zyaire was she could possibly save her life by telling them. It was harsh, but they were making every effort to make sure Teresa was not hiding anything from them.

I walked all the way into the room as Teresa hugged her mom and sobbed. "What if something bad has happened to her, Mom?" she said.

"Teresa, nothing bad has happened to Zyaire. They will find her soon, I promise," her mother said.

I looked on, cynically thinking to myself how irresponsible it was for people to make promises during a crisis that they had no idea if they could keep.

They say a mother knows when something bad has happened to their child, like they develop some sort of sixth sense. Nevertheless, I felt nothing of the sort. No assurance that she was safe and no dreadful feeling that she was in harm. I just felt lost and engulfed by my pain and fear of the unknown. Maybe this was because I had spent the last few years obsessing about my daughter's image, instead of finding a way to connect to her and embrace our differences. Maybe there was no sixth sense now that she was missing because I had no sixth sense concerning her when she was here. Truth be told, she was an enigma to me.

Detective Chavez entered the room with John, and the other officers briefed him on their conversation with Teresa. He told John and me that they were going to have some popular runaway areas checked out, but they could not treat this investigation like a missing person case because there seems to be no foul play.

"This seems to be a runaway case, folks," he said bluntly.

"So what you are saying is that you are not going to look for my granddaughter, right?" my mother asked.

"No, we are going to look for your granddaughter, but we can't deploy the same type of teams we would if it were, say, a kidnapping. However, I will have some officers look around popular areas. We will report it as a runaway case, and we will put a description out of her in case someone sees her."

John and I remained silent. I assumed, like me, he was emotionally drained, and still in shock from all that had happened over the last eighteen hours. I finally stood up and shook Chavez's hand.

"Thank you, Officer. Please let us know if you hear anything."

My mother walked the officers to the door. Teresa and her mother left out with them. They decided it was best they be at home in case Zyaire did make her way there. Teresa promised, me before leaving, that if Zyaire contacted her she would notify us immediately. As the officers, Teresa, and her mother pulled off, my father pulled up. My mother had tried to get him on the phone earlier but could not. He was spending the day with his mother in the nursing home. She had turned ninety-seven years old today. He must have heard my mother's frantic message on his phone when he left and came right over without calling.

I stood at the doorway as Maurice Mitchell jumped out of his car and rushed to his wife's side, who was standing out front. "What is going on, did they find her?" he asked my mother frantically.

She looked at him, and he saw the brokenness in her eyes and immediately knew the answer. He hugged her tightly, and she, not knowing I was looking on, let out the sobs that she had been holding back all afternoon.

"It's okay, honey. We will find her," my father assured her.

He held her there for a while, and I found myself envious of the love that was between them. John and I once had that kind of love, but it had been years now since we had shared that kind of connection. My father, on the other hand, would hold my mother for as long as she needed to be held. He was Diane's rock, and the only man she could ever truly depend on since she grew up without a father. They had been together since high school, and he knew everything about her. She did not have to be strong around him. She could fall apart, and he would pick up the pieces. They were soul mates who had started out as friends many years ago. The way they fell in love was simple but beautiful. They stood outside one day talking alone for the first time. They usually hung with a group of friends, but on this particular day, everyone had gone off in their own separate directions, leaving just the two of them standing in the school's parking lot.

It was a gorgeous day, the sun was shining, and a young Maurice, who was much taller than Diane, was staring down at her as they spoke. They discovered from their conversation that they both had a love for music and writing poetry. My father dared my mother to recite one of her poems, and she complied after he agreed to recite one of his first. After he was through clumsily spurting off the words of his latest poem, my mother gracefully spoke the words of a piece she had written called "Forbidden Love." My father once said he was entranced by the dulcet tone of her voice as the words danced off her lips like musical notes. When she was finished, there was a brief moment where both their eyes met and locked. Neither of them said anything of the explosive feeling they felt at that time, but they became inseparable, finding any excuse to run into each other in the halls, and plotting opportunity after opportunity to be alone. Later they admitted to each other that it was in that moment that they had first spent alone when they had fallen in love with each other. It was just that quick and simple, yet perfect.

I continued to eavesdrop on them from the doorway. My mother filled my father in on everything that happened so far: the police showing up, Teresa and her mom coming by, the police saying it was a runaway case, and finally my reaction to finding out Zyaire was missing. They both spoke of how they grieved for me.

"To find out your husband is a cheating scumbag, your best friend is a deceptive witch, and your daughter has run away all in twenty-four hours is more than any one person deserves," my mother said unapologetically.

My father smiled as he looked down at her. "Calm down, tiger," he said.

He knew how feisty she could be and how protective she was over her family. Her belief that I had betrayed her mother by not naming Zyaire after her as I had promised was the reason she and I had been at odds for so many years. That all seemed silly now, and I could tell, like myself, my mother was having deep regrets over the time she missed with me.

"I am not going to let what happened in the past keep me from comforting my daughter now, Mauri," my mother said, calling my father by the pet name she has used for years.

"Good." My father smiled. He always hated the tension that had grown between my mother and me. He often felt he was being put in the middle of our longtime feud. I was realizing now how unfair that had been.

"Let's head back inside," my mother suggested.

"Wait," my father said and pulled a handkerchief out from his pocket. He wiped my mother's face with it. "One more hug before we go in?" he asked. My mother buried her face into his chest as he tightly held on to her.

I quickly went back inside, and ducked off into the kitchen, where I found John sitting alone. By the time my mother and father had made it back there to join us, they came face-to-face with a verbal explosion. "You're right, this is all your fault, you are a worthless cheating prick!" I wailed at the top of my lungs.

"I did not sleep with her, if that is what you think!" John declared.

I laughed heartily. "You must take me for a complete and utter fool, and now our daughter is missing because of you. She could be hurt, or worse!" Tears filled my eyes. "I may never be able to tell her how much I love her because of you." I kept thinking about how hard I had been on Zyaire over the past year. I wanted her to be a sophisticated and proper young lady, but now all I wanted was for her just to be here.

"Don't blame this all on me," John shot back. "Lately, you don't even treat her like a daughter, you treat her like she is one of your little pet projects, like she needs fixing or something!" he yelled.

"How dare you!" I screamed and lunged toward him. My father quickly grabbed me before I could reach John, and it was a good thing he did. I wanted to strangle him.

"Stop it!" my mother yelled to the both of us. She turned to John. "John, my daughter is right, you are a worthless cheating scumbag, and when this is all over, I am going to tell you how I really feel about you, but right now my granddaughter's missing, and that has to be our number one focus. We have to find her." My mother's voice cracked with her last words, and my father put his hand on her shoulder.

The doorbell rang, and we all rushed to the foyer. I made it there first and swung the door open without even asking who it was. There was a petite woman in a gray suit and glasses standing there, and not Zyaire as we all hoped.

"Can I help you?" I asked. The woman standing there looked familiar, but I could not remember why.

"Yes, I am here to ask you a few questions," she said.

She looked back and spotted John standing behind me. "Oh, Mr. Ryan, you are here too, I have some questions for you as well."

"Who are you?" I asked.

"Did the police send you? Do they have any idea where Zyaire is?" my mom chimed in desperately.

"Yes, I am here on behalf of Plymouth police department," she said with a raised brow. "I am Detective Lindsay Grey." She held out her hand and I shook it.

"Well, come in, please," my mom said, stepping out of the way and shoving all of us backward in the process. We all headed to the living room and sat down.

Detective Grey pulled out a tape recorder from her purse. "You don't mind if I record this, do you? I want to make sure we do not miss anything that may help us find your daughter." Everyone agreed it was fine that she recorded our conversation. We wanted to do anything that would help find Zyaire.

Grey started in immediately with the questions. "So, Mr. Ryan, I understand you have been unfaithful to your wife, have you guys worked things out?"

John was visibly uncomfortable with the question, but he answered anyway. "No, but we are both dedicated to helping find Zyaire," he said. The questions continued and they did not get any less uncomfortable.

"Mrs. Ryan, was Zyaire very upset about your husband's cheating?" the detective probed.

"Yes, she was very upset when I last saw her. We both lay right on that couch and cried last night," I explained. "We hugged until we fell asleep together. When I woke up, she was gone. I figured she was upstairs sleeping, but I guess she wasn't." I choked up a little while talking, so I grabbed a tissue from the box on the coffee table and wiped my eyes.

My mother stood up. "I am going to get some water for everyone," she announced. "I will be right back." She left the room, and I excused myself to follow her. We both headed toward the kitchen.

"Detective Grey looks familiar, doesn't she?" she asked once we crossed the kitchen's threshold.

"I thought so too when I first saw her. She must be one of those people with a familiar face," I suggested.

"Hm," was all that my mother said before reaching under the countertop to grab a serving tray, and began to place bottles of water on it. She was quiet as she attentively placed each bottle onto the tray one by one.

I looked on, examining my mother's face, wondering what she was thinking. "Oh my god," she hissed suddenly and startled me in the process. She took off, leaving the tray behind, and dashed down the hall back toward the living room. I ran behind her in a panic, wondering what had just gone on in her mind.

"Get out of my daughter's house right now!" she yelled when she entered the doorway of the living room.

"Mom, what are you doing?" I asked furiously.

"You don't recognize her?" she asked.

I eyed Detective Grey intensely. It was not long before the lightbulb finally turned on. "Oh my gosh, get out of my house!" I demanded.

"Mrs. Ryan, I only want to ask you a few more questions. Don't you want to get your story out there? This could help you find Zyaire. How long has she been missing?" Detective Grey spoke quickly, trying to get out every word.

"Get out of this house right now, or I will call the police," my mother threatened. John and my father looked on confused. Detective Grey stood up, and my mother and I led her to the exit. "Would you like to give a statement, ma'am?" Detective Grey asked my mother before she slammed the door in her face.

"The nerve," my mother said, looking at me with both her hands placed defensively on her hips. We both walked back into the living room where a very confused John and my father were waiting.

"Oh!" my mother said, realizing they were in the dark about what just happened. "I guess you guys are wondering what that was all about?" she asked.

"Yes, please tell us," my father insisted.

"That was no Detective Grey," I said.

"She was Lindy Marks from *The Informant*, the celebrity gossip magazine," my mother emphasized.

"She is their top online writer. I thought she looked familiar when she walked in, but I did not figure out who she was until Mom asked me for the second time if I recognize her."

"Oh my gosh," John said, rubbing his temples. "We just told her that Zyaire is missing," John recalled.

"And why she is missing," I added.

"Yes, and I am sure it will be on the Internet by this evening," my mother reckoned.

Right then and there we all decided that what gets out to the public was not important right now. The important thing was finding Zyaire. John called the security gate, and they explained that Lindy Marks had claimed to be family, and that is why they let her in. John instructed them not to let anyone else in without their permission, unless it was Zyaire. We all sat at the kitchen table and discussed plans to help find my daughter. As much as we all wanted to get around it, I knew it was time that we all faced the inevitable.

"We may have to involve the media," I finally declared.

Chapter 14

He Gives Me Butterflies

(ZYAIRE)

When I walked out of my new beautiful prison, as I called it, I was taken aback. The halls were brightly lit by elaborate chandeliers that hung from the artistic ceilings. I was surprised to see electricity. My room was lit by only lanterns.

I anxiously squeezed Acaeus's arm.

"Are you nervous?" he asked.

"A little," I replied, clenching his arm even tighter.

I thought to myself, if I had to be kidnapped by anyone, I was sure glad it was Acaeus. As we strolled down the hall, he pointed out certain things of importance to the castle. It was as if we were in a museum and he was my personal tour guide. There were beautiful paintings up and down the halls, and sculptures adorning almost every doorway. I took notice of several pictures depicting the same beautiful woman, so I asked Acaeus whom she was. "She is the founder of this world," is all he said, and we continued down the hall. We reached a narrow hallway, and Acaeus led me down it.

A few yards and a quick turn to the left led us into a large kitchen where a woman was busy preparing a meal. She bowed when

Acaeus entered the room. "Sir," she said and then went back to what she was doing. The aroma in the room was intoxicating, and I could feel my stomach rumble. Acaeus walked up to the tall woman whose brown hair was neatly pulled into a tight bun. She was more than modestly pretty, and her delicate hands were busy at work cutting vegetables on a wooden cutting board.

"Adelphie, stop for a minute if you please. I want you to meet someone," Acaeus said, interrupting her. Adelphie wiped her hands on a towel and greeted me with a large smile. "Adelphie, this is Zyaire, she is going to be my guest for lunch today. Zyaire, this is Adelphie. She is the castle's head cook. The youngest we've ever had, the best we've ever had, and the first female, might I add," Acaeus bragged.

I was not sure how to greet her, and was relieved when Adelphie held out her hand to shake mine, just as a person would have done in my own world.

"Zyaire, it's nice to meet you. I am preparing a special meal for the birthday boy that I am sure you will love."

"It's nice to meet you too, and I am starving so I can't wait to eat," I admitted again.

"Well, do not worry, Adelphie is quite good, and noble too," Acaeus said. "She first took this job temporarily while our cook at the time was out for medical reasons. The first six months she worked here, she gave her whole salary to her parents to buy equipment and help build a ramp for their home to accommodate her younger sister, Kate, who was unfortunately paralyzed after being thrown off her horse. Adelphie's family is well-loved and hard workers in our land. They have worked in our factories for years, and were instrumental in the building of our railroads. The king offered to pay for little Kate's expenses, but the Floros, Adelphie's family, are prideful people who don't believe in handouts. Instead, Adelphie offered her services as a cook to help her parents. When our head cook decided not to return and retired instead, the king asked her on permanently, and we have been enjoying her wonderful food ever since." Acaeus smiled at Adelphie and she blushed in response to his praise. "And that is actually why I am here," Acaeus continued. "How long until our delicious lunch will be served, Adelphie?"

"Well, sir, seeing as it was a late request to serve lunch," Adelphie jokingly pointed out, "it should be ready between fifteen to twenty minutes."

"Great, that is plenty of time," Acaeus declared and grabbed my hand, pulling me quickly from the kitchen and down the narrow hall.

"It's plenty of time for what?" I asked, as my feet swiftly treaded the ground, trying to keep up with him. Acaeus did not answer, so I blindly and maybe even giddily followed him. He dragged me down the halls, and I ran trying to keep up with him. We laughed whenever one of us slipped as we turned the corners of the large castle.

"Where are we going?" I shouted to him as he continued to pull me down hall after hall.

"We're going to the one place that just may be more beautiful than you." Acaeus flirted, looking slightly over his shoulder. Then he stopped abruptly and stared directly at me. I smiled at him, and stared deep into his eyes. "Well, maybe not as beautiful as you," he finally declared, and off he went once again, continuing to drag me by the hand. I could not believe what was happening to me. This was by far the biggest adventure of my life, even more exciting than the expeditions at sea that I'd been on with my father.

We finally stopped again to exit through a side door. I was out of breath and breathing deeply by the time we reached there, but Acaeus, obviously more fit than I, didn't look like he had done more than a light skip. We walked outside, and there was a beautiful garden, different from the one I saw from my room's window earlier. Situated in the garden was the largest greenhouse I had ever seen. I stood there and took in the beauty of my surroundings.

"This is beautiful. My mother has a friend who would love this. She owns a flower shop." I kneeled down and smelled the petals of a flower like none I had ever seen before. Its scent was sweet. "This would make the perfect perfume," I said, smiling at Acaeus.

He leaned down to smell the flower too. "You're right, it does smell pleasant." He walked ahead of me. "Come this way, I want you to see something else." I scurried to his side, and he reached down and grabbed my hand. Whenever he touched me, no matter how slight, I felt butterflies. When we reached the greenhouse doors, Acaeus stopped to make an announcement.

"Now this may not be as lovely as you, but it runs a close second," he said, smiling at me.

He swung open its doors, and I immediately felt the warm controlled temperature that was always present in other greenhouses I had visited. There was also one thing I did not expect when I walked inside, beautiful butterflies that gracefully flew all about. I had never seen anything like it. Gigantic beautiful multicolored butterflies filled the room's air. One came and landed directly on my shoulder, and I laughed in delight. Their colors were magnificent. I looked up at the ceiling, watching the gorgeous winged insects as they soared through the air.

"It's a butterfly house," Acaeus said.

"It's so beautiful. I have never seen butterflies this big before."

"You know what makes it even more special?" Acaeus asked.

"What?"

"This butterfly house was designed and ran by a woman named Agathe. She was completely blind."

"That's so sad," I said.

"Maybe, but she was really at peace with it. She went blind as a child, but had long before developed a love for the beauty of nature. Look around," Acaeus said, stretching both his hands wide and spinning in recognition of all that surrounded us. "She designed all of this in her mind, and then commissioned it to be brought to life."

I just stood there in awe of all the perfectly sculpted statues, flowers, plants, and the beautiful colors that surrounded me. It was poetry without words.

"Look, come here, let me show you this." Acaeus grabbed my hand again and led me to the other side of the butterfly house. "Take a look at that," he said, pointing up at branches that sprawled from several trees. I looked up and saw large chrysalises lining the trees' branches.

"Oh my God, look, that one is hatching, I think." We both walked closer to the tree.

"It is hatching," Acaeus confirmed. We stood and watched as the butterfly slowly emerged from the chrysalis.

"This is so exciting," I declared, bouncing up and down like a young schoolchild.

Acaeus laughed at my childlike behavior. "You know I planned this whole thing, right?" he said, insinuating that he knew we would be able to witness the last stage of the butterfly's metamorphosis.

I nudged him slightly in the side with my elbow. "You did not, you big liar." The butterfly was finally free from its chrysalis, but it just hung there.

"I guess it's not ready to fly yet, and we need to get to lunch. We can come back to check on it after if you like?" Acaeus asked.

"Sure, let's do that. I am so ready to eat." My stomach grumbled at just the thought of food.

We walked back to the other side of the castle. It was a longer trip since we weren't running this time. I was surprised at how quiet it was. There was no one in sight.

"Is it always this quiet here?" I asked.

"No, quite the opposite actually, but the king is away on a retreat, so all the people who are usually here working are off visiting their families, or attending to him there. My family is away with him on the retreat as well. When they get back, we will celebrate my birthday, but for now, I am happy just to be with you."

"Will I get to meet the king?" I asked.

"I am sure you will," Acaeus answered.

I smiled and stared out the windows as we strolled down the halls together. The views reminded me of a trip I took to Greece when I was fourteen. Aphrodan was definitely historic, and it had the richness that could be found in places like Greece, but it also had an overflow of modernization that I hadn't expected.

When Acaeus and I entered into the dining room, the table had already been set for two. It was a long table, and my place setting seemed a mile away from his. We both took a seat, and Adelphie walked in shortly after balancing two plates on the palms of her hands. She placed my plate down first since I was closest to the entrance she came in. I immediately smelled the aroma from the baked chicken covered in a butter sauce.

"Yum, smells good," I said, complimenting Adelphie.

"I hope you like it," she cheerfully replied.

Adelphie came back with drinks, and then left Acaeus and me alone. Lunch was delicious, and I wasn't modest about how hungry I was. I cleared my plate, and when Adelphie did come back and offered dessert, I did not turn it down as my mother always told me I should.

When we were finished eating, we returned to the butterfly house to find the newly morphed butterfly had already flown off. We looked around for a while to see if we could spot it, but there were so many beautiful butterflies flying freely that it was impossible to tell them apart.

"Let's sit down for a minute," Acaeus suggested. We both took a seat on a wooden bench that was in the center of the room.

"So what do you do? You are so young and already have people calling you 'master' and 'sir,'" I asked, remembering how Marco had referred to Acaeus when I first woke up.

"Marco is a little intense, but he means well." Acaeus laughed. "I am a general, as I told you before, but you probably don't remember. You were kind of out of it. I am one of ten to our army."

"You're pretty young to be a general, right?"

Acaeus shrugged and laughed. "That's what you said when I first told you too."

"Did I? That is so embarrassing." I laughed.

"I am the youngest we've ever had, so it is an honor."

"How many people live here in Aphrodan?"

"Well, Aphrodan is divided by the North and South. The North's population is approximately ten thousand, whereas the South's is only half that amount. That is why we are known as the dominate region. Something the king of the South has always hated."

"So there are two kings here?" I asked, confused.

"Yes, a king of the South and a king of the North."

"I can't believe there are so few people here, no wonder there is no airport," I pointed out, now remembering some things from our first conversation.

"I am sure the human world is interesting and full of many people, but we are cut off from it."

"Apparently not," I said, pointing to myself, and smiling. "So what do you do for fun, march and do army drills?" I teased.

"And don't forget standing at attention," Acaeus joked. "I am sure I like a lot of the same things you do. I like to go to parties and dance. I like going to plays, hunting, swimming, riding, and fishing."

"Oh, I am the best fisherwoman, you have no idea," I bragged.

"Well, maybe one day we should go on a fishing trip at the lake and see who can catch the most fish."

"So there is a lake here?" I asked.

Acaeus laughed. "Not this again. Your opinion of Aphrodan isn't much, is it? I have to take you on a tour so you can see that we are a civilized group of people."

"So you mean you don't eat dirt and live in caves?" I smiled.

Acaeus got lost for a moment looking at me.

"Your smile is radiant," he finally said.

"How about we go on that tour right now?" I suggested, while embarrassingly ignoring his last comment.

"Not now, but soon maybe," Acaeus said.

The doors to the Butterfly House flew open and Marco entered. "Is everything okay?" Acaeus asked.

"Can I speak to you in private please, master?" Marco asked.

"Marco, I told you, Acaeus is fine, you don't need to call me 'master,'" Acaeus said, embarrassed. "Wait here, I will be right back," he said to me before walking out with Marco.

I stood up, deciding to try one more time to find the newly morphed butterfly while I waited for Acaeus to return.

ACAEUS

I walked out of the room with Marco, leaving Zyaire behind.

"What is it?" I asked impatiently.

"I have just received word that the king will be returning in the morning. He knows the mortal is here."

"Is that why he is coming back early?"

"I am not sure, but I would think so."

I paced back and forth for a moment. "How did he find out, Marco?"

"I don't know, sir, we told as few people as possible."

I sighed deeply. "Obviously not few enough," I huffed. "I was hoping I could figure out a way to send her back before he returned. Now her fate may be left up to the ridiculous laws of this land."

"I'm sorry, Acaeus."

"Don't be, it's my fault. I should not have brought her back to the castle. I knew the risk, but I could not bear to leave her in the dungeon. She's..." I paused.

"Beautiful, sir," Marco finished.

I made no admission to his suggestion.

"Make sure you don't tell anyone else, and make sure the others who know tell no one either. The last thing we need is King Abas finding out about her."

"Yes, sir. It would be a bad thing for the king of the South to know," Marco affirmed before bowing and walking off.

I gathered myself before walking back into the Butterfly House. I wanted to make sure the stress of the news I had just received was not showing on my face.

"Is everything okay?" Zyaire asked when I walked back in.

"Everything's fine. The king is returning in the morning."

"That's good, right?" Zyaire asked.

"It's great," I lied. "Although I was enjoying having the castle all to myself," I admitted. "Are you ready to go?" I asked, holding out my hand to Zyaire.

"Yep, I'm ready." Zyaire took hold of my hand, and we headed back into the castle.

"I've never met a king before," she said as we strolled down the halls once again heading back to the Gold Room where she was staying. "What do I do when I meet him? Should I bow, or curtsey?" she asked.

"Well, for one thing, you never look directly at him, or blink in his presence, that would be considered treason and a mandatory ten-year prison sentence."

"Really, it's treason to blink?" Zyaire asked, flabbergasted.

"No, not really." I laughed.

Zyaire shot me a disapproving, but playful, stare. "That is *not* funny. I would have been standing there looking at my shoes and trying my best not to blink. Do you know how hard that would have been?" she complained.

"Yes, and I could see you now." I stood perfectly in place, looking down at my shoes and not blinking. We both laughed, and our voices echoed off the castle's walls. Zyaire swung at me playfully, but I ducked and ran down the halls. She took off after me, and we both took turns chasing each other until we got to the Gold Room's doors. She made me feel like a kid again, a feeling I welcomed since my obligations as the king's nephew had forced me to grow up far too quickly.

In the Gold Room, we both took off our shoes and lay across the bed. Zyaire began speaking almost immediately, which I liked because I'd never had someone who I could talk to for hours on end without ever getting weary of the conversation.

"Tell me something you haven't told me already." Zyaire asked, her eyes full of curiosity.

"Like what?" I replied.

"I don't know. Something about you or your family."

I took a moment to think of something she'd care to know. Then, it hit me.

"To be honest, there is something that I've put off telling you since you've gotten here," I admitted.

Zyaire's eyes opened wide. "Really? What is it?"

"Well, you know how I've always told you I'm a General?"

"Yes, the youngest there has ever been," Zyaire recalled.

"Wait, you're not going to tell me that you're not actually a General, but some poser, are you?" She asked.

"No, it's not that at all. I really am a General, it's just that I'm not only a General. I also have another important role in this castle." I hesitated when saying the next words.

"The King is not just my ruler. In fact he's much more than that. He's also my uncle. The King and my mother are sister and brother."

I wouldn't have thought Zyaire's eyes could have gotten any wider then they already had, but they did.

"Wait, that means you're royalty. Why didn't you tell me?" She asked.

"I intended to at the right time, but I was honestly enjoying the moment. People tend to change when they find out I'm part of the royal family. I was enjoying you being comfortable enough to be yourself around me."

"Wow! I have so many questions that I want to ask you," she said, staring blankly at the ceiling.

"Like what?" I asked curiously.

"Well, for one, in my world my family is well known. We are considered famous. Mostly because my family is rich. It has been this way on my mother's side ever since my great-grandmothers parents opened a clothing store that became a huge success. My father's family is also well off, and for me, being a part of two families as well-known as they are has been complicated at times, but I couldn't imagine what it is like for you, I mean your family is royalty. Which means you must be held to some pretty unbelievable standards, right?"

I nodded my head in recognition of her assumption.

"So, tell me, what is it like being the nephew of a King?"

"It has its perks, but it also comes with a lot of responsibility. Being a member of the Royal Family is a job from birth. You don't have the privilege to be young and free like other children. From my youth I was expected to act a certain way, look a certain way, and even be a certain way. Essentially, my life was not, and still is not my own. The way of the crown is all that matters."

"Ok, so those are the downsides, but what about the perks, there must be a ton of those," Zyaire said.

She then turned from her back, and onto her side, leaning up onto one elbow, and giving me her full attention.

I pondered for a moment before speaking. "Let's see, the perks. Well, one perk is getting to live in this beautiful Castle. I grew up in this castle, and as a boy even though I had a lot of pressure on me, living here was the biggest playhouse any child could ever dream of. I had the most elaborate birthday parties as a kid. My favorite was one where a host of entertainers came with all sorts of trained animals, and performed with them. There were also teams of acrobats, both men and woman, young and old, and they performed daring feats with ropes, and rings of fire. It is still one of my favorite things to see."

"You mean a circus?" Zyaire asked.

"Is that what you call it where you are from?"

"Yeah, I use to go there every year with my family until I was about ten or eleven years old. Where I am from no house would ever be able to hold an event that big. Instead it is put on at large arenas."

Well, here we call it "The Show." It has now been incorporated into our "Founders Day" Celebration each year."

"Who is the founder of Aphrodan?" Zyaire asked.

"Our world was founded by one of the great Goddesses, her name is Aphrodite."

Zyaire suddenly sat up in full attention. "Wait, what did you say?" She asked bewildered.

"I said our Founder is the Goddess Aphrodite," I confirmed.

"Wait, you don't mean Aphrodite, as in Aphrodite, the Goddess of love?" she further inquired.

"Yes, how did you know that?" I questioned, amazed.

"She is a part of our curriculum in school. It is a period we study called Greek Mythology. It is said to be made up of myths and fables, not real people or real gods."

"And they talk about the Goddess Aphrodite?" I asked.

"Yes, but no mention of Aphrodan. Aphrodite was the goddess of love and beauty, and the daughter of Zeus, but none of that was supposed to be real," Zyaire said.

"Yes, Zeus is powerful beyond measure. He once tried to destroy our world. And I assure you, they are very real. Aphrodan wouldn't exist if it weren't for the Goddess Aphrodite."

"Aphrodan, Aphrodite, your world was named after her," Zyaire suddenly realized.

"Yes, it was."

"So, all this time, what I have thought to just be Greek Mythology, something we were forced to learn in school, and told it was solely based off the ancient fables of the Greeks, was in actuality real stories about real Gods and Goddesses?" Zyaire was obviously flabbergasted by the look on her face.

"Yes, this world, and the Gods you have been learning about are all real, and still very much alive."

"Alive?" Zyaire queried.

"Yes, the Gods are immortal. Unlike us, they don't just have longer life spans, they are eternal."

Zyaire sat there silent, trying to take in all that she was now discovering.

"You know, we learn about your world in school too," I admitted.

"Really? What is it, like a Human Studies course?

"Well, they call the course, "Earth Studies", but yes. Speaking of that, maybe you can tell me about some things that we thought to just be fables?"

"Ok, like what?

"There is one fable that is told, and it is that mortal doctors peel away their patients face to make them look younger, and sometimes they even suck fat out from their bellies to make them thinner. Is this true?" I asked.

"Unfortunately yes," Zyaire laughed.

"Oh my goodness. Who would want to subject themselves to that?" I asked.

"You wouldn't believe how many people actually do. It used to be that only famous people did it. The ones who were always in the spotlight, but now there are people who will flush their life savings down the toilet just to be able to pay and look like what our world tells them is beautiful. I think it is very superficial, and brought into play by the overwhelming pressure put on our society based on the standards made by the woman and men of Hollywood." Zyaire explained.

"Well that's very conscious of you. But what is Hollywood?" I questioned, confused.

"Oh yes, good old Hollywood, it is where all the famous people who make our movies and films live."

"Oh, I understand, so your people see them as perfect and strive to be like them?"

"Exactly." Zyaire confirmed.

"Well, don't you ever change, because I think you are perfect just the way you are," I said, adoringly looking into Zyaire's beautiful eyes. She blushed and shyly looked down, breaking our gaze before quickly changing the subject.

"How do you guys stay so in touch with what is going on in our world?" Zyaire asked.

"We are not in touch anymore and haven't been for decades," I explained. "Aphrodan once had a constant view of the mortal world. Two sorcerers, Artemas and Clytia, created the Ring of Vision, which allowed them to see into the mortal world. The problem was, centuries ago any contact with the mortal world was forbidden, so they successfully hid the Ring of Vision until the pocketbook, the pocketbook you traveled here in, was discovered and it was decreed that all sorcerers cease from performing any magic, or it would be punishable by death. Eventually a surprise raid on the homes of certain sorcerers whom were suspected of performing illegal magic was done and that is when the Ring of Vision was discovered."

"Wow, so what happened to it?" Zyaire asked.

"Well, because our region discovered it, it was placed under the protection of the North's king. The Ring of Vision, however, has its limitations, and it only shows limited views of the mortal world. Only displaying what it deems necessary at the time of request." By the end of my story, Zyaire's eyes had grown heavy. I glanced toward the window and realized we had talked the sun down. I offered to leave so she could get some sleep.

"No, I'm not sleepy," she insisted, either not wanting her time with me to end, or not wanting to be left alone in a strange world.

I kept talking, but before long, she could no longer fight her weariness. She dozed off in the middle of me telling her about my first fishing experience. I pulled the covers over her, and ran my fingers through her dark wavy long hair. She was so beautiful to me, and not just physically. That would be obvious to any man.

"I'll take care of you," I whispered into her ear as she slept. I did not yet know how, but I knew I would risk anything to protect her if I had to. No matter how enormous the risk, I would not let her fall prey to the South Kingdom, or mine.

Chapter 15
The Treaty
(ACAEUS)

I barely slept the night before, and I awoke early eager to see the king. When I got to his study, I slightly knocked on the door, jarring it open before entering. "Can I have an audience with you, your majesty?" I asked, walking in.

I had left Zyaire cozy in her bed last night, and now I needed to know what would happen to her. My uncle sent away his advisors at my request so we could talk alone. He always met with his advisors once a week to seek advice on how he could serve his people better, and improve the problems of our land. He was a king who was dedicated to the well-being of his people.

"Have you kept this quiet from as many people as you could, nephew?" King Aimilios inquired.

"Yes, of course, Uncle, I have told no one other than those you already know of."

The king sighed and rubbed his fingers through his hair, as he often did when he was deep in thought. "You weren't even born the last time a human entered our world, nephew. Wonderful things came from that, but I can assure you it was not without complications," he admitted somberly.

I looked on as he stood up and walked toward the picture window and took in the view that overlooked the castle's grounds. He stared out at the sky without saying another word. Therefore, I decided to interject. "You mean Lillian, right, Uncle?" I asked nervously.

He quickly turned around and looked at me, bewildered. He never spoke about Lillian to me before and was surprised to hear me mention her name.

"Please don't be upset, my lord," I quickly stated in response to his reaction. "My mother, your sister, told me very little about her. She said I was never to bring it up to you, and that others knew not to do so as well. I did so knowing this was a source of pain for you, but since you brought it up first, I thought it would be acceptable to speak about. Please forgive me if I overstepped," I pleaded.

"No forgiveness is needed, nephew. I am not naive. I know this is a topic of interest to all the people of Aphrodan. It is certainly no secret. Indeed, it was good of your mother to tell you about her; after all, they were good friends. Lilly, that's what I called her," King Aimilios reminisced. "My beautiful Lilly," he said, as a mixture of pain and adoration fell on his face. "She brought so many wonderful things to our world," he added and walked off to stare out the window again.

I dared not say a word, I wanted the king to go on, and he did.

"She used to say, 'I am going to revolutionize Aphrodan,' and she did in many ways. Despite the fact that we were more superior than the human world in many ways, she brought wonderful ideas here that made our lives exciting." He paused again, and I remained silent, hoping he would continue. I wanted to hear him talk about his love for Lillian, as my mother had told me about, but he did not; instead, he changed the subject.

"So tell me about the girl. Is she well?" he asked.

"She is fine, uncle, fiery and beautiful," I said, smiling. "But she was also very weak when she first arrived. She slept for two days straight."

"That is to be expected. The transport leaves them very weak. She will be fine," King Aimilios assured me. I approached the next subject carefully.

"You're majesty, what will we do with her? She is afraid and wants to go home." Now I paused, choosing my next words wisely, hoping not to offend the king with my desires, knowing all too well the law of the land. "If it be in your majesty's wishes, can we send the girl back home the way that she had come before anyone else knows of her?"

King Aimilios turned from the window. I could see he was under much stress. "I wish it was that easy, nephew. Maybe if the girl could be transported tonight, it would be even more feasible. The problem is she can't be transported while the pocketbook is sealed."

"I don't understand, Uncle, what do you mean sealed?"

King Aimilios sighed again, but this time more deeply, more agonizingly. "Let's sit down," he said and walked over to the two dark leather chairs that were in front of the burning fireplace. "Nephew, you were only recently named as one of my ten generals. The youngest among them, only seventeen years old, and now you are eighteen. Yet there are many things you still do not know."

"I have diligently studied my position and the history of our land," I said proudly.

"Even still, you do not know it all," King Aimilios declared. "There are some facts that have been removed from our history, for what is said to have been for the betterment of our society. Many things have been deemed myths, especially how our world came into existence. However, the divided appearance between the North and South has never fallen to doubt. We, the North, are considered the people of the day because it is daytime longer on our side of the land. Eighteen hours of daylight and only six hours of darkness. Our separation also runs in our appearance. The people of North Aphrodan's skin is bronze, and our eyes and hair are dark."

"Except in my case," I interrupted, pointing both fingers at my piercing green eyes.

"Yes, you are different in that regard, but still one of us nonetheless," King Aimilios said before continuing.

"The South is considered the people of the night because their land experiences 18 hours of darkness. In addition, their appearance is in contrast to ours with their lighter skin tones, light eyes, and golden hair. This separation based on our appearance is something I have always wished to change. The king of the South, however, is pleased with our separation. One land, one people, would mean one ruler, and he will not put his throne, or the future throne of his descendants, on the line."

"Uncle, tell me the secrets of this land," I pleaded. "I won't tell a soul," I promised.

"I don't have time to tell you them all," King Aimilios declared, "but I will say this, as you know, we are the forgotten descendents of Aphrodite, the Greek goddess. She had many lovers—many human lovers. Some of which she successfully hid the presence of. It is believed, she hid them here on the land of Aphrodan—a land she founded and named in her likeness. It is said she bore many unknown children in this land by these lovers, and we are the descendants of them. All the people of this land are considered to be half mortal and half immortal. This is why we are called *mid-mortals*. We are able to die, but we live a much longer life than full mortals do. It is also said that at one point those who lived in the land could travel freely through a secret passage Aphrodite had created leading into the human world."

"The Gate of Passage," I interrupted.

"Yes, the Gate of Passage," King Aimilios confirmed. "Her father Zeus, who was the god over all the gods of Olympus from which Aphrodite came, was said to have discovered this land that she hid, and planned to kill every person who occupied it. He was a jealous ruler, and despised the fact that the goddess Aphrodite had thought herself so great that she would create a world with people who saw her as the head and not him. He was intent on destroying it. Instead, Aphrodite begged that her father spare the people of Aphrodan whom she had grown to love immensely, and they her. In exchange, she agreed not to return to the land, and took a lifelong vow of celibacy to show her father how penitent she was. She agreed to return to Olympus with her father, and remain there with him for eternity. Zeus, a father who always wanted to be in control of his beautiful and headstrong daughter, accepted her terms but banned any further travel through the Gate of Passage so that no one could any longer venture from Aphrodan into the human world freely. He created two great beasts to guard the Gate of Passage that is located deep in the Black Forest. They are the same Black Lions that live in the Black Forest today. As you know they are strong, beautiful, and intelligent creatures, and the female has since birthed their own descendants. Nevertheless, their beauty should never deceive one. Any person who dared venture into the Black Forest to gain access to the Gate of Passage stood no chance against these ferocious beast, whom exacted death without pause. Therefore, all this remained so for many centuries, until Zita, the great sorcerer, coming from the bloodline of many great sorcerers, dwelled on the land. As you know, she created an entrance into the human world disguised as a handbag. Zita was the longest living descendant in Aphrodan, far exceeding the two-hundred-year natural life expectancy of us Aphrodites. She was 502 years in age when she created the new passage. She successfully and secretly traveled into the human world for years, until General Abderos became suspicious of her frequent disappearances, and he asked for my permission to search her quarters, which I granted. They discovered in her journals the details of her travels and the means. They waited to arrest her when she returned, because it was against the laws of the land to attempt travel into the human world—a promise Aphrodite ordered the people of the land to keep many centuries ago. However, Zita was clever, and she had plans in case something like that ever happened. When she returned and discovered that she was being sought for arrest, she hid in the Black Forest."

I swiftly interrupted, "The Black Forest? Were the Black Lions present at the time?" I asked, bewildered.

"Yes, they were there," King Aimilios answered.

"That's impossible, Uncle. They would have eaten her alive."

"Do you know the full history of the Black Lions?" King Aimilios asked me.

"Well, I would never presume to know more than you, your majesty, but I have seen them from afar, from atop the cave, the same cave we found the girl in," I replied.

Then King Aimilios went on. "It is well known that the Black Lions were put on the land by Zeus, the father of our founder and true queen, Aphrodite. What is not well known is that when Zeus first discovered the world, he secretly placed the Black Lions there to destroy anyone who tried to travel. Many lives were lost before Aphrodite discovered what her father had done. When he took Aphrodite from our world, he left the lions in the land, as a constant reminder of his wrath, and the blood that was shed by his doing. No one dared enter the Black Forest again."

"Until Zita," I interrupted.

"Yes, until Zita. She was very powerful, and it has long since been rumored that she possessed a greater percentage of immortality than anyone else in Aphrodan. It is further rumored that her mother, who was also a sorceress, conceived her with another sorcerer from the South. This mingling of blood is said to have made her more powerful than even her ancestors before her. Romantic mingling between the North and South was and is forbidden. It is also believed that she bewitched the lions and lived amongst them until the next first full moon of autumn."

"Why did she stay until the first full moon in autumn, why not leave right away?" I asked, puzzled.

"Zita was unable to create a continuous opening between Aphrodan and the human world as Aphrodite had. She could only travel and return one time a year. The first full moon in autumn opens the realm she created, and passage is possible."

"So she would have to stay in the human world for a whole year before traveling back?" I asked.

"No, there was a departure and return time that was possible within a short time frame. That cycle sometimes changed, but I have never seen it exceed forty-five days in time, and usually it was much shorter."

"What decided the time of return, Uncle?" I eagerly asked.

"The handbag," King Aimilios said pointedly, "or pocketbook, as Lilly liked to call it. When it was time to travel back into the human world, the pocketbook would glow from within, with a great blue light. When the blue light was present, return travel was possible only within a twenty-four-hour period. We learned this from Zita's journal."

"And what if someone decided to stay and not travel back?"

"At the end of the twenty-four hours the light from the pocketbook would no longer illuminate, and then the traveler would have to wait until the new autumn year to return. But there were consequences for that," King Aimilios added. "There was a ten-year life penalty if a mortal did not travel back to their own world during the twenty-four hour window. Spending one year in Aphrodan would take ten years off a mortal's life expectancy. Zita herself had placed this curse on the pocketbook, presumably as a way to exact revenge on anyone who dared steal it from her."

King Aimilios stretched his legs under the table. An injury he sustained while on retreat was still healing. I took that time to interject.

"So when Zita came back to Aphrodan, she could not just return back to the human world once she figured out that she had been discovered?" I concluded.

"Yes, that is right, nephew. She would have had to hide in the forest for a whole year to gain entry into the human world once again. Some believed she had never left the forest again, and still lived there amongst the lions. Even so, the cave that leads out to the lion's den was constantly guarded since it was the drop-off point when one enters back into Aphrodan. Unfortunately, that fact was not discovered until more than a year after her escape, since most of her writings were well hidden. She had ample time to leave and come back by then. During the course of all this, King Abas and I were involved in heated discussions. As king of the South, he was furious at the deceit of Zita, and he blamed the North for not keeping a watchful eye on her sorcery. He captured and tortured many of Zita's family in an attempt to get her to come forward. He used torture chambers to force them to talk. Not even children were spared from his treacherous wrath. However, they knew nothing, but he would not stop. He shaved the heads of the women he captured, even the young girls, and then the men were beaten close to death, allowed time to heal, and then beaten again. One woman he held captive was with child and almost lost her baby because of the conditions she was kept in. All of this because he felt the discovery of Aphrodan by humans would be the end of our world. I was beyond disgusted by his tactics. There was nothing that could justify what he did to the good people of that family. However, I agreed with his fear regarding the unknown. The human world and its people were a mystery to us all.

The South was already at odds with us, being jealous that most of the desired crops, natural elements, and livestock were abundant only on our side of land. Through our agreement of the potential dangers Zita had brought to our land, we created a peace treaty. In the treaty, first before anything, I arranged for the immediate release of Zita's family. The treaty also opened the door for trades of goods and food between us, and requested travel between the North and the South. It was also agreed under the treaty that if Zita were captured, the pocketbook, which was the means of entry into the human world, would be destroyed, and so would Zita. If by chance Zita had in fact been back in the human world, and one of the humans were to discover the handbag and enter into Aphrodan, then the handbag would still be destroyed as planned, and so would the human."

As I listened to King Aimilios I cringed at the thought of what this treaty could mean for Zyaire.

King Aimilios got up and poured a glass of water from a pitcher situated on a small table near the door.

"This is where Lillian comes in, right, Uncle?" I inquired.

King Aimilios sat back down and took a sip of water from his glass. "Yes," he said, pausing for a brief moment before continuing. "It was early in my reign when what Zita had done was discovered. I was a young man, like you. As you know, the Black Lions killed my father while he was hunting. His horse galloped into the entrance of the Black Forest that connects only by a bridge to our forest. The Black Lions were far off from the location of the Gate of Passage, and when they saw my father, they attacked immediately. A Southerner, who was also hunting in the forest at the same time, reported the means of his death. My father liked to hunt alone. He said it was a time of peace away from his duties as a king. His death was a shock to everyone, and it catapulted me into a position much sooner than I had expected. Therefore, I have made some mistakes. Some I regret, and some I do not. Some say Lillian was one of those mistakes, but for me she is one I will never forget, or regret."

Before he could continue, a knock came at the door. I got up and opened it to find Marco standing on the other side. He was developing a knack for interrupting at the most inopportune times. "Marco, come back later," I persisted. I was anxious for my uncle to finish the story.

"I am sorry, Sir Acaeus, but this is very important," Marco pleaded.

"Okay, come in, but make it quick."

He entered and bowed before King Aimilios. "Your majesty, welcome back," he said before continuing. "I have been told that the news of the human girl has begun to spread. It is believed the South now has knowledge of it."

King Aimilios stood up and angrily slammed his fist on the hard oak table to his right. "How is this possible, can no one keep their mouth shut?" he yelled.

"I don't know, my lord, but I have said nothing to anyone," Marco insisted.

"This changes everything," King Aimilios declared. "We must now send word to the king of the South that we have the girl in our possession."

"My lord, no," I pleaded. "Why, all this fear over a mortal? Are we not the dominate species, promised exceeding wealth, health, and intelligence beyond what a mere mortal can fathom. Are we not the children of the goddess Aphrodite?" I exclaimed, trying to convince him that there was no true danger where Zyaire was concerned.

"Acaeus, you know of our treaty and its contents. I am obligated to honor it," King Aimilios reminded me.

"If you tell King Abas, then you have sentenced her to death. Please don't do this, maybe he does not know yet." I tried desperately to change the king's mind. We both turned to Marco for answers.

"How sure are you that the South knows?" King Aimilios asked.

Marco turned toward me. "I'm sorry, Sir Acaeus, but we are convinced in our findings. The news came from a reliable source in the South," Marco confirmed.

I dropped my head into my hands.

"Then it is settled, we must send word to the king of the South, or it will seem we are hiding her, and that will jeopardize our treaty with them. It has been destroyed once, I cannot let it be destroyed again, and I owe that much to the good people of the North," King Aimilios declared. "Where is the girl now?"

"She is asleep in the Gold Room, your majesty." Marco replied.

"Forgive me, your majesty," I pleaded once again. "But this is a young girl, she is innocent, if you tell King Abas, he will demand her death," I reasoned.

"If I don't tell him, he will find out anyway. My first duty has to be to this kingdom. I cannot risk the lives of thousands just to save one," King Aimilios stated. "I cannot do that to my people in such times as these."

"But what about your conscience, Uncle, and your heart, don't you have a duty to them as well?" I replied.

"I can see you have quickly grown fond of this girl, but you are crossing a line into matters you should not comment on, nephew," King Aimilios warned.

"I beg your forgiveness, Uncle, but I cannot be a part of this," I exited the room swiftly and stood outside the door. I knew from the look on my uncle's face as I exited that he was grieved by my words. Surely he understood all too well his position and he was already contrite in the outcome that might lie ahead, but perhaps now that he was older and wiser, and more stubborn, he would refuse to act out of impulse as he had in his youth concerning Lillian. I would not let Zyaire be a victim of his test of wills. There had to be a way to save her and prevent the people of the North the cost of war.

I listened outside the door as the king continued his conversation with Marco.

"Marco, let my companions know I will be preparing to head to the South later."

"Should I tell them the purpose of your visit, my lord?"

"Yes, tell them I am going to visit King Abas," he dolefully replied.

Chapter 16

Meant to Be

(ZYAIRE)

I slept peacefully through the night. The bed was so comfortable I didn't want to get up. Acaeus kept popping his head into my room quietly. I was always a light sleeper, so each time the door cracked my eyes wearily opened. I was too tired to actually lift my head and acknowledge he was there, so each time, thinking I was still asleep, he left. Finally, I guess he decided to check and make sure I was still breathing. I didn't notice the door opening this time. He patted me softly on my shoulder to wake me. I was startled, but then grinned when I saw that it was him standing over me.

"Are you always a late sleeper?" he asked.

"Not usually," I said through a yawn. I stretched my arms wide; then suddenly I realized he was looking at a sure-to-be-disheveled me. I quickly covered my face and turned away. "Don't look at me. I'm sure I look like crap," I said, embarrassed.

"I don't think you could look like *crap* even if you tried, Zyaire," Acaeus assured me. Then he leaned over to where I had turned away, and I quickly turned my head back in the other direction. We playfully went back and forth like that for a short while. Then he gave me a playful pat on my right thigh. "Come on, get up! We have things to do. Tonight is my birthday dinner," he announced.

"Am I invited?" I asked.

"Hmmm let me think," Acaeus teased.

"Fine, I will just go to some other general's birthday party," I declared.

"Of course you are invited. My parents can't wait to meet you," he finally said.

"What about my clothes?" I asked.

Apparently, he had already thought of everything. "You are to be treated like royalty today," he declared. "I have arranged for an attendant from one of the stores to bring over some clothes for you to try on. You should like that, right? I know you told me last night that your family owns clothing stores. I hope our clothes are suitable for someone of your expertise."

"I am sure they will be fine. Truth is I am not exactly the fashion type. I do think it would be much more fun if we go out and shop, don't you? Then you could take me sightseeing," I suggested.

"Not today. The king is back, and there is a lot I have to do before dinner."

"There's a lot to do before dinner? What about breakfast, and lunch?" I asked.

"You slept through breakfast, Sleeping Beauty, and lunch has long been over."

Just then, I smiled at him.

"What has gotten you smiling?" he asked.

"I'm smiling at you. Sometimes you speak so proper and adult-like. I like it though. You're so different from the boys at my school."

"Well, I am glad you like how I speak. I hope you like other things about me too," Acaeus said, stroking my hair and looking into my eyes. I was still underneath his gaze. Everything he said seemed to make me melt into a puddle. As much as I was missing home, I was actually dreading the idea of ever having to leave him. It was crazy. I barely knew him, yet he was kind and gentle to me. I knew he wasn't one of those boys my father had warned me about, the boys who only have one thing on their minds. I wanted to ask him if there was anything he liked about me, but I was too nervous to do that.

"I want to take you somewhere before dinner if that is okay with you?" Acaeus asked.

"Give me a moment, let me check my calendar." I pretended to open a calendar and glance through it before finally closing it. "What do you know, all my pocketbook travels have been temporarily put on hold, so I am free?"

Acaeus laughed at my playfulness. "Is half an hour enough time for you to get ready?" he asked.

"Make it an hour, and we have a deal." I put out my hand for Acaeus to shake. When he did, a little shock shot between us. "Ow," we both said and burst into hysterics. When we finally calmed down from laughing, Acaeus tenderly gazed at me again.

"I will be back in an hour," he said.

"Okay, I'll be here. No escapes, I promise."

Acaeus began walking out the door.

"Wait," I said, stopping him in his tracks. He turned back to face me. "I can't help but wonder, why are you being so nice to me?" I asked.

He grinned and declared, "I like making you smile." He then paused for a moment as if he knew what was to follow, and without fail, I smiled affectionately at him. Satisfied, he turned and walked out the door, closing it behind him.

I stood up, and paced the floor for a moment before I picked up a pillow and hugged it over my heart. I took a deep breath, then exhaled as I did a freefall onto the bed backwards. I imagined that, like the movies, Acaeus still stood outside the door, his back leaned up against it, smiling and delighted just as I was.

I spent the whole hour getting ready, which was new for me. I usually got dressed in no time flat. However, I found myself wanting to use every minute allowed to look my best for not just him, but myself too.

Acaeus was prompt in returning to my room; he brought me a snack to eat. "Here you go," he said, handing me a silver tray with all sorts of fruits and cheeses neatly organized on it. "This will sustain you before dinner, eat up," he commanded.

I ate the strawberries, grapes, and then I began eating the cheeses. They were delicious. "Wow, this is some of the best cheese I have ever tasted," I said, biting into a cheese that Acaeus called graviera.

"Well, legend has it that Aristaios, son of Apollo and Cyrene…"

"I heard of them at school," I said, interrupting him.

Acaeus continued. "Well then, it was said that Aristaios was sent by the gods to give the gift of cheese-making to the Greeks. The gods called it "a gift of everlasting value," Acaeus recalled.

"That's so cool," I said, grabbing for a hardened piece of Feta cheese. I plopped it into my mouth, and before swallowing, I stood up and said, "I'm ready, let's go!" I was excited to find out where he was taking me.

ACAEUS

This time, when we entered the hall just off from her room, the castle was busy, and many people were walking up and down. They all stopped and greeted us with a quick bow and a hello as they strolled by. They looked at Zyaire curiously, but not shockingly. They obviously knew of her presence in the castle.

"Everyone is staring at me," Zyaire whispered.

"Why wouldn't they? Look how beautiful you are," I said as if it were a matter of fact, and it was. She did look beautiful. She was wearing a floral dress with quarter sleeves and an asymmetrical hemline, the warm colors perfectly complimented her skin tone, and the fitted cut of the dress showed off her petite yet curvy physique.

"Acaeus, it is nice to see you again," Mr. Lambros said, stopping us as we walked down the hall.

I held out my hand to shake his. "Mr. Lambros, it's nice to see you as well. I see your eye has healed quite nicely."

"Oh, yes, and I have learned my lesson to never kneel down behind that horse again." He laughed.

"Now are you sure it was the horse and not Mrs. Lambros who gave you that dark eye?" I teased.

"Yes, quite sure," he said, and we both laughed.

"Oh, forgive my rudeness," I said, turning to face Zyaire. "Zyaire, this is Mr. Lambros. He is a racehorse trainer, and is currently training the king's newest horse to be raced."

"It is nice to meet you, Zyaire," Mr. Lambros said.

"It is very nice to meet you too," she replied.

"Well, I will let you two continue on," Mr. Lambros stated. "It is nice seeing you again, Acaeus, and it is very nice meeting you, Zyaire."

I wished Mr. Lambros a good day then took Zyaire by the hand to continue on. Before long we reached the open room that would lead us to our adventure.

"This is the Great Hall," I told Zyaire.

She looked around at all the pictures that adorned the walls. "Who are all these people?" she asked.

"The kings and queens that have ruled the North."

"What was right there?" Zyaire asked, pointing to a large empty space that was vacant between the portraits.

"That space held the portrait of our last queen," I told her.

"And…why is it no longer there?" she asked, intrigued.

"The king ordered it, as well as had every other portrait of her taken down. It was just too hard for him to bear seeing her once she was gone."

I changed the subject, pointing to another picture that adorned the walls. "Look there," I said, pointing to a picture of our current king.

"Is that your king?" Zyaire asked observantly.

"Yes, you are correct. That is my uncle, and king."

"He has kind eyes," Zyaire stated.

"He is very kind actually," I said before grabbing her hand firmly. "Come on, let's go." I led her to the French-style doors that led outside the castle. "Are you ready for another adventure?" I turned and asked her before we could open the door and cross over the threshold.

"Sure," she replied reluctantly.

I could see how anxious she was to see what was on the other side of those doors in the way she tapped the heels of her shoes up and down on the floor. Finally, I flipped on a light switch that was to the right on the wall before swinging open both doors simultaneously for effect and walking outside. The sun had not gone down, yet mysteriously for centuries this part of the castle always remained in darkness, which made the scene that much more magical. It was a garden maze. Beautiful lights lit up the bushes and trees surrounding it. A large gazebo stood at the east end of the garden. It was lit elegantly with blue and clear lighting. To the left was a creamed marble fire pit. Centered right before the entrance of the maze was a dazzling wishing fountain. The water was crystal blue, and in the middle of the fountain stood three sculpted swans standing together in a circle with their wings spread out. Water magnificently flowed from their beaks. The ground was paved with smooth, colorful stone anywhere nature's life did not stand. There were two entrances to the maze, both tall bushes pruned into rounded archways. I pulled two coins out of my pocket and handed one to Zyaire. This prompted her to look at me curiously. Without any explanation, I closed my eyes for a brief moment then threw my coin into the fountain.

"Your turn," I said gesturing for Zyaire to do the same. "Make a wish," I urged.

Zyaire closed her eyes, made a silent wish, and then threw her coin into the fountain with mine. "Did you wish to go home?" I asked, and held my breath as I waited for her response.

"Surprisingly, no," she admitted. "I am having fun with you, Acaeus. You are intriguing, and I enjoy your presence," she said honestly.

"Aha! Now who sounds all adultlike," I teased. That remark landed me a quick swat at my arm with the back of her hand. "You are quite abusive, aren't you?" I laughed.

"Only when teased," she said with a devilish grin.

"Okay, the adventure begins now," I said and whisked her away by her hand, just in front of the archways.

"What are we doing?" Zyaire asked, her curiosity now getting the best of her.

"In a moment, the lights will flicker, and that means the clock has started. You will enter the maze through the left, and I through the right. The goal is to get to the middle before the time is up. You will know you are there because you will see a beautiful sculpture of the goddess Aphrodite."

"You mean the goddess of love?" Zyaire interrupted.

"Yes, that's right. I am still amazed that you know who she is," I stated.

"Yep, the good old Greek mythology class has taught me a lot."

I was intrigued and wanted to ask more about what she had learned, but I would have to save my questions for later.

"Let me finish explaining quickly. We don't have much time before the lights will flicker." I continued. "When the lights flicker, you only have ten minutes to reach the middle of the maze. If you have not reached the middle in ten minutes time, the lights will all go out, indicating your time is up. Only a pathway of lights leading out of the maze will light up once the allowed time has passed. If you make it to the middle where Aphrodite stands, you will find a glowing scepter in her hand. Pull the scepter to expose the hidden switch that will turn on the lights to exit the maze. Are you up for the challenge?" I asked.

"Of course," Zyaire said confidently.

I could tell by the trembling of her hand that deep inside, she was actually nervous. It was a huge maze, and even I questioned if I could actually make it through it in such a short amount of time.

"You know, they say if two people make it to the middle together before the time is up, then they are destined to be together. It is said Aphrodite herself created the maze."

"So how many girls have you tried going through this maze with?" Zyaire asked me, now nervously running her fingers through her hair.

I smiled at her adoringly, and looked into her big blue eyes. "You're the first," I declared. Just then the lights flickered, and with one quick and final glance at each other, we both took off through our separate archways.

In the beginning, I could hear Zyaire desperately prowling through the maze, assumingly hitting one dead end after the other, as she blurted out "Shoot! Shoot! Shoot!" over and over again. The sound of her fast-paced rustling soon stopped, and I could hear her as she slowed her steps and carefully picked her direction. "That's right, Zyaire, slow and steady wins the race," I thought. After a while, I could not hear her at all.

I concentrated on the task. I started out slowly and struggled, hitting dead end after dead end; however, I was resourceful because of my military training that taught me to navigate my way out of sticky situations. I soon discovered there was a pattern in the maze, and I decoded it—left, right, right, left, left, right, right. Once I knew the maze's secrets, I glided through it with no problem until I reached the middle and noticed that the texture of the terrain in front of me had changed. I picked up a very large boulder that sat alongside the bushes and threw it at the ground in front of me. It quickly sank.

My mind raced. "Oh my god, it's a booby trap." I yelled out desperately, "Zyaire, Zyaire!" but my screams were to no avail. She could not hear me, as she was traveling on the other side of the Maze Garden. I picked up another boulder and threw it further than the rock before it. It hit the ground and made a thud, letting me know the ground there was solid. I backed up and sprinted forward before jumping, gliding through the air, and eventually landing on firm ground.

I perilously glided through the maze, taking no account to what other traps might lie before me. I was grateful when no other obstacles presented themselves. I repeated the maze's pattern several times before finally turning the corner to where the beautiful golden statue of Aphrodite stood. I scurried to the other side of the finish line, but it was blocked. I could not gain access from where I stood. I pulled at the scepter that sat in the hand of Aphrodite, hoping to find the switch that would turn on the lights to the maze, but it was jammed, and unable to be moved. I tugged at it ferociously without progress, as it would not move even an inch. I screamed out in frustration and ran back to the place where I believed Zyaire was to exit. However, it was completely closed off.

"Zyaire, Zyaire, can you hear me?" I yelled again, but there was no reply.

Time was running out quickly, and guilt began to settle in as I thought about Zyaire sinking into the ground. "Oh god, I didn't know," was all I could say. The details of the maze had been kept a secret for centuries. If I had known there was a danger in it, I would have never exposed Zyaire to it. I yelled out to Zyaire one more time, and again, met with no reply. I turned and looked upon the statue of Aphrodite. She was beautiful to behold, and I stared at it for a brief moment before nervously pacing around her. I knew all too well the lights would soon go out, and I would just have to wait until then to find Zyaire. Impatiently, I continued to pace around the statue of Aphrodite until I became resolved that Zyaire would not make it before the lights went out. I prayed that perhaps she never made it to the middle of the Maze where the quicksand was present. Maybe she would be waiting for me when I reached the front, I hoped.

I sat on the concrete bench that rounded the area and waited for the lights to turn out. It is amazing how long minutes can seem when one is waiting. My hope was shattered, and I hung my head between my legs, as regret began to fill my thoughts. What had I done to this poor young girl? This beautiful young girl. She might be dead, and it would all be upon my head to bear. The dread of it all brought me near tears. Then I heard a rustling sound just outside the finish line. I jumped up anxiously.

"Hurry up, Zyaire," I screamed out, hoping it was she.

A moment later, a hidden door behind the bushes slid its way open, and Zyaire rounded the corner into the home where Aphrodite stood. Just after her feet planted on the ground, the lights flickered and then went out. The glow from Aphrodite scepter shined bright and Zyaire's face gleamed in all its glory. I stood silently looking at her. She was out of breath, and her hair was unkempt, but she was alive, and had made it before the lights turned out. Her dress was torn, and there was a little bit of dirt on her cheek, but standing there, she could not have looked more beautiful to me. I knew I should not feel this way about her, or anyone for that matter. My life had a purpose, and that purpose did not include love. Besides, she was a pure mortal, and it was possible that she could be put to death, making it even more unwise for me to become attached to her, but as her blue eyes sparkled in the dim light, my soul became connected to hers, and I knew there was no turning back. I was in love with her.

I slowly walked toward Zyaire, and she toward me. We embraced, and I wanted to kiss her, but did not. Instead, I held her for a while. "I can't believe you made it," I whispered in her ear.

"Me either." She chuckled.

"Was there quicksand on your side?" I asked.

"Yes," she said, clinging to me even tighter at the mention of it.

"I am so sorry. I had no idea there was a trap in the maze, or I would have never sent you through it," I assured her. We finally eased out of our embrace, and I looked down at her and smiled. We were both overwhelmed and could not seem to find the words to say to each other at that moment. I could certainly not tell her how I was actually feeling. We stood in the dark with Aphrodite's scepter providing our only light.

"How did you get past the quick sand?" I asked her.

"When I got to that part of the maze, I heard a stream from behind the bushes. I stopped for a quick moment to look at it, and I noticed it was overflowing, and the dirt looked mushy, but I still walked on, and my foot sank deep into the ground. I panicked for a moment, but my foot only sunk deeper." I looked down and noticed Zyaire's right foot and part of her leg was covered in dirt. "Then I remembered," she continued. "I watched a video one time about how to get out of quick sand. I guess it pays to be a geek sometimes," she joked. "I remembered that you should never struggle or it would make you sink faster. I looked around for something to grab on to so that I could pull myself out, and I noticed a thick branch extended from one of the bushes. It was not close enough to reach out and grab, I had to maneuver around on my left foot and stretch my body out to reach it. I sank further at one point, but I finally grabbed it, and was able to pull myself out."

I breathed a sigh of relief and hugged Zyaire. "I am so relieved you are all right," I said. "So how did you finally get past the quicksand once you were free?" I asked, finally letting her go.

"Well, if you stop hugging me, I will tell you, silly." She threw me a quick smile then, and I was impressed that she still had her wits. "So," she continued, "I tried to pick up a boulder to see if it would sink—"

"I did that too," I interrupted again.

"But I couldn't," Zyaire continued. "It was too heavy for me to carry. I had to take my chances. I took off my shoes, and I went back far enough to pick up speed. I ran and jumped. I was praying that I made it across the whole time." Zyaire laughed. "I fell on my behind when I landed, and that's how I tore the dress. I know I look a mess right now." She ran her fingers through her hair.

"You look fine. I didn't know the little mortal had all that spunk inside her," I teased. I reached over and pulled at Aphrodite's scepter. This time it folded down effortlessly, and there exposed was the switch. I flipped it up, and the garden lit up again in all its glory.

"We better get going, or we will be late for dinner," I said.

"Oh, my god I totally forgot about dinner. I have to change first. I can't meet your parents looking like this." Zyaire pointed down to her torn dress.

I grabbed Zyaire's hand and began to lead her out of the maze.

"We made it," Zyaire said, looking up at me and smiling. I knew she was remembering what I had told her before we took the maze's course. The legend was if two people made it through together, they were destined to be with each other. We walked out of the garden hand in hand, and I knew legend or no legend, I would be bonded to her forever.

Chapter 17

I Will Protect You

(ACAEUS)

When Zyaire and I got back to the Great Hall's doors, I heard someone yelling my name. "Wait right here," I said and walked toward the sound of the voice.

"What are you doing here, Yanni?" I asked my best friend who was standing outside the gate that surrounded the garden. "You know it is after hours for travel," I warned. Yanni was from the South of Aphrodan, and after a certain time, travel was forbidden between the two kingdoms.

"Of course I know, why do you think I am out of breath? I could only travel up to a certain point before I had to take the rest of the journey on foot. I hauled my behind over here before anyone could see me," Yanni explained.

"This must be important if you are willing to take such a risk. So what is it?" I asked.

"King Aimilios is over at the South meeting with King Abas. There are rumors that the North is harboring a female mortal here. Is it true?" Yanni asked.

Yanni was the son of King Abas, so he received information first-hand. Our friendship at one time would have been against the law, but since the treaty between the South and the North, communication was no longer forbidden, although certain kinds of fraternizing remained a crime. No one from the North could enter into a romantic relationship with anyone from the South, and vice versa. This was on account of King Abas's fear that mingling between the two sides could one day cause an uprising, which he knew all too well he was sure to be the victim of. The king of the North was greatly loved, even by the people of the South. It was often rumored that they wished for a king like ours.

"Who told you about this?" I asked.

"My father told me, of course, so is it true?" Yanni asked again.

"Come here," I said in a whisper and gestured for Yanni to walk further away from where we stood. "What is your father saying about this?" I asked desperately.

Yanni's expression grew dim. "He said he is going to make sure King Aimilios made good on the treaty this time and killed the mortal. He is there telling King Aimilios this right now."

I wrenched my clothes and clenched my teeth. I was trying my best to hold in the actual fury I wanted to release. Zyaire was in the distance, and I wanted her to know nothing of this absurdity.

"No, he can't do this, they can't kill her," I said through a raised, but hushed voice.

Then I heard a noise just behind me, and both Yanni and I turned around to find Zyaire standing there. Her face was pale, and she was gazing at me with a look of betrayal.

"I'm going to die?" she asked, barely able to raise her voice above a whisper.

Yanni was speechless when he saw her. He looked her up and down, observing the nature of her injuries from the maze, but when he looked back up at her face, I could tell that even he could not help but recognize Zyaire's dazzling beauty as he stared into her piercing blue eyes. I approached her swiftly.

"No, I won't let that happen," I promised.

"You lied to me. You told me I wasn't in danger!" Zyaire wailed, tears beginning to stream down her cheeks. I stared away, looking down toward the ground, ashamed, knowing that her words were true. I did not tell her that she was in danger. I could not. I only wanted to protect her from how she was feeling right now. I hated myself in that moment, knowing I had failed her.

"So is this dinner even about your birthday, or is it my last meal?" Zyaire asked, terrified.

"I won't let it come to that," I promised again.

"Stop it!" she yelled, then slightly doubled over, and rubbed her stomach, as it seemingly grew nauseous. "Stop making promises to me that you can't keep." Zyaire then glared at Yanni, who was still standing on the other side of the gate. "Who are you? Are you here to take me to die?" she asked.

Yanni's handsome pale face grew even paler. "No, I'm Yanni, Acaeus's best friend. I just came to tell him the..." Yanni paused and stared into Zyaire's watery blue eyes. "I'm sorry," he said, seemingly wishing like me that there was something more that he could offer other than his apology.

I walked over and stood face-to-face with Zyaire, putting both my hands on her shoulders, commanding her attention. "Listen to me. I promised that I would protect you, and I intend to keep that promise."

"Why would they want to hurt me? I haven't done anything wrong."

"It's complicated, and I will tell you all about it, but right now we have to get back into the castle and have dinner as planned. Our best defense right now is to stay calm," I reasoned.

"How can I stay calm after hearing that I am going to be killed?" Zyaire asked.

"That won't happen," Yanni blurted out suddenly, and Zyaire and I both turned around and looked at him.

"I will talk to my father. I will get him to change his mind about this. I will help you. You have my word," he promised. The words had for sure come out of Yanni's mouth before he had even thought about it. Obviously, seeing Zyaire agonizing, he could no longer take it. He could see the fear in her innocent eyes, and it had undoubtedly touched him.

"That's a great idea, Yanni," I said. "Your father respects your opinion. He will listen to you."

"I am petrified that my life is now dependent on someone I don't even know. But what choice do I have now? I have to trust you, Yanni," Zyaire said. She turned and looked at me. "Acaeus, I still trust you. No matter how illogical that might be, since you have already lied to me. And if Yanni is your best friend, I trust him too."

In that moment, I could only stare at Zyaire in amazement. Her strength and trust in me deemed me beyond words.

"Thank you for trusting me. I'll come back tomorrow so I can let you know what happened," Yanni promised. "I have to go now before someone realizes I am gone." He turned to walk away, but Zyaire stopped him in his tracks.

"Wait," she yelled out to him. She walked up to the gate, and he met her there. She reached out and grabbed his hand. "Please, convince your father not to hurt me. I will go home and never come back here. I won't tell anyone about Aphrodan. It will be like this never happened," she promised.

I could see the desperation in Zyaire's eyes, and it killed me. Her face was still pale, and her lips shivered as she spoke to Yanni. "I'll do my best to get through to him," Yanni promised before ducking off into the night.

ZYAIRE

Acaeus reached out and grabbed my hand. I was still standing at the gate and staring out into the night. "I am going to talk to King Aimilios when he gets back from the South," he said, attempting to assure me. "Surely he will listen to me once I tell him…"

"King who?" I interrupted. I had never heard Acaeus refer to the king by his actual name before and was shocked when I heard the same name my great-grandmother had mentioned in her letter.

"King Aimilios," Acaeus continued. "He is the king of the North, and King Abas, Yanni's father, is the king of the South. I will talk to King Aimilios. I will get him to meet with you. I know if he spends some time with you, he will not allow anything to happen to you, no matter what that ridiculous treaty says."

"What treaty?" I asked, still in shock after just finding out that my great-grandmother's lover was the king of a secret world.

"There is a peace treaty between the South and the North, the second of its kind. The South and the North have never gotten along. They were always at odds. However, years ago, they signed a peace treaty centered on their agreement that a mortal entering Aphrodan would be dangerous to our world. Both kings agreed that if a mortal entered the world, they would be..." Acaeus paused.

"Put to death," I finished.

"Yes," Acaeus admitted somberly. "When a mortal did finally enter Aphrodan, King Aimilios broke the treaty when he decided to spare her life. I am confident he will spare yours too, Zyaire. Who would want to hurt you?" Acaeus said, as he affectionately chucked a finger under my chin. Then he gently rubbed my back to comfort me. He knew how I was feeling in that moment.

I closed my eyes, inhaled deeply, and allowed Acaeus to comfort me. He held me in his arms, and I fell deep in thought. I was sure that my great-grandmother was the mortal that King Aimilios had spared, and almost as equally, sure that he was the man my great-grandmother spoke of in her diary. I would have to read more to be certain. Until then, I would say nothing to anyone. If Yanni's and Acaeus's attempts to save me fails, then it may be the love between King Aimilios and my great-grandmother that I would have to count on to save my own life. All I could do now was hope that Yanni and Acaeus would pull through for me, and if they didn't, maybe my great-grandmother's love would.

Chapter 18
Choosing Sides
(YANNI)

More than two hours had passed before I finally arrived back at the South of Aphrodan. Fantastic fireworks lit the sky as they had most evenings, a tradition frequently followed by our people to bring beauty to our long nights. I had to stop frequently and hide for fear of being recognized, which prolonged my return. I snuck back in through the back entrance of the castle. I spotted King Aimilios and some others leaving when I arrived. I wasted no time and went straight to my father's quarters. I wanted to know what he and King Aimilios decided to do with Zyaire.

"Father," I said, entering into his study and finding him sitting at his desk with just the desk lamp on.

"Hold one second, son, let me finishing signing my approval for this execution."

"You're executing someone again, Father?" I asked bewildered.

"Yes, son. If I don't heavily enforce the laws of our land, who will? Some people foolishly think that they have a right to their own beliefs and opinions despite my explicit orders. If you want to rid the kingdom of such tyranny, you make an example of someone."

My father continued to look down, placing his signature on several pages.

Finally, my father, the king, looked up from what he was doing and stared at his son. "Where have you been? I sent for you, and no one could find you," he asked.

"I was out in the garden reading," I lied.

"Ah, my son, the scholar," he exclaimed.

"Why were you looking for me, Father? I see King Aimilios was here. Is something wrong? What will he do with the mortal?"

My father stood up and switched on the lights in the room. He was draped in a long sleeveless mink vest, large gold chains dangled from his neck, and elaborate rings shined from the knuckles of his hands. His head was still covered by his golden crown bearing fifteen priceless jewels. These days you would only see King Aimilios wearing his crown during ceremonial occasion, yet my father still wears his crown each day, as a way to remind his people of his authority over them.

"As you already know, a mortal has once again penetrated our world, and this time I am going to make sure the North honors our treaty and the mortal is put to death," my father said. "That pocketbook must be destroyed for the last time. It is a threat to our world and everything we know."

At that moment, I knew I was speaking to the king, and not my father. King Abas was determined in his words, and my face grew dim hearing them.

"So what does King Aimilios say about this?" I asked.

"He claims he wants to honor the treaty this time around, and that he came to me today out of respect and good faith to make me aware of the situation, but Aimilios is weak. Kindness is his infirmity, but not mine. If he refuses to destroy the mortal, I will not hesitate to invade his castle, seize her, and execute her myself." King Abas's words were sharp and devastating for me to hear.

"But, King, if you do that, you know we would then be at war. Surely, there is another way to settle this if King Aimilios does want to spare the mortal. Why not just send her back?" I suggested.

"Because the pocketbook would go with her," King Abas yelled, pounding his fist on his desk. He stood up and began to pace.

"I swear, if Aimilios backs out of this treaty by breaking one of its conditions, I will make him food for the Black Lions just as his father was."

My father's hazel eyes blazed in fury. His large and intimidating frame shook with animosity as he paced up and down the floor. I was a dead ringer for him. We shared the same light hair, pale skin, square jaw, athletic frame, but our personalities could not have been more different.

King Abas was stern, intimidating, and ruled with a heavy hand. In contrast, while King Aimilios's subjects were loyal out of love, King Abas's subjects were loyal out of fear. Yet they adored me, heir to the throne of the South. My gentle nature, humor, and reasonable outlook were favored amongst the Southerners; and they silently longed for the day when I would become king. Many subjects have told me as much.

"My king, don't you think it's best we wait before we declare war against the North?" I again reasoned. "We don't even know what King Aimilios will do, and I'll be honest, Father, the thought of taking an innocent life doesn't seem fair to even me."

My father looked at me in disgust. "I let your mother become too involved in your upbringing. She has made you weak and soft. Your emotions make you vulnerable. How can you be the future king of the South if you cannot stomach what is your duty. Your duty is to protect our rulership at all cost. Do you understand that if the North gets close with this mortal, they can learn secrets from her that will allow them to overthrow our kingdom? Wake up, son, you are not a child anymore, and you are either with me, or against me. But choose now because if King Aimilios lets this mortal live, I will draw a line in the sand, and blood will be lost, one way or the other."

Then my father approached me, and I stood face-to-face with him as he continued. "You are the future heir of the South. I need you by my side to be my eyes and ears. Tell me now, are you with me or against me?" He held out his hand to his son, and servant. I paused for a brief moment, knowing my decision now could determine my future rein over the South. After little thought, I reached out and shook my father's hand firmly.

"I am with you, I promise," I said.

My father pulled me into an embrace. As the king hugged me proudly, the only thing present in my mind was the beautiful, innocent face of Zyaire, and the thoughts of how just hours earlier I had made a promise to her that I now could not keep.

"Tomorrow, I want you to leave early and travel to the North," My father demanded. "I was never keen on your friendship with Acaeus, but I knew one day it would serve us well. I want you to find out from him what they are planning to do with the mortal, but be discreet. I want him to believe he can trust you. So talk to him as if you are on his side. If they are planning to save the mortal, the sooner we know, the more likely we will be able to devise a plan to get that pocketbook and destroy her ourselves."

I wrenched at his words, but I wanted to please him. "Yes, Father. I will leave first thing in the morning," I said.

I left my father's study and walked the long halls to my bedroom. I could not get Zyaire's face out of my memory. Her brilliant blue eyes and her innocent expression haunted me as I strolled down the long, dim corridor leading to my room. My agreement with my father to betray Zyaire as well as my best friend was weighing heavily on me. When I entered my room, I stood at the tall mirror adjacent to my bed, and my striking reflection that resembled my father's stared back at me.

"You're not a child anymore, Yanni," I admitted to myself aloud. "You're the heir of the South, the black lion of the kingdom—fearless and deadly." I pounded my chest. "You are a man, true to your purpose, and a staunch defender of Aphrodan in its entirety. Your position cannot waver. Your path has already been chosen." I looked at my reflection as its expression changed from worried to determined. "You are the future king," I proclaimed. Then I stood there for a while watching as my eyes grew more intense. I knew, in that moment, that in a short course of time, my intentions would be made clear, and my life would change forever.

Chapter 19

A Party to Remember

(ZYAIRE)

I had always been told that I was mature beyond my years, but when Acaeus left me alone in my room to get cleaned up, and dressed for the party, my first instinct was to throw a tantrum once that door closed. I wanted to literally throw myself on the floor and cry, kick, and scream like a toddler. However, I chose to live up to the mature facade that everyone else believed I actually possessed. Like many times before, I was actually scared to death, but I pulled myself together as I had on many occasions after my parents' infamous fights, and went on as normal.

After a quick bath, I put on the brand-new dress that was left on my bed for me when I'd returned. Acaeus had thought of everything…except the chance that I might find out what was really going on around here. On our way back into the castle from the garden, when we passed through the Great Hall, I again noticed the empty spot on the wall. I now wondered if the picture that once hung in that spot was my great-grandmother's. Then that would make her a queen, and I had no reason to think that she was ever that. The more pieces I put together, the more anxious I was to know how much truth was in my suspicions. I went to grab my great-grandmother's diary to read while I waited for Acaeus, but a knock came at the door before I had a chance to pull it from underneath the bed. When I opened the door, instead of seeing Acaeus whom I was expecting, I was met by two little twin girls instead.

"Are you Zyaire?" they asked in unison.

"That's me, and who are you two?" I asked cheerfully.

"We are Acaeus's sisters," one of them said. "We came to take you to his party," said the other.

"Aw, how sweet," I regarded. "Wait right here just a second and let me grab one thing, okay?"

I darted back into my room, grabbed the sheer scarf that accompanied the primrose-colored dress I was wearing, threw it over my shoulders, then hurried back to the door where the girls anxiously awaited my return.

"Okay, I am all yours," I said. Each girl grabbed one of my hands and led me down the halls. We went in a different direction than the one I had been through with Acaeus. "I have never been to this part of the castle before," I said as we continued to walk hand in hand.

"The party is in the north wing of the castle," one of the girls said.

"In the ballroom," the other chimed in.

Realizing I didn't know their names, I finally asked, "What are your names?"

"I am Alena."

"And I am Alyssa."

"We are six years old," they once again spoke in unison.

Besides from a slight difference in their height, the twins looked exactly alike. Both of them had their thick, black hair pulled to the top of their heads in an adorable bun. They wore matching pink frilly dresses that flared out at the bottom. Their eyes were a beautiful shade of brown, and delicate light freckles were speckled on their cheeks.

As we neared the location of the party, I could hear loud voices and music escaping from the closed double doors. It made me think of my party. I could only hope that no disaster would happen at Acaeus's party, as it did mine. The girls each grabbed a separate moon-shaped handle of the door. The handles of the doors were shaped just as the handle of the door in the dungeon when I first arrived in Aphrodan. When they pulled the doors open, the music became louder, yet the laughter that filled the air quickly came to a halt as everyone stared in our direction. I noticed Acaeus from across the room, and he quickly rushed to my side. He grabbed me by the hand, signaled the music to stop, and spoke openly to the crowd. The room was filled with people both young and old.

"Attention, everyone, I am sure you all know by now that we have a visitor amongst us. Well, this is she. Please welcome the beautiful Zyaire, who is going to be my guest for the evening."

"Kalosórisma!" the crowd all cheered.

"That means 'welcome,'" Acaeus leaned in to tell me.

"Thank you," I replied then curtsied. I had no idea why I curtsied, but it just seemed like the right thing to do at the time.

"Now that we have gotten that out of the way, and you have all gotten your eyeful, let's party," Acaeus said; then he screamed out "OPA!" before the music started again. The crowd mirrored his enthusiasm, repeating "OPA!" loudly before returning to their mingling. I had heard the word "opa" before during my stay in Greece. I knew it was a word used to signify praise or applause. Once again I was amazed to see how similar Aphrodan was to the world I lived in. There was even a DJ bumping his head up and down as his selection of music blared through the speakers. This was no medieval times as I had first imagined it to be. History and modernization were both beautifully woven into this one world. The DJ's ears were adorned with large headphones, just like I'd see back home, and as I glanced around the room I saw a young boy sitting off in the corner alone with ear buds in his ears, busily playing what seemed to be a hand held video game. The room was lit with shining lights fixated in the ceilings supplied by electricity, unlike the all candle lit room that I was a guest in.

"Let me take you to meet my parents," Acaeus said, interrupting my thoughts.

"Okay," I replied bashfully.

"You are not nervous, are you?" he asked.

"Just a little. I have never met royalty before. Well, besides you," I corrected.

"We are no different than you. Don't worry, they will love you, and you will love them."

He led me across the ballroom floor to where the head table was set up. Unlike all the other round tables in the room, the head table was rectangular and stretched across the front of the room from almost beginning to end. The table was decorated handsomely with fresh flowers, fruits, and greenery draped across the front and corners. As we walked closer, Acaeus's parents noticed us approaching and stood up.

"Happy birthday, son," his mother said, her eyes beaming at him, and then me.

"Yes, happy birthday, Acaeus. I see you were finally able to make your way up here through the crowd, son," his father said.

"Is that your way of telling me I kept you waiting, Father?" Acaeus smiled. Then he greeted them with a shallow bow of his head. "Mother, Father, thank you for your well wishes. I would like to introduce you to my guest, Zyaire." Acaeus gently nudged me forward with a hand against my back. "Zyaire, this is my mother, Princess Carissa, and my father, General Corban."

"It's really nice to meet you, thank you so much for having me," I said with a shaking voice.

"It is our pleasure," General Corban said. Smiling broadly, he reached out, took my hand, and kissed it.

"You are an enchantingly beautiful girl, Zyaire," Princess Carissa said, grabbing hold to just the fingers of my hand after her husband and delicately shaking it with a gentle movement.

"Thank you, Princess Carissa," I said, blushing.

"Oh, just call me Carissa please. There is no need for such titles here. After all, these are the days of the new moon," she said, smiling. I wasn't sure what that meant, but I smiled back.

Acaeus's mother was an attractive woman, and his father was also handsome, but their looks were nothing in comparison to Acaeus. In fact, he did not look much like his parents at all. Like Acaeus, his parents were charming and friendly, but their appearances were very different from his. Acaeus was tall, yet both his mom and dad were average in height. His mother actually leaned more on the short side. In them, Acaeus's large green eyes were replaced with eyes that were small and dark brown in color. They were both pleasant enough to look at, but they did not have the strikingly good looks that Acaeus had. Alena and Alyssa, his twin sisters, looked much like their parents. They were the doll-size figures of their mother, all the way up to their button noses and their thick black hair. But not Acaeus. He was different. He was perfection.

After Acaeus and I went down the line of people sitting at the table, and he had introduced me to them all, we went and took our seats with his parents. One sat on each side of us.

"Zyaire, I am so sorry my brother, the king, could not join us tonight. He is still very weary from his travel. Perhaps you will meet him another time," Princess Carissa said.

"Perhaps," Acaeus said abruptly then changed the subject. He was right to recognize that any mention of the king would remind me of the danger I was in. Before the situation could become awkward, Alyssa and Alena came bumping behind us, crowding between both Acaeus and myself.

"What are you two up to?" Acaeus said, tickling them both and making them laugh hysterically.

"Alena and I want to sit here with you two," Alyssa said, jumping up and plopping down onto Acaeus's lap. Alena followed and climbed into mine.

"Wouldn't you two much rather stay over there with all the other kids at the table I had set up especially for you?" Acaeus asked.

"No," they both whined.

"We want to sit here with you," Alyssa said, "and Zyaire," Alena followed. She lay her head on my shoulder and hugged me tightly.

"Well, I guess that means you two do not want the chocolate cake that is coming to your table after dinner. I will send word to the cook not to send your pieces out," Princess Carissa interjected. She started to put up one finger in the air before both the twins looked amusingly at Acaeus and me, their small eyes opened as big as they could get them, and together they chimed, "Goodbye!" They quickly jumped out of our laps and dashed back to where they came from. We all laughed.

"Chocolate is always the best bribery," Princess Carissa said, still laughing.

"Yes, it always works on you," the general said to his wife, and picked up a small chocolate appetizer that sat on the table in a small stacked tray filled with treats. He brought it up to her lips. She took a bite and then gave her husband a lingering tender kiss on his mouth before finally setting his lips free. They gazed at each other lovingly as they pulled away.

"See, I told you," General Corban said, smiling.

"Don't you two get all mushy on us," Acaeus said.

As I watched them, and watched Acaeus looking on at them, it reminded me of the days I used to watch my parents during moments like that. Those days had long since gone, and only memories now replaced them.

The music and chatter continued even after the food was served. It was all delicious, but I was amazed by a dish that they called saganaki. It was a melted cheese dish. By way of tradition, it was flambéed at the table by our server. As the flame was lit, everyone screamed out, "Opa!" The taste of the dish was just as exciting as the theatrics.

After dinner, the music became livelier, and Acaeus got on the dance floor and did a choreographed dance with his father, and then his mother. Soon after the crowd joined in. The sound of beating drums and high-pitched instruments thumped into the large ballroom. I stood with the group of onlookers and clapped my hands in rhythm as they did. Acaeus's eyes eventually locked with mine, and I smiled at him. He was so handsome and full of life. It wasn't just his looks that made him so attractive; it was who he was, the gentleness in him, and the kindness he shared toward me, a girl he barely knew. I looked out in the crowd and spotted him twirling a little girl around in a wheelchair. I knew right away that it was Adelphie's little sister, Kate. They looked just alike. Acaeus was being so sweet and gentle with her, making her laugh as he twirled her across the dance floor. He signaled for me to join him, but I shied away, shaking my head. He would not take no for an answer. He came toward me with his hand out.

"Come on, take off your shoes, and let's dance."

"Take off my shoes?" I asked in rebellion.

"Yes, be carefree, and just dance with me." He looked at me with that "trust me" look again, and I slid off my shoes and let him lead me on to the dance floor.

I had years of dance lessons, but this was his world; he was the instructor and I was his student. He glided me up and down the floor. Our rhythm was fast, yet smooth. I kept up with him as best I could. I threw my head back and laughed aloud when he twirled me around without pause; then he pulled me in closer and rocked with me from side to side. He entranced me—enchanted even. I had been so enthralled by the adventure that I had completely forgotten the imminent danger that I would soon face. Then I heard a loud crash coming from the corner of the room. Startled, I was jerked out of my trance. Chants of "Opa!" followed the crash, and another crash soon followed that. It was the sound of plates being purposely broken onto the floor. I had seen this happen at a party we attended at a restaurant when I was in Greece with my parents, but I was still surprised to see it happening here in Aphrodan. Two plates were handed to Acaeus and me. He looked at me for approval.

"Sure, let's do it!" I exclaimed. We smashed the plates onto the floor, and then Acaeus swooped me up into his arms and led me away so I would not step on the glass with my bare feet. There was something fun about breaking things, especially since I grew up in a house where my mother was always screaming, "Don't go near that!" whenever I came slightly close to any of her priceless items scattered throughout our house.

"Let's break more," I said, my eyes gleaming like a kid experiencing something exciting for the first time. Acaeus laughed at my childlike behavior as he led me in his arms across the dance floor. When we reached the carpeted area of the ballroom, Acaeus put me down gently.

"I love this carefree side of you, and I love that you bring out this carefree side of me," he said, looking down at me.

"Well, it's kind of funny," I said. "I didn't have this carefree side before I got here, or before I met you."

Our tender moment was accented when a beautiful woman who stood in the middle of the dance floor began to hum into the microphone she held in her hand to the sound of the sweetest music I had ever heard. Handsome couples filled the dance floor around her, and for the first time I noticed there was not an unattractive person in the whole room. I had never seen so many beautiful faces in one place. I stepped back into my shoes, and Acaeus led me out onto the floor. We danced, and every connection I thought I felt the day I danced with Tyler at my party seemed bleak in comparison to the way I was feeling in that moment.

As the night wound down and Acaeus wandered off to thank everyone for coming, I tried to forget what happened in the garden, but my mind frequently strayed. I was afraid of what might happen to me and wondered if I would make it out of Aphrodan alive. At the end of dinner, the head cook, Adelphie, brought out a beautiful cake in honor of the birthday boy, but Acaeus, sensing the growing anxiety in me, apologized to everyone, and opted for us to eat our pieces later. Before leaving, he cut the first piece, which was traditional in Aphrodan, just like in my world; then he discreetly asked Adelphie to have two pieces sent to the Gold Room.

In the Gold Room we were lying there silent for the moment until there was a knock on the door.

"You may enter," Acaeus called out.

A tall, slender man entered the room delivering a tray with two very large pieces of cake on it and two glasses of sparkling water. Acaeus placed the tray on the nightstand next to the bed and picked up a plate to offer me.

"No thanks, I am not in the mood for cake," I said.

"You are actually in the perfect mood for cake," Acaeus replied. "So come on, eat it. Sweets always make people feel better. Besides, it is my birthday, and it would be bad luck if I ate my cake alone," Acaeus said, smiling.

"Bad luck?" I laughed. "So what will happen to you if I don't eat it?" I asked.

"I could endure misery, pain, sickness, a life of boredom, or perhaps eternal years of my mom dressing me. Who knows! Do you really want me to eat this alone and have to find out?" he joked.

I let out a hearty laugh. "How do you do that?" I asked.

"Do what?"

"Make me laugh when all I should be doing right now is crying."

"I told you that I would protect you, and I meant it. I would head a war to save you if I must." I hoped it would not come to anything like that.

"Well, if you can make me laugh at a time like this, then no army has a chance against you. You would just charm them to death," I declared.

"So you think I'm charming?" Acaeus asked.

"That's not what I meant," I replied.

"So you don't think I'm charming? Is it the whole 'my mother dressing me' thing?" he asked, smiling at me again, and once more staring into my eyes as if he was hypnotized by them. I stared back at him, smiling, and then I changed the subject. I was too embarrassed to tell him yes, I did find him immensely charming, and handsome, beautiful even.

I cleared my throat and looked away briefly before returning my gaze to him. "Your mother seems very proud of you. I can't tell you the last time I made my mother proud," I said.

"Well, I will not believe that. Look at you, Zyaire, you are smart, you are fun to be around, you are strong, and beautiful." Acaeus put his hand on top of my hand. "I am sure your mother is very proud of you."

"Well, I would give anything to see even her disapproving look right now," I admitted. "Not that I don't enjoy being here with you," I quickly explained.

"I know," Acaeus said with understanding. "I am going to talk to King Aimilios. He is long back from the South by now. He is a good person, and I don't believe he will let anything happen to you. I know you are in a place that is unfamiliar to you, and I know you must be terrified, but I need you to put a little bit of trust in me. I won't let anything happen to you, I promise."

I laid my head on Acaeus's shoulder, and he gently massaged my scalp with his fingers, just like my father used to do when I was worried about something as a kid. He used to say my hair was soft and smelled like the petals of roses. We stayed like that for a moment, sharing one piece of cake, and then talking about our families. I only spoke briefly about my father and made no mention of the disaster that took place my last night in Massachusetts. After seeing how in love Acaeus's parents were, I was even more embarrassed to talk about it.

"Do you have a lot of friends where you're from?" Acaeus asked.

I sat up and crossed my legs Indian style. If I had lain there much longer with him rubbing my head, I would have fallen asleep. "I used to, but I cut a lot of them off. Now I mostly hang with my best friend, Teresa," I said.

"What is she like?" Acaeus asked, obviously trying to keep my mind on home.

I smiled. "She is crazy, in a good way. She's funny, pretty, carefree, kind, and very flirtatious. She can talk me into doing practically anything. She is just that persuasive." I laughed thinking of Teresa and how she could always talk me into doing the craziest things. "One time she convinced me to join our school talent show with her. I hate putting myself on display, but she shamed me into doing it, since all the proceeds from ticket sales would go toward helping fund the completion of an animal shelter that was being built."

"Oh, I see, so animals are your weak spot?" Acaeus asked.

"Yes, and get this, for our talent she was a rapping magician, and I was her hype man apprentice. It was hilarious. Oh wait, do you even know what rap is?" I asked, remembering where I was.

Acaeus returned my laughter. "Yes, Zyaire. There is nothing your world is privy to that my world has yet to discover. After all we are the dominate species," Acaeus bragged.

"Is that so?" I asked, challenging him.

"Yes, we are the descendants of a Greek goddess. We are educated, inventive, witty, vivacious, cunning, powerful, handsome, and seasoned. We live long lives so we have time to acquire things far beyond mere mortals' beliefs. Our oldest living is 302 years old. Your world celebrates when a human merely passes the age of one hundred. And even still…" Acaeus tone changed and he looked at me tenderly, and defenseless. "And even still, when I am around you I feel dominated, I feel weaker."

His words made me weak, and then we were silent for a moment after that, but the atmosphere was loud around us. I could hear his heart and mine beating in unison. Finally, he interrupted the silence.

"You were telling me about Teresa, and I took you away from your story. I apologize."

I really missed my best friend, and could only imagine what she would do if she was here right now. For one thing, she would be yelling for me to kiss Acaeus, and telling me how hot he was. She would probably storm over to the South herself and give King Abas a piece of her mind.

"What about you?" I asked. "I bet you have many friends."

"I have many acquaintances, but as far as real friends, just Yanni, who you met earlier. Our friendship is unconventional because we are from opposite sides of the kingdom, but we just clicked immediately. He has this subtle sense of humor that I just get. Yanni is also very confident and strong-willed. He likes to do things his own way, which I too can completely relate. More importantly, he is loyal. He knows things about me that no one knows. I trust him with my life."

"And mine?" I asked.

"Yes, and yours," Acaeus assured me. I let out a deep yawn and stretched my arms.

"You're tired, I should let you rest," Acaeus told me. Like before, I did not want to let him leave my side, but I was tired, and there was something I wanted to take care of once he was gone.

"Okay. I'll let you go, but how do I find you if I need you? Do you stay here in the castle?" I asked.

"Yes, but my room is in the west wing of the castle, so it's all the way on the other side. However, there will be a guard outside your door tonight. I assigned him. He is loyal to me. If you need me, knock on the door and ask him to send for me, and I will come to you."

"Does that mean I will be locked in again?"

"It's the king's orders now, but don't worry. I will talk to him when I leave you." Acaeus rubbed his hand across mine. "I have never felt this way about anyone before. I feel like I have known you forever. Like we existed together in another world, and now we have met again." He inched closer to me on the bed, and my heart sped up as the space closed between us. I stared into his eyes and he into mine. He reached his hand out, and stroked my cheek, and I rolled my head, rubbing my face against his hand. My eyes briefly closed before staring back into his. Acaeus stood up over me and kissed me softly on the forehead.

"Good night, Zyaire."

"Good night, Acaeus."

He took one more look at me then blew out all but one of the lanterns that were lit. Then he grabbed the tray sitting on the nightstand before he walked out the door.

When Acaeus left, I sat there looking pensive for a moment. I could hardly believe all this was happening to me. Yet my thoughts went quickly from feeling like Cinderella at the ball to a prisoner of war.

The last few days were met with a whirlwind of events. It started out great. I could still remember the high I felt when I walked into my party with Black-Eyed Peas's "I Have a Feeling" blasting through the speakers. I could not have guessed that hours later I would be having my heart broken by my father and my mother's evil best friend. Not to mention being sucked into a pocketbook, meeting the guy of my dreams, and now learning my life was in danger. "If only I could get to the wizard," I thought, feeling like Dorothy in the far-off world of Oz. "He would know the answers."

Suddenly realizing I was finally alone, I jumped up and ran to the door. I listened to see if I could hear anyone on the other side of it. There was dead silence. I ran back to the bed and bent down to pull out the box containing my great-grandmother's diary. I needed to know everything that happened between her and King Aimilios. It could save my life. I turned past the first page that I had already read and found the next entry dated September 24, 1952. I lay back on the bed to read my great-grandmother's words:

> *"Today started off as a beautiful day. Aimilios gave me the most wonderful gift—a gorgeous, white horse. I named her Lillie belle, after my name and favorite flower. Aimilios and I went riding together in the afternoon, and it could not have been more romantic. We stopped and had a picnic in the largest most exquisite field I have ever seen. In fact, there were flowers growing there that I have never seen in just one part of the world. North Aphrodan is rich in nature. Its earth grows*

fruits and vegetables that America only sees specifically in one region; yet, in Aphrodan it all came together in one place.

We took our shoes off and walked around the field for a while. The grass felt like heaven between my toes. We stopped and picked two mangoes off a tree that I would have expected to see growing only in India. Then we ate it sitting under the protective leaves of a Japanese maple tree. We laid our blankets there and relaxed in the shade. Aimilios was most handsome in this element. At that moment, he was not a king but a man who loved and adored me. He stared into my eyes as we lay there, and he told me that he loved me more than he loved himself. I had to pinch myself, or I would have believed it only to be a dream. Here I was in this enchanted world with a gorgeous king who loved me dearly. If only it was all as simple as that afternoon had been.

When we returned to the castle, General Abderos was waiting for us. He told us that there were rumors that King Abas, ruler of the South, was preparing to go to war against us. The goal of this war was to kill me. I had never been so terrified in all my life, and so burdened with guilt for the possible danger my presence was bringing to Aphrodan. Of course, that night Aimilios comforted me. He told me that our army was much stronger than the South's and that they would never risk going to war with us. I was still shaking with fright, so he held me, rubbing his hands up and down my arms and legs, his touch arousing every part of me until our passion could no longer be contained. He made what could only be called love to me, and it, like every time before, was dazzling. We lay there afterward, silent for a moment, our legs intertwined, and staring into each other's eyes. I will never forget the words that he said when he finally did break our silence: "You're beautiful. You are by far the most beautiful woman I have ever looked upon, but that is not why I love you. I love you because you are intelligent, brave, caring, and witty. You make me smile and laugh. With you, I forget I am a king, and remember what it is like to just be a man. I have never adored anything as much as I adore you, and I won't imagine my life without you in it."

The next thing he said to me I answered without hesitation. He sat up and grabbed my hands, demanding my full attention. His hands were shaking a bit, and his palms were clammy. I had never seen him nervous before this. "Will you pledge yourself to me," he asked. "Will you marry me?" I, without a moment of doubt, said, "Yes!"

That is right, today, September 24, 1952, I have agreed to be the wife of King Aimilios, sovereign ruler of the North of Aphrodan—this strange yet wonderful world that I have literally been dropped into. It's needless to say, I could not be any happier."

I reread the last sentence while lying there still, and deep in thought. The empty spot on the wall could have once been the picture of my great-grandmother. Before long, my daydreams were distracted by the sound of a key turning in the knob of the door. I was terrified of who could be on the other side, and all I could think to do was run and hide. I tossed both the diary and the box underneath the bed, not bothering to put them back the same way that I found them.

Then I ran into the closet and closed the door, leaving it slightly cracked. I could hear my heart pounding rapidly, and the beats increased by the moment. I peeked out as the door opened slowly. A shadow cast across the floor before the figure entered the room. I held my breath afraid to make even the slightest noise. The shadow grew smaller as the person inched past the doorway. My fear increased as I stood in limbo wondering whether this would be the moment my life would end. Was this an assassin coming to fulfill the treaty? Would I ever see my friend and family again?

Just as tears began to fill my eyes, they were halted by a familiar voice saying my name in a whisper, "Zyaire, Zyaire."

It sounded like Acaeus, but the person who entered the doorway was dressed in all black, and a hood covered his head. I dared not move until I was sure it was him.

"Zyaire, where are you?" the male voice asked. Closing the door behind him, the image walked toward the bathroom and swung the door open. It then hurried toward the window and looked out. The voice of the male figure got desperate.

"Zyaire, where are you?" he asked then pulled the hood from his head, revealing the face of Acaeus. I came out from the closet, and Acaeus looked at me puzzled.

"Don't look at me like that, you are the one standing there looking like the Grim Reaper," I huffed. "What are you trying to do, scare me to my death?" I asked.

"Who is the Grim Reaper?" Acaeus asked, getting more confused by the moment.

"The angel of death. The one who wears all black and a hood, and he carries a scary-looking scythe in his hand. He looks exactly how you looked with that hood on," I explained.

"A scythe? Like the god Chronus used to carry?" Acaeus asked, still confused.

"Ew, you mean the one who ate his children?" I asked.

"He didn't actually eat his children. That was just a tale. The tale of him eating his children was only supposed to be taken in a poetic sense, for time devouring all things. You know like the old saying, 'Nothing lasts forever.'"

"Right, well, I meant you look like the Grim Reaper because you are wearing all black and have a hood over your head, and you snuck into here like you wanted to kill me just as a Grim Reaper does."

Acaeus smiled at me in amusement. "Okay, so that clears one thing up. Now why were you in the closet?" he asked.

"I was hiding. I didn't know who was coming in the door. Knowing someone is out to kill you makes you a little jumpy, who would have known? And in spite of my insecurities, I happen to like my body, and I don't want it maimed, hung, or killed," I stressed.

Acaeus laughed at me rambling. "You know, you are very cute when you're mad," he said and walked over to give me a hug. He squeezed me gently in his arms. "I'm sorry I upset you."

"I'm sorry too. One more second and I would have wet my pants," I admitted. We both laughed aloud, and Acaeus hugged me again. I buried my face into his chest. He smelled so good, and I took in his scent with a deep breath. "Wait, why are you here?" I asked, pulling free from his embrace. "Did something happen?"

Acaeus took a deep breath, as if he was dreading the words he had to say to me. "I talked to King Aimilios. I tried to get him to come and visit you, but he won't."

"Why won't he see me?" I asked. Acaeus turned his back to me and paced the floor for a moment.

"Just tell me," I demanded. "I want to know everything. This is my life on the line. Please don't keep anything else from me," I pleaded.

Acaeus grabbed me by the hand and led me to the bed so we both could sit down. He took a deep breath before talking. "I asked King Aimilios how things went with King Abas, and he told me that he still expected him to honor their treaty agreements."

"Meaning the treaty that says I have to be put to death?"

"Yes, that ridiculous treaty." Acaeus looked me dead in the eyes. "You told me not to hold anything back, so I am telling you everything."

"Go ahead, what else did he say?"

"He said we could not afford to break our treaty with the South again, that their army has grown stronger over the years, and if we break from the treaty by keeping you alive, a war would ensue, and the North is not guaranteed to win."

"So that's it, he wants me dead?" I asked.

"Not exactly, he said he would attempt to dissuade King Abas from taking your life, and perhaps maybe just imprison you."

"What?" I exclaimed and burst into tears. "No, I can't go to prison. I just want to go home. He has to see me. He has to let me talk to him, and explain that I will never come back here."

"My heart breaks at the thought of never seeing you again, Zyaire, but if that is what it would take to keep you safe, I would welcome the heartache. I begged him to see you. I even accused him of not seeing you on purpose so he would not have to see your face in his mind every night knowing what he had done to you. He told me to remember my role, and that it was not wise to speak to my king that way. He was right. It is very dangerous and disrespectful to quarrel with a king. I had nothing left to say at that point, because I already knew what I must do."

Acaeus walked over to me and placed his hands on my shoulders. "I won't let them kill you, or even throw you into prison, which is still death. There is only one way to save you, and that is to get you out of here tonight."

"How would we do that? Where would we go?" I asked, bewildered.

"There aren't that many places where we can go that they won't look for us," Acaeus admitted. "I have some ideas, the last more dangerous than the first."

"I trust you," I said, a single tear trickling down my face. "But I'm afraid. If they catch us, what will happen to me?"

"They won't, because we are going to leave now while the sun is down. They won't expect it."

"But we can't hide forever," I reasoned.

"And we won't have to," Acaeus declared. "Before we leave, I am going to grab a few things. Food, supplies, clothes for you and me, water, packs for us to carry on our backs, and the pocketbook."

My eyes opened wide. "You're going to steal the pocketbook?"

"Yes, we need it with us so you can get back home."

I threw my arms around Acaeus. "Thank you."

"You're welcome," he said, hugging me tightly and then pulling away. "Okay, I need you to listen carefully, the sun will not stay down for much longer."

"Is it that late already?" I asked.

"North Aphrodan only has six hours of darkness," Acaeus explained. He reached down and took a pocket watch out from his pants.

"Take this," he said and handed me the shiny gold watch. "When it reaches 2:45, I need you to come out of the room and turn to the right. Walk down the hall until you get to the fourth corridor on your left. Turn there, and at the end of the corridor you will see a set of doors. Go out those doors and wait for me there. Do not go down the steps. Just sit down on the ground right outside the doors. Sometimes the guards run searchlights over the entrances to make sure the area is secure, so I want you slouched down behind the banister that surrounds the steps, okay?"

I nodded my head in agreement.

"So repeat it for me. Where are you going to go when you leave the room?"

"I am going to take a right when I come out of the room, go down the hall until I reach the fourth corridor on the left. At the end of that corridor is a set of doors and I will go out those doors and wait for you."

"Sitting down slouched behind the banister," Acaeus reminded me.

"Yes, I will wait for you sitting down and slouched behind the banister."

"Also, remember you have to leave here at 2:45 exactly, because the sun rises at 3:30."

"Okay, I will remember."

Acaeus hugged me one more time. "You can do this," he said before walking out the door.

I paced the floor nervously. I looked down at the pocket watch. It was 2:00 a.m. Only forty-five minutes before Acaeus and I would attempt a great escape. I knew those forty-five minutes would feel like eternity, so I took out my great-grandmother's diary to pass the time. The next entry was October 1, 1953:

Aimilios surprised me with the most wonderful gift today. He calls it the Gold Room. A beautiful room he designed just for me detailed with my favorite color, gold! I am lying on the bed now as I am writing this. It is the most exquisite bed I have ever laid in—even more exquisite than my beloved bed at home. It is the perfect mixture of soft and firm. The room is well lit by lanterns, a touch he knew I would love since I told him how much I love to relax in the softness of candlelight. There is not a lamp in the whole room. The fireplace is directly across from the bed, and on each side of it is a sculpture, one of a man and one of a woman. He said he had it made especially for me. The two angelic figures represented us. The bathroom has a handsome soaking tub. I can't wait to soak in it when Aimilios is off doing his kingly duties. I could go on and on describing the room's beauty, the gold-painted walls, the beautiful vanity, and artistic dressers, or the unique headboard on the bed, but what took my breath away was on the outside of the room. Just outside of my window is a beautiful lily garden, my favorite flower. The assortments of colors are magnificent. I have never seen anything like it. Aimilios himself designed the beautiful landscape. We are finally going to be married tomorrow, and this, he said, was his first gift to me. It is where I will put on my wedding dress, and where I will, for the first time, say goodbye to being a bachelorette. Married life, happy wife, here I come!

As always the end of the entry was signed *"Lilly."*

I slowly gazed at the room as if I was looking at it through new eyes.

"She slept here. My great-grandmother slept in this room," I said, standing up and slowly walking up and down the room's floors. "These were her floors, designed just for her." I remembered the brush that sat on the vanity. I went over and picked it up. "This was her brush," I said. I slowly brushed through my thick black hair and then placed it back on the vanity. Then it finally hit me like a ton of bricks, my great-grandmother had in fact once been the queen of North Aphrodan.

I looked at the watch. I had twenty minutes before I would have to leave. I was still wearing the maxi dress I had changed into earlier. I had taken off my sandals, but went ahead and put them back on. As I bent down, a chill ran across my arm, and I wondered if it was the ghost of my great-grandmother. The thought did not make me afraid. I grabbed the bag that the clothes were brought to me inside of, and put the dress I was wearing when I arrived in Aphrodan inside. I also grabbed the diary and tucked it underneath my dress inside the bag.

Climbing up on the bed, I laid my head on the propped pillows. My feet slightly hung over the bed's side. I lay there silently, nervously thinking of the escape Acaeus and I would soon pursue. I watched as the hands on the pocket watch ticked away. When it reached one minute before the destined time, I jumped to my feet and grabbed the bag I intended for travel. I went to walk out the door, but first looked back at the room that had been commissioned especially for my dear great-grandmother. I felt connected to her in a way I had never had the chance to be. I went to walk out the door again, but doubled back once more. I walked to the vanity, grabbed my great-grandmother's brush, and threw it inside the bag. It and the diary were now special to me, and I was not going to leave Aphrodan without them.

The lights in the hall were dim, and I wondered if that was a usual occurrence, or had Acaeus made it that way so I would go unnoticed? I slinked down the hall, staying close to the walls on my right. My feet were moving swiftly but threading lightly as they hit the floor. When I was just about to pass the first corridor on the right, I heard voices and saw the shadows of people about to exit from a door in front of me. I quickly turned off into the corridor and peeked around the corner. I saw a male and a female walk down a few feet and then turn to go inside another room. Wasting no time, I immediately came from around the corner and resumed my journey to the fourth corridor on the left. When I reached it, I turned and looked back before sprinting across the hall. I jogged down to the doors that Acaeus mentioned. Then I opened it quickly and walked outside.

I looked out at the dark sky that was filled with stars. It was beautiful. A light appeared in the distance, and I quickly ducked down behind the banister as I was told to do. The light shined over my head and I crouched down even further, trying to ensure I was not seen. The luminous searchlight lingered there for a moment, and I feared I had been discovered. My heart began to do that oh-so-familiar race again, and I thought for a moment to just run from where I was and never turn back. Then I heard Acaeus's voice in my head, "You have to trust me," so instead I sat very still with my head down until the light finally moved on. I stayed like that, hoping Acaeus was not caught stealing the pocketbook and that he would come for me soon. I realized that we had not discussed what I was to do if he was caught and never showed up. I prayed it did not come to that, because if he didn't show up, I had no idea what I would do.

Chapter 20

Hope for Zyaire

(GERALDINE)

"Wife of John Ryan threatens to cast her line into a different sea," is what I heard my mother read aloud before I entered the kitchen. She had not left my home since Zyaire went missing a few days ago, and she vowed not to leave until she returned. When she looked up and saw me walking through the door, my mother quickly turned the page of today's paper.

"There is no need to hide it, Mother. What brilliant title did they come up with this time?" I asked, already knowing the answer. I walked over, turned the paper back to the previous page, and read its headline. I chuckled even though it was not amusing. "Well, they are getting pretty clever with tying his life as a fisherman into these titles."

The media was buzzing with the news of John's affair and Zyaire's disappearance. I made a decision to use the media to my advantage and scheduled a press conference for 10:00 a.m. The mood in the house was somber. Zyaire's phone was found under her nightstand late last night, and all hope of getting a message to her that way was lost. I checked her outgoing and incoming calls to see if she had been in contact with anyone prior to going missing, but the last call she made was to her father before the party had even begun. He had not answered. The last incoming call before she went missing was from Teresa, but they were missed calls that were placed in the early morning hours after Zyaire's party.

Things were intense, but I had stopped blaming John and had actually begun to feel a little sorry for him. The night before, I found him sitting in the living room in the dark, holding a picture of Zyaire and crying. I walked over and put my arms around him. No matter what he had done to me, I did not wish this pain on anyone, not even him.

"We will find her," I told him. "Alive," I added.

Then he grabbed my hands and told me how sorry he was for everything. I listened, but did not make any comment. I was not ready to forgive him yet, or talk about what drove him to do what he had with my once best friend.

The doorbell rang, and Mary Josie stopped cleaning and left the kitchen to get it. When she opened it, I could hear her greeting John.

"Good morning, Mr. Ryan." It must have been strange for her having him ring the doorbell instead of using his own key to come in.

"Hi, Mary Josie, good morning," John said.

"Mrs. Ryan is in the kitchen," Mary Josie informed him.

John walked back to the kitchen and found my mother and me sitting at the table having a cup of coffee. Mary Josie came in behind him.

"Would you like a cup of coffee, Mr. Ryan?" she asked.

"Yes, thank you, Mary Josie."

John sat at the table next to the women I was sure he believed hated him, but we both greeted him pleasantly enough. "So is everyone ready for this press conference?" he asked.

"Ready as one could be," my mother replied.

"Where is Dad? The media will be here soon," I asked.

"He is upstairs getting dressed. He should be down soon." Before my mother could get her last words out, my father walked into the kitchen and joined us.

"I am down now," he said pleasantly. He walked over to give his wife and then me a kiss on the cheek. "Good morning, everyone," he said, acknowledging Mary Josie and John as well.

"Coffee, Mr. Mitchell?" Mary Josie asked, holding the pot in the air.

"I will have some tea if it is not too much of a hassle, Mary Josie."

"Yes, Mr. Mitchell, no problem."

Mary Josie had returned from hiding the moment she heard Zyaire was missing. No matter how uncomfortable she was in stressful situations, she would not abandon us when we needed her the most. Besides, she loved Zyaire and saw her as a little sister. She was heartbroken and terrified when she heard that she was missing. It made me appreciate her in a way I had not allowed myself to over the years.

"So how long until the vultures arrive?" my father asked.

"They will be here soon. Mary Josie has set up chairs in the family room," I replied. Mary Josie also set out coffee and muffins for the press as well.

The doorbell rang and Mary Josie left the kitchen again to answer it. Dorian Jackson, the public relations representative that I hired for John a few years back, had arrived as scheduled just before the media. I had asked him to come to make sure the questions did not get out of hand and that the press obeyed the rules that we had put in place.

Mary Josie started to pour him a cup of coffee, but before she could fill the mug, the doorbell rang again. This time, when Mary Josie returned to the kitchen, she announced that Kate Channal from Channel 7 News had arrived. She was the first to arrive from the press, and her camera operator was right behind her, ready to film the conference. Mary Josie escorted them into the family room as she was instructed. Before she could make it back to the kitchen, the doorbell rang again. I stood at the end of the hall when she opened it, and three reporters and their crews were standing there. She led them into the family room as well. Everyone sat around, drank coffee, and ate muffins while the rest of the media arrived. The crews took time to set up. Promptly, at ten o'clock, our family was seated and the press conference began.

I started by reading a statement on behalf my family:

> Today we are here, letting the media into a very private matter in our family, in hopes that it will bring our beloved daughter and granddaughter Zyaire home. Zyaire went missing a few days ago, and we have not heard from her since. We are hoping that the public can help us find her.

I held up a picture of Zyaire.

> This is my beautiful daughter Zyaire. She was last seen wearing a multicolored cocktail dress that she wore for her sweet sixteen birthday party. We believe she was wearing this dress when she left because it is unaccounted for. If anyone has any information of her whereabouts, we are asking that you contact us immediately. We have set up a hotline for any calls offering tips to where she may be. Please call 1800-555-1212, or e-mail us at hopeforZyaire@gmail.com.

The next words I spoke were meant for my daughter, and I braced myself before speaking, something I had to do often these last few days.

> Zyaire, if you are out there and are listening, we are very worried about you, and we all love you very much. Please, I am begging you to come home where you belong.

My throat got very dry, and my voice began to crack.

> Daddy and I love you, and we miss you so much. Come home to us please.

Tears fell from my eyes and rolled down my cheeks. I looked over at my mother, and her eyes began to water as well. When I was done reading, Dorian Jackson came and stood next to the family.

"At this time, the family will be taking a very few questions. Please follow the instructions that the family has put forth so we can have a smooth experience and let the family move on with their search for their daughter," he said.

Kate Channal was the first to ask a question. "Mr. Ryan, can you tell us the height and weight of your daughter to help those who may be looking out for her?"

"Yes, Zyaire is 5'3" and 115 pounds. Also her hair is long, black, and wavy."

Jackson called on another reporter for the next question. "To the grandparents, I understand Zyaire went missing after her sweet sixteen party and you were present at the time. Is there anything that she could have said to you the last time you saw her that may help determine her whereabouts?"

"No, everything was hectic after the party, and we left before being able to say goodbye. I was here the next morning when it was discovered that my granddaughter was missing," My mother wiped a tear from her eye. Having to relive that moment was obviously as hard for her as it was me.

"Mrs. Ryan," another reporter called out of turn, "do you have any reason to believe she may have left the state?"

"I certainly hope not. She has never travelled alone before, and I seriously doubt she is anywhere outside Massachusetts." I had said the words, but I did not know if I truly believed them.

Chapter 21

The Great Escape

(ZYAIRE)

I sat still, crouched on the cold ground. The temperature had dropped from earlier, and a cold chill ran up and down my arm. My mind began to wonder in the silence. I thought about home and how much I missed my parents—even my dad. I wondered what they were doing right now, and if they were worried about me. I was sure they were, and I suddenly realized they probably thought I had run away.

"I got to get home," I mumbled. I bounced my knee up and down nervously. "Where are you, Acaeus? Please come soon."

I buried my head into my lap trying to stay as warm as possible. My feet were cold. I wished I had not been wearing sandals. I thought to take out my great-grandmother's diary and read it to pass the time, but I did not want Acaeus to show up and see me with it. I wasn't ready to let him know that I had discovered it. I began to worry at the thought of Acaeus being caught while trying to steal the pocketbook. The guards could be inside looking for me right now, I thought. I rocked back and forth partly because I was cold, but mostly to calm my nerves. It was not a freezing type of cold I was feeling, but more like a chill. It seemed as if I had been waiting there forever, but when I looked down at the pocket watch Acaeus had given me, only ten short minutes had passed. "Boy, how time stalls when you're not having fun," I thought to myself.

I lifted my head for a moment to look around. Everything was still and quiet, so I buried my head back into my lap. As soon as I did, I abruptly heard a noise. Someone was on the other side of the door. I could only hope it was Acaeus, but why was he stalling? Why hadn't he opened the door yet if it was him? I braced myself to run when the door began to swing open, but it was Acaeus who quietly walked through the exit.

He quickly kneeled down beside me as the searchlight once again loomed above. We sat there still and quiet until the searchlight finally passed.

I reached out and hugged Acaeus. "I was afraid that you got caught and you weren't coming."

"There would be no way that I would ever leave you here like this. Getting caught was not even an option," he assured me. I tightly hugged him again.

"What do we do now?" I asked.

"I need you to change your clothes."

"Here?" I asked, shocked.

"Yes, here. I will not look. I promise." Acaeus handed me a pair of black jeans, a black tank top, and black sneakers and socks.

"I am sensing a theme with all this black," I observed.

"Yes, the theme is going unnoticed when trotting across the castle's lawn."

"Good idea," I agreed and pulled my sandals off.

Acaeus turned around while I changed clothes, and he quietly whistled. I guess that was his way of blocking out that I was undressing behind him. When I was finished changing, I tapped him on the shoulder. "You can look now," I said.

Acaeus turned around. “How do girls do that?” he asked.

“Do what?”

“Change so quickly, and in the smallest of spaces?”

“It’s a gift, I guess.” I shrugged.

Acaeus handed me a hooded sweatshirt to complete my outfit, and I happily put it on. The night was humid, yet an awkward chill breezed over me repeatedly. It was cozy being in the overgrown sweatshirt.

“Are you ready to do this?” Acaeus asked. I nodded my head.

“Did you get the pocketbook?” I inquired.

“Yes, it wasn’t easy, but I got it. It’s in here.” Acaeus pointed to one of the two black backpacks he brought along with him. “Here you carry this one,” he said, handing the lighter of the two backpacks to me.

I put the backpack on and a look of worry fell over my face that did not go unnoticed by Acaeus. “I promised you that I would protect you, and I will. I promised you that I would get you home, and I will,” he confirmed to me again.

Then he grabbed me by the hand just as the searchlight passed over us. After peeking over the banister to make sure the coast was clear, he signaled to me, “Let’s go.” We ran down the steps, staying low to the ground, and sprinted across the lawn before the searchlights could make its rounds again. When we got to a locked gate, Acaeus took out a set of keys to open it. When on the outside, he locked the gate behind him.

We walked for at least a quarter of a mile before the castle was out of our sight. This was my first time out from the castle grounds—well, my first lucid time out from the castle grounds since I had been to Aphrodan. The city was beautiful, and vehicles lined the streets. They looked different from the ones back home; they were sleeker and looked beyond our time. Aphrodan was more modern than I had imagined it to be, yet history was nestled throughout. Alongside the shiny black tarred streets were cobblestone sidewalks. I looked to the left of me, and on a well-maintained parking lot surrounded by smooth sidewalks, and grass medians, stood a ten-story building appearing to be made completely of glass. Through the windows, I could see multiple desks and untucked chairs swiveled in front of them presumably from the workers as they left in a hurry to end their day. Yet to the right of me stood a beautiful ancient temple, raised from the ground, its elegant proportions illuminated by the lights that surrounded it. When we turned the corner, a swarm of people met us. I nervously inched in close to Acaeus and looked down at the ground.

"It's okay, they don't know who you are," Acaeus whispered.

"Are you sure?"

"Yes, see, no one is even looking at us."

I lifted my head and watched as the people went about their nightly business paying us no attention. The place was buzzing like a busy downtown New England Street in the heat of the evening. The women were dressed in stylish clothes, and the men were equally fashionable. I watched as some people strolled down the street with phones up to their ears, chatting away just as I would expect to see in my own world. I was in awe. However, there was still something different, regal, and classical about them all—the way they dressed, the way they walked, the sophistication of the women, the distinguished looks of the young men.

"Why are so many people out so late?" I asked.

"It is the youth of North Aphrodan you are seeing. There is not much time to enjoy nightlife here, so on weekends they stay out late until the sun begins to come up. This part of the city is lined with hops, so it's popular."

"What are hops?"

"They are strips with multiple places that play music and serve drinks. People hop from one place to the other, so they call them hops."

"They don't actually hop, do they?" I asked.

Acaeus chuckled at my question, and we both laughed hysterically at the thought of it.

"Could you imagine a bunch of people just hopping down the street?" I asked, still laughing.

Acaeus suddenly fell deep in thought.

"What are you thinking about?" I asked.

"I am thinking about how my time with you is ending. It feels like you were sent here just to bring laughter into my life and to show me what it means to be connected to someone in a way I have not before."

"What do you mean? You are connected to your family and friends, right?" I asked, confused.

"It is hard to explain, Zyaire. I guess all I can say is that I am different from other people my age. I have a purpose, with that purpose comes great responsibilities, and those responsibilities do not allow me the luxury of true connections—soul-tying connections, that is. If it was up to me, I would have you stay here with me forever as my greatest friend, but I know that would not be very wise because your safety is more important to me than anything, even my own desires."

I wanted to ask him so much about all that he had just said. What was his purpose? Did he mean being a general? Moreover, did he really only see me as a great friend, because I saw him as so much more. For once, I did not let my curiosity get the best of me. I just grabbed his hand tighter and walked with him in silence.

We travelled past the crowd of people and turned the corner down a dark alley. The alley was completely empty except for a motorcycle sitting alone and propped up next to the wall of a building.

"Good, it's here," Acaeus noted.

"Are we riding on that?" I asked.

"Yes, you don't have a problem with motorcycles, do you?"

"I don't know, I've never been on one before."

Acaeus handed me one of the two helmets that were hanging from the bike. "Put this on, in case we crash." My eyes widened. "I am just joking, I am a safe rider, I promise."

"How did you get this here?" I asked.

"Marco brought it here for me."

"Can we trust him?"

"Yes, but even still he doesn't know where I am taking you," Acaeus assured me.

"Where *are* you taking me?"

"Somewhere private that no one else knows about other than me. It is an abandoned cabin that I found hidden deep in the forest some years back. It once belonged to a sorcerer. I go there when I need time to be alone. We will be able to wait safely there until you can leave."

"What are we waiting for?" I asked.

"The pocketbook, only it can tell us when it is time for you to go. Until then, we hide and wait."

Acaeus climbed onto the bike, and I got on behind him and hugged his waist tight. He revved up the engine. "Are you ready?" he yelled to me over the noise.

"I guess so," I responded nervously.

We sped through the streets of Aphrodan. I really liked the excitement I felt from being on a motorcycle with the wind in my face, gliding in and out of the little traffic that was on the road, and my arms wrapped around Acaeus. Soon we were on a long stretch of road, and the sun had started to come up. It was a perfect view of the sunrise as we slowly drove toward it. In the distance, in the slopes of hills, I pointed excitedly at what stood before me.

"Wait, can we stop?" I yelled. Acaues pulled the bike over to the side of the road, and I looked on with marvel. "Is that an open-air theater?" I asked.

"Open air?" Acaeus asked, confused.

"Yes, a large theater that is in open space, like in times of Ancient Greece where they had performances in honor of the god Dionysus."

"You mean a theatron?" Acaeus asked, pulling his helmet from his head. "You sure know a lot about a place you've never been. Come to think of it, Zyaire, you know a lot about the gods that people of your time have never even met," Acaeus pointed out, amazed.

"I told you, it was a class I had in school. We never thought any of what we learned was real. Do they still perform here?" I asked, still enchanted by the theater.

"Only on special occasions, like during the festivals, or for the king's birthday."

"I would love to see that someday," I declared.

Acaeus smiled at me before putting his helmet back on his head. I gripped his waist again, and I held onto Acaeus tighter as he increased speed on the bike.

We finally turned off the road and drove down a dirt path that led us into what Acaeus called the North Forest. When the path ended, Acaeus stopped, and he and I jumped off the bike.

"Where is the cabin?" I asked.

"It is deeper in the forest. We are going to have to hike from here."

"What about your bike? Are you just going to leave it here?"

"No, I am going to walk it part of the way and hide it somewhere on the way to the cabin."

Acaeus and I took the long walk through the North Forest. On the way, Acaeus hid his bike as he had intended. The trees in the woods were tall—stretching almost to the sky, it seemed, as I looked up in amazement. I spied a tiny creature that I had never seen before as we walked. Its face was similar to a chinchilla, but its body resembled a rabbit. It even hopped. Then we passed a waterfall running into a lake below it. The water was crystal clear and beautiful. I squealed in delight when I saw what looked like two swans sitting at the edge of the stream, gold in color.

"What are those?" I asked, enchanted by the beautiful creatures.

"They are goldies, Aphrodan's native bird. They are believed to be mystical, and legend has it that if one were to eat from your hand, you would be granted prosperity and an extra twenty years onto your predestined life span. The legend says an extra twenty years is added for each Goldie that eats from your hand."

"That's so cool!" I said, and caused Acaeus, once again, to smile at my youthfulness.

"Hey, 'cool' is a mature word."

"Yes, very mature, and cool," Acaeus said, still smiling.

More than an hour had passed by the time we reached the log cabin. I thought it was cute. It was painted brown; a job Acaeus said he'd done himself to help camouflage it in the woods. A sturdy, sheltered porch was on the front with two wooden rocking chairs sitting on each side of the cabin's door. Inside was a fireplace with logs already cut, and set beside it. The furniture was what one would expect to see in a cabin: a brown, orange, and tan striped couch that pulled out into a bed; a reclining chair that matched the couch; and a small wooden table next to the window. There was no electricity of course, so Acaeus had hung lanterns all around for light.

When the fire was finally lit, Acaeus and I sat down on the couch together. I finally had a chance to relax, so I laid my head on his shoulder. The pocketbook sat on the table. I looked at it wondering when it would beam with the blue light, as Acaeus told me it would. On one hand, I could not wait to get home where I would be safe and get to see my family again; on the other hand, I could not imagine being anywhere else than right there, lying safely in Acaeus's arms. It seemed silly, but I felt like I had found at sixteen what most women look forward to for most of their lives. Was it even possible to truly love someone at my age? I wondered. Then I suddenly shivered as a chill swept across my shoulders, and Acaeus tightened his arms around me to keep me warm. An unexplainable feeling swept over me at the sensation of his embrace. At that moment, I knew it was not only possible but also factual; I was in love with Acaeus.

Chapter 22

Decisions, Decisions

(YANNI)

I awoke early as my father had instructed me to, and took the long ride on my motorcycle to North Aphrodan. Acaeus and I had purchased our motorcycles together. Mine was white and red, symbolizing the colors in the South Aphrodan symbol, and Acaeus's was yellow and white, symbolizing the colors in the North Aphrodan flag. I was not proud of the mission I had been assigned, and the thought of betraying my best friend and Zyaire had kept me up for most of the night. Somewhere between sleep and restlessness, I had become resolved with my purpose, and I was ready to do as I was destined.

This time when I arrived in the North, I did not have to make my presence discreet. It was during the accepted time of travel outlined in the North and South's treaty. When I finally reached the castle, I went to the guards at the front entrance for an announcement of my arrival to Acaeus. The guards sent word for Acaeus to come out to meet me for entrance into the castle, which was custom.

I waited for a long while for Acaeus to come out to greet me, but instead I was met by Marco.

"Marco, my friend, where is Acaeus?" I asked.

"Please come inside, Prince Yanni. I will explain everything," Marco assured me.

When inside, Marco entrusted me with information that Acaeus had given him to relay. "Prince Yanni, Acaeus asked that I give you this." Marco handed me a sealed envelope. I looked at it curiously. "It is a letter, Prince Yanni, written by Acaeus."

I began to open the letter, but Marco stopped me, putting his hand swiftly over mine.

"Prince, forgive me for touching you, but he told me to tell you to make sure you opened this in private, out of the castle," Marco instructed.

"Where is he?" I asked.

"That's all I can tell you right now," Marco whispered.

"Yanni, how nice to see you," a voice said from behind us. I slipped the envelope inside my jacket before turning around.

"King Aimilios, I wasn't expecting to see you, but it is wonderful all the same." I smiled and bowed in recognition of the North's sovereign.

"Where is Acaeus? I am sure you are here to see him, right?" the king asked.

"He has gone visiting for the day, your majesty," Marco replied before I could say a word.

"Yanni, I am sure your father has made you aware of the mortal amongst us."

"Yes, he has made mention of the girl," I said casually.

"Marco, since Acaeus is out visiting, where is she?" King Aimilios asked, concerned.

"She is asleep, your majesty. Acaeus has left me with the duty of looking over her until he returns. I just came down for a moment to greet Yanni."

"Very well then, Yanni, it was nice seeing you. I will be seeing your father later," King Aimilios said before turning to face Marco.

"Marco, when Acaeus returns, tell him I wish to see him, and you should hurry back to your post. We would not want the mortal to slip away," the king urged.

"Yes, your majesty," Marco agreed. Marco and I both bowed as the king departed.

The moment the king was out of sight, I turned to Marco ready to interrogate him. "Marco, my friend, am I to believe Acaeus has gone visiting and left Zyaire here alone?" I asked, puzzled.

"Prince Yanni, please just go and read the letter, it will answer all your questions," Marco insisted.

I saw how nervous Marco was and decided not to press him any further. "If this letter doesn't answer all the questions I have, I will be back," I warned Marco before turning to exit the castle.

When outside the castle's gates, I rode to a secluded area to read the words Acaeus had left for me. I opened the letter and read each word attentively.

> *Yanni, I am writing you because above anyone, I know I can trust you, my best friend, with this information. I now know your king is determined to kill Zyaire, and my king is unwilling to do anything to prevent it. I have now done the only thing I had left as a choice to do; escaped the castle grounds with Zyaire and the pocketbook. I do not want to put you at odds with your king and father, but there may come a time that I will need your help. I hope you will be there when and if I do. When the pocketbook opens the gate of passage, Zyaire will return to her world, and my fate will then be determined. My affection for her exceeds any treaty, and I will not let her die knowing I could have protected her. I can now only hope that the*

mind of this pocketbook grants her access swiftly, because the longer it keeps her here the more likely our whereabouts will someday be discovered. Until we meet again. Acaeus

I slammed the letter shut and crumpled it with my hands. "Ah, Acaeus, your nobleness borders idiocy," I huffed. I sat there thinking for a moment, my head buried into my hands. I knew that if anyone could figure out where Acaeus had gone, it would be me. Just as Acaeus knew what he had to do, I was just as convinced of my purpose. Therefore, I jumped on my motorcycle and headed out on a quest to find Acaeus and Zyaire.

I searched the North of Aphrodan, looking in every secluded and secret place. I even visited the homes of some mutual acquaintances of ours and subtly asked if they had seen Acaeus around town last night with a girl. No one had, and as the day grew late, I thought to give up my search. It was not until I remembered a conversation Acaeus and I once had that I was compelled to go to the woods. I remembered Acaeus speaking of a place deep in the North Forest that he would often go to escape the pressures of life at the castle.

When I reached the forest, I had no idea which way I would go. It seemed endless in all directions. I eyed my surroundings, looking to the east and west and finally at the ground around me. I stared at the dirt beneath my feet and recognized the imprint embedded in the soil. It was motorcycle tracks. I followed the tracks until they disappeared. Then I looked around, but there was no sign of Acaeus or Zyaire. Just then I saw something shining in the distance as I made my way through the shrubbery. I found Acaeus's bike lying flat against the ground with the sunlight reflecting off its shining rims.

"Acaeus, you are making this far too easy." I laughed, shaking my head.

I left Acaeus's bike there and walked back out to where the tracks ended. I then followed the path just in front of it until I came to a waterfall. I saw goldies surrounding a lake and walked down toward them. I pulled up some honeysuckle plants that surrounded the lake and tried to feed a goldie from my hand, hoping to get a blessing of prosperity and longer life. I tried on several of them, but none would eat from my hand.

"Despicable birds, how dare you not eat from a prince's hand," I squealed. "But you are very beautiful," I admitted. I finally gave up hope of further prosperity or longer life, and I continued back on the path I hoped would lead to Acaeus and Zyaire.

After hiking for more than an hour, I reached an area of the North's forest where I could smell chimney smoke. Off in the distance, I saw the smoke rising out from the tress and into the sky. "Amateur." I laughed, referring to the poor job Acaeus did of hiding the location of him and Zyaire.

I walked a path toward the direction the smoke was coming up from and was led to a small log cabin. I tiptoed up to it and went around the back. When there, I peered into a window and saw Acaeus and Zyaire fast asleep on the sitting chair together, with Acaeus holding Zyaire in his arms.

I did not bother to go inside. I had gotten what I wanted, and now knew the whereabouts of Acaeus and the mortal, something both castles of Aphrodan would soon be anxious to know as well.

Chapter 23

Time to Face the Music

(GERALDINE)

Even though John and I were on edge from the previous day, we had somehow managed to sleep for most of the morning, something we both had not done since Zyaire went missing. The sleeping pills prescribed by our doctors were definitely helping as aid to our slumber. After yesterday's press conference, we spent the remaining part of the day and evening passing out flyers in Plymouth and New Bedford. It was late when John and I had returned home, both emotionally drained. Mary Josie had stayed late and made us a cup of chamomile tea to help calm our nerves before heading home.

My mother and father had finally gone home too at the insistence of me and John. I said I needed a night alone in the house—an idea I figured out was foolish only after they had pulled off in their car. After pedaling around with the idea in my mind, I had finally put my pride aside just as John was about to leave for the night and asked him to stay there with me. I still was not ready to share a bed with him, so John slept in the guest room. Just having him in the house gave me some comfort.

Despite the coma-like state the prescribed sleeping pills and exhaustion had put us in, John and I were forced to get up when my mother called to let us know she and my father were on their way over. We had an appointment this morning to meet with a foundation that helps families look for missing children. The foundation usually helped in cases of foul play only, but from all signs, Zyaire's disappearance appeared to be a runaway and not a kidnapping. Their involvement in her case just proved that money and celebrity could go a long way—a fact that my mother usually loathed; she felt that all people should be treated equally despite their financial situations. In this case, she was willing to take any help in finding her granddaughter, including throwing the weight of her name around. She would have to fight the good fight against discrimination later.

My parents arrived only seconds before Jessica Jennings, the president of Hand-to-Hand Foundation, pulled into the driveway. We waited for her at the door, then we all walked into the house together. John and I thanked Jessica for coming. Jessica had started the foundation twenty-five years ago when her own daughter had gone missing. It was two years later when amazingly her daughter was found halfway across the country. She continued the foundation, knowing all too well the pain a parent feels when their child's well-being is in question.

Mary Josie had prepared a light breakfast in the kitchen, and we all sat together, ate, and discussed the plan of action to get the word out about Zyaire's disappearance to the public. My family's celebrity status would aid in that part of things. Jessica discussed a plan to use their volunteers to put up posters in and around town with pictures of Zyaire, asking if anyone had seen her on the night she went missing.

"It could create a trail that may help lead to her," she explained.

"What about an award?" John asked.

"Yes, we would definitely be willing to offer an award to anyone who helped bring our daughter home," I agreed.

"How much of an award would be acceptable in this type of case?" my mother asked.

"Of course money would be no object when it comes down to our granddaughter," my father chimed in.

"Money is always a good motivator to get the public talking, but it also brings in a flood of bogus tips. We would have to be prepared to handle that," Jessica explained.

She discussed how to utilize the 800 number and the e-mail already set up by us in conjunction with the award.

"As I stated, certain complications come from tip lines and e-mails, especially when a reward comes into play," Jessica warned. "However, the benefits outweigh the risk," she concluded.

"I think this all is a good start. I feel more confident that we can find her," I said.

"Well, again I want to warn you that many false tips will come through the hotline, and when you are so hopeful of a tip and it turns out to be false, it can be really hard, but don't worry, my team will help in following up on them all. If you like, we can wait to make you aware of the tips that seem promising, and filter out the ones that are a dead end. It is important to entertain every tip though, because you never know when the day will come that a tip will actually pay off," Jessica said.

This was a fact that Jessica knew all too well. It was a tip that led to the return of her own daughter. We spent the rest of breakfast mapping out our plans going forward. Everyone loved Jessica and her sincerity. We were happy to have her as well as her team on board in the search for Zyaire.

When Jessica left, John, my parents, and I all went into the family room to wind down. We would all be going out again today to pass out flyers in another part of town and were bracing ourselves for the long day that was ahead. John and I were sitting next to each other on the couch. I was holding a picture of Zyaire in my hand, and my head was resting on John's shoulder. I looked up and caught my mother peering over at us. She just smiled and looked away, resting her head on my father's shoulder as I was doing on John's. John and I both looked down at the picture of our daughter somberly. Whether we liked it or not, this tragedy had begun to bring us closer over the last few days. With John home all the time, I was reminded of the good man he used to be. I reluctantly hoped that he would become that person again, and maybe I could become the person I once was as well. The truth was we had both changed for the worst in many ways.

The phone rang and I answered it. It was Teresa. She had been calling several times a day since Zyaire had gone missing, hoping to hear that she was found. Each day so far she was given the same reply, "No new news on Zyaire yet." She and her mother would be going out with the family today to help pass out flyers. I confirmed the time and place we would meet and thanked Teresa again for helping. When I got off the phone, I decided to tell the others what I had been thinking ever since we did our interview the other day. I sat up straight and began speaking without bothering to first get everyone's attention. However, my words to follow demanded it: "So I have been thinking about this a lot, and I think it is time we expand our search outside of Massachusetts." Everyone looked at me shocked at my sudden admission. I sighed deeply, and continued, "I think it is time we all face the fact that it was very possible, likely even, that Zyaire is nowhere near home anymore."

Chapter 24

The Kiss

(ZYAIRE)

All of King Abas's attempts to rid Aphrodan of me so far have failed. I guess love does conquer all.

I read my great-grandmother's words in her diary with intrigue, but I quickly closed the cover and stuffed it back under the clothes in my bag when I heard Acaeus stirring on the couch.

"Zyaire," he called out, wondering where I had gone.

"I'm right here," I responded, and he turned to find me sitting at the table.

"How long have you been up?"

"Not long, just staring out the window. These woods are amazing. The animals and even the insects are beautiful, so unique and colorful."

"You know, they say these woods are enchanted."

"Are they?" I asked, intrigued.

"Possibly, but the Black Forest is for sure."

I got up and went to sit next to Acaeus on the couch. "What *is* the Black Forest?" I asked.

"It is a large forest that extends from the North to the South. The entrance of the Black Forest starts where the North Forest ends. In fact, a drawbridge in this forest connects to that very entrance. Of course, it is never let down since no one travels into the Black Forest anymore.

"Let's go see it!" I exclaimed.

Acaeus laughed at my eagerness. "We can't. Entering the Black Forest is dangerous. It is guarded by a pride of Black Lions, and they do not exactly welcome visitors. They are very protective of their land, and they will not hesitate to defend it."

"Nice try, very spooky, but there is no such thing as Black Lions." I smirked and got up to get myself one of the canteens of water from off the table.

"Bring me one of those too, please," Acaeus said. I handed him the water and sat back down next to him on the couch. "I am actually serious," Acaeus continued. "Aphrodan has a lot of interesting history that you don't know about, and the Black Lions are part of that history. I assure you, they are very real. I have seen them. And you almost walked right into their territory the day you first arrived here," Acaeus pointed out.

"What do you mean?" I asked.

"I never did tell you how I discovered you in the cave that day, did I?"

"No, you didn't, so come on, tell me, tell me, tell me," I chanted, drumming up a smile from Acaeus.

"There is a spot from the top of the cave that you can look down onto the Black Lions' land, and more often than not you will find them there guarding the cave. The people of this land will not go anywhere near them, and most believe it is bad luck to even look upon them, but I go there because honestly, they intrigue me. They are beautiful to see, and that day I was surprised to see the leader of the pack standing in an open area. Basil, as he is called, eyed me far above him at the top of the cave, and he stared directly into my eyes. It was startling, but amazing. Just then, I saw a blue light bursting from an opening of the cave. I entered the cave from the north side of it to see where the light was coming from, and there you were, jumping up and down into the air." Acaeus laughed. "What were you doing by the way?" he asked, amused by my odd behavior that night.

"Don't laugh at me," I said. "I was trying to go back to where I came from!"

"And you thought you could jump back to your world?" Acaeus laughed.

"No, fly!" I said and gave him a playful poke in his side. I began laughing too, realizing how funny I must have looked jumping into the air.

"Okay, okay, finish telling me the story," I urged. "That encounter is actually a bit fuzzy to me," I admitted.

"You were quite out of it." Acaeus remembered. "Okay, so I saw you jumping up and down into the air, and I guess you heard me at some point because you looked around and asked was someone there. I dared not reply. Then I saw you make your way toward the wooden door, and that's when I grabbed you before it was too late."

"Before it was too late for what?" I asked, still confused.

"That entrance has not been used for centuries, ever since the Black Lions had been placed into the forest. That door actually leads right onto their land. And I had just moments before seen the leader of the pack standing a few yards away from that very opening."

I got chills at the thought of how close I had come to standing face-to-face with Basil.

"I grabbed you, and you fainted in my arms, and the rest is history," Acaeus said, smiling.

"So the Black Lions live in the Black Forest, but you said they were placed there. Who placed them there?" I asked.

"That's a story for another time," Acaeus said. "Right now I am hungry, and I am sure you are too."

Acaeus got up and walked over to the table. I followed him. He pulled out a jug of water from a stash he had already had there at the cabin, and then he took out toothpaste and two toothbrushes from our packs. We both brushed our teeth in a steel basin. The cabin had no running water or electricity, but Acaeus had obviously been there often and was used to surviving under those conditions. When we were finished, he opened the cabinets, and they were stocked with nonperishable food items.

"We have this if we need it," Acaeus declared. "But for today, we are going to fish for our food." He opened another cabinet which was taller than the others and pulled out two fishing rods. They were beautiful rods.

I admired the one he placed into my hand. "So are you ready for that bet?" I asked, referring to the bet we made that I could catch more fish than him."

"What do you want if you win?" Acaeus asked.

"A kiss," I murmured before I could even realize the words were coming out of my mouth.

Acaeus even looked shocked at my admission. I did want to kiss Acaeus, and I had thought about it many times, but I was now embarrassed that I had actually blurted that out. It was silent between us. Acaeus looked into my eyes admiringly from the short distance now between us. He began walking slowly toward me, and my heartbeats sped up as his gaze locked in with mine. My hands shook nervously as he got closer. Acaeus stared at me as if I was the most beautiful thing he had ever looked upon, and that said a lot since Aphrodan was filled with so many attractive people and breathtaking sights.

He slowly leaned his head down toward mine, and I took a deep breath, and then exhaled before tilting my face slightly to the side. I closed my eyes, and everything I gave off was to show him that his kiss would be welcomed. Acaeus stroked my hair with one hand and slowly brought his lips within inches of mine, so close that I could feel him breathing next to me. I nervously bit my bottom lip as the electricity increased between us. Finally, I lifted my chin and our lips met. His kiss was soft, gentle, and tender. I felt like I was floating off the ground as he pressed his mouth firmly against mine. Without him saying it, I could feel all the love he had for me in his kiss. When our lips finally separated from each other's, I leaned my forehead against his chest, and Acaeus pulled me in close and embraced me. He had not known it, but he had just given me my first kiss.

ACAEUS

Zyaire and I used the hour hike back down to the lake which we had passed on our way to the log cabin, talking about our lives and how much we were going to miss each-other when she went back home. When we arrived at the lake we set up equipment and started a fire. We decided to cook what we caught right away since we had no way of preserving it. Once we were settled in, we put bait on our hooks and cast the lines far out into the water. The lake was large and reached eight hundred feet at its deepest point. Aphrodan was lacking in nothing. The lake was abundant with different species of fish.

"Aren't you afraid that someone will come here and see us?" Zyaire asked.

"Not today, it's Monday, and in Aphrodan citizens do not work or labor on Mondays," I explained.

"Why don't you work or labor on Mondays?"

"It's considered a sacred day. Aphrodite founded Aphrodan on a Monday. Also, it was a Monday when she was banned from Aphrodan. It is a day of reflection and a day of honor for our world's founder and true queen. Work of any kind is forbidden, and entrance into the woods is revoked."

"So we are breaking the law right now?" Zyaire asked.

"I won't tell anyone if you don't?" I smiled.

"Wait! Wait! I have something," Zyaire screamed. She planted her feet firmly on the ground and began to slowly reel her line in. "You are getting your butt whipped already," she teased.

I laughed and tried to distract her, but Zyaire was focused, and she artfully reeled her catch in. It was a big one. I could see it trying to pull away from her line.

"Do you need my help?" I asked.

"Not a chance, this one is all mine."

I was impressed at how Zyaire was handling her catch. She slowly reeled it in, patiently stalking whatever was caught at the end of her hook, and tiring it out before she finally brought it the rest of the way in. A large lake trout wiggled on the end of Zyaire's hook. I quickly grabbed a large net and scooped the fish up into it.

"Oh my, that has got to be at least fifteen pounds," I presumed.

"Should we quit now, or do you want to keep feeling the pain of losing," Zyaire said, feeling quite proud of herself in that moment.

"Don't claim victory so fast," I said as I began to feel a pull on my line. "It feels like a big one, you're going down, mortal," I declared. I reeled my line in, and when I pulled it from the water, the puniest fish I had ever seen dangled from it. Zyaire burst into laughter, and I took off after her dangling the still wiggling wet fish on the end of my hook. We both laughed as we ran around after each other.

"You call that a catch? How pathetic," Zyaire goaded me.

I finally caught her and gave her a huge bear hug. "I got you!" I exclaimed.

"You may be better at catching fish, but I am better at catching you." I gave her a kiss on the cheek, and she blushed. I swear that I could not remember a time that I had laughed so much. To think that a pocketbook would determine when that laughter would end was somewhat depressing.

After we were tired out from our antics, Zyaire and I sat around the fire and enjoyed her catch. It was plenty for both of us to eat, and I had brought some homemade bread along that I managed to grab from the castle. When we finished eating, we both sat there full and satisfied. "Let's go see if a Goldie will eat from our hands," Zyaire suddenly suggested. She broke off a piece of the bread, crumpled it in her hand, and jumped up on her feet to head toward the Goldie's before I could even reply. I stood up and reluctantly followed after her. At first, Zyaire approached a Goldie with much trepidation. "They don't bite do they?" She asked, standing a few feet away from a Goldie that was resting peacefully on a grassy path that surrounded the lake.

"No, they are very gentle actually. They are more afraid of you, then you of them I'd guess."

"Ok then, here goes," Zyaire said with her hand outstretched as she took light steps towards the first Goldie. When that one didn't eat she began going up to one after the other before finally getting frustrated with it all and giving up.

"Okay, your turn," she said, frustrated that the birds did not grant her prosperity and longer life as I had told her about.

"No, it's frivolous, let's just go. If they didn't eat from your hand, I am sure they won't eat from mine either," I reasoned.

"No, you have to go," Zyaire insisted and shoved bread crumbs into my hand.

"This is crazy, you know. It is just a myth, I should have never told you about it," I said.

"Well, you did, so try it please," Zyaire begged.

I reluctantly lowered my hand toward one goldie, and without even a moment of hesitation, it came right over and ate from my palm, then another came over and began to eat too, and another.

Before we knew it, there were four goldies eating from my hand. I threw the crumbs to the ground, as other goldies began to walk toward me.

"This is ridiculous," I said and briskly walked off. Zyaire followed behind me.

"What's wrong? Why are you upset? You just gained eighty more years of life, and if you had stayed a little longer, more was to come." I was silent, but Zyaire rambled on. "It's strange right? The way they acted toward you, I have never seen birds act like that. They were drawn to you." I was still silent, so Zyaire grabbed me by the arm and stopped me from walking any further.

"What's wrong, why are you acting like this?" she asked.

"It's just a stupid myth, it doesn't mean anything," I said and kept walking.

"Okay, so maybe it is just a stupid myth, but it was still pretty amazing, right?" she said.

I stopped and looked at her, realizing I was overreacting to the situation.

"Yes, it was amazing," I said, smiling, and grabbed her hand to continue walking. I could see by the look on Zyaire's face that she was completely bewildered by my reaction. But she said nothing more about it as we kept walking. We went back to our spot by the lake and gathered all the things we'd brought with us. The mood was a bit awkward as we headed back toward the cabin. We both added tidbits of conversation here and there to fill the silence.

We were almost to the cabin when I needed to take a moment alone to relieve myself. "Can you wait here for one moment? I will be right back," I said.

"Okay, I am just going to take a rest right here on this rock while I wait." Zyaire sat down on a big rock to await my return. I started to walk off, but she stopped me. "Hey, there are no big animals that I need to look out for, are there?"

"No, you are perfectly safe in these woods," I assured her.

I walked off far enough into the woods so that Zyaire could no longer see me. I had overreacted about the goldies. Zyaire had no reason to be suspicious of me, or who I really was. On my way back I picked some dandelions to give to her as a way to show my regret for how I'd behaved, but when I got back to the spot where I left her, she was no longer there. I looked around the whole area in a panic before I saw her standing a few feet away holding flowers in her hand and smiling. As I got closer, I noticed the colors of the petals were red and lime green.

"Zyaire, no, drop those!" I yelled from the distance.

"Ouch!" Zyaire yelped as the flower's thorn pierced her as they fell to the ground. I ran to her quickly.

"Oh no, let me see that," I said. I was worried and I grabbed her hand to examine her injury.

"It's just a prick, don't worry," Zyaire said. Blood trickled down her thumb, and my face drenched in concern.

"What's wrong, why do you look so worried, haven't you ever seen a little blood before?" she asked. Then she suddenly wobbled to the side and braced herself so as not to fall. "I feel dizzy," she said as I grabbed her by the arm to keep her from falling.

"Sit down," I instructed her. "That flower is poisonous. I have to try to squeeze the poison out quickly.

"Poisonous!" Zyaire said terrified as she sat on a stump embedded into the earth. "How poisonous is it?" she asked.

"Dangerously poisonous," I reluctantly informed her. I quickly took out the first aid kit in my fishing pack. Then I pulled out tweezers and pulled out a thin piece of the thorn that had been lodged in her skin. I began squeezing the pus from her thumb and absorbing it into a gauze.

Zyaire was rapidly becoming more ill, and her breathing began to sound labored.

"Acaeus, I can't breathe very well," she said, gasping for air, tears welling in her eyes. I worked more desperately then trying to squeeze the poison from her hand. Zyaire became nauseous and began to vomit profusely before stumbling off the stump flat on her back and convulsing.

"Zyaire, stay with me!" I pleaded.

I got on the ground and laid her head on my lap. Zyaire's eyes could barely stay open, and I continued to beg her to stay with me, but she did not. Instead, she fell unconscious into my arms.

I screamed out in agony at the empty forest. "I won't let her die! Do you hear me out there? I will not let her die." I grabbed Zyaire's arm and felt her pulse. It was weak, but there. I whispered into her ear as I cradled her in my arms. "I won't let you die, Zyaire." Everything I lived to protect in that moment was cast away. The secret of my identity, the promises I had made before I knew her, the purpose of my existence in Aphrodan, it all meant nothing to me in that moment. I had promised I would protect her, and so without any further hesitation, I did.

Chapter 25

The Dreary Bush

(ACAEUS)

Nightfall had come and gone seven times. I paced around the sitting chair as Zyaire lay there without movement. She had been unconscious for seven days now, but her breathing was back to normal, and her pulse was strong. I could not understand why she was still unconscious. I had done what was needed to keep her alive. Now I was growing increasingly nervous and wondered if she would ever wake up. I carefully lifted her head and sat down next to her. I placed her head back down on my leg, and I rubbed her head.

"I should have never left you alone. I am sorry. I should have warned you about the dreary bush, and this would have never happened," I whispered to Zyaire as I stroked her hair.

The dreary bush got its name from its poisonous outcome. The bush bloomed the most beautiful puffed flowers one could ever see, but its stems were lined with poisonous thorns. The poison was the most lethal of any poison in the land. Just one prick and it could take down the strongest of men. However, because of its beauty, every home in Aphrodan yearned to have a vase filled with the deadly flowers that bloomed from the dreary bush on its table. Even still, the only table you would find the beautiful flowers were on the tables of the kings of the North and South, and the richest citizens of Aphrodan. You see, there was only one man who was willing to risk his life to covet the flower, and his services were far too expensive for even people of the middle class to afford.

I rubbed Zyaire's head for a long time, trying to stay awake. I wanted to be alert in case she needed me. It had been a long seven days, and I was exhausted. I stared at Zyaire for a long while as she peacefully slept, but before long, I dozed off too without even realizing it.

The sun peeped through the windows of the cabin, and the birds sang their glorious morning songs. Something seemed right in the air, as if a miracle was on its way. When I'd awoke from my sleep suddenly, I found Zyaire still in dreamland. I tapped her shoulder and called her name several times, but there was still no response. Now my worry turned to grief, as I feared she would never wake up.

"Maybe I was too late," I murmured, disappointed in myself, "I should have acted faster." I eased Zyaire's head off my leg and back onto the soft cushion. I painfully inched up, my leg numb from the position I laid in all night. I stretched and then sat back down onto the arm of the chair before I got up again to open the window. The sound of the birds calmed me. Their song was particularly cheerful this morning. I sat back down next to Zyaire on the couch. With my eyes closed, I swayed my head back and forth to the birds' uplifting melody.

I had been so engulfed in the hopeful sound of nature's songstress that I barely felt the gentle hand touch my lower back. Zyaire touched me with more force on her second attempt, and I turned around quickly to find her staring up at me.

"You're awake!" I exclaimed and kissed her forehead in delight. "I thought I'd lost you."

"What happened?" Zyaire asked.

"You pricked your finger on a very poisonous flower," I explained.

She thought for a moment before responding. "I remember now. I got very sick, and I couldn't breathe," Zyaire recalled dreadfully.

"That's right," I said, looking down at her. 'But it is over now, and you are going to be fine.

Zyaire smiled at me. "I had a dream about you," she said, her voice very weak.

"You did? What was it about?"

Zyaire let out a whooping cough, and I got up to get her a canteen of water.

"Here, drink this. You're probably very dehydrated from vomiting and going without water," I explained.

"Great, how embarrassing, I forgot about that part." Zyaire cringed.

"You shouldn't be embarrassed, I assure you. Besides, I am just happy that you are alive, vomit and all," I teased.

"Yuck, that's gross!" Zyaire reached up and gave me a weak and playful tap on my shoulder; then she let out a lingering dry cough again.

"Drink that water," I urged. She took small sips and closed her eyes with each swallow. A pleasant look dawned on her face as if the water felt good going down her dry throat.

"How long was I unconscious?"

"A whole week," I revealed.

"A whole week?" A look of disbelief came over Zyaire's face. "Are you joking with me?" she asked.

"No, I wouldn't joke about something like this. It has been a whole week, and it was a hard one," I admitted. I suddenly let out an unconscious sigh of relief.

"What happened exactly?" she asked, still confused. "Wait, first, let me tell you about my dream," she said, sidetracking from her original request as she so often did. “I heard you in my dream. You told me you wouldn’t let me die, and then you healed me.”

I was caught off guard by her words. “What do you mean when you say I healed you?”

“I can’t explain it exactly. You just touched me, and I was healed,” she said.

“Well, I wish it was that easy,” I said, now uncomfortable with the direction of the conversation. I stood to my feet. “I carried you back here after you passed out, and eventually your breathing became normal, and your pulse was stronger. I guess I squeezed most of the poison out, but it took time for your body to recuperate from the toxins that did get in.”

Zyaire slowly reached up and pulled me back down to sit. She put her arms around me. “Thank you,” she murmured.

“For what?”

“For taking care of me like you said you would.” Her voice was still low, weak, and her tone was innocent and childlike.

“I would do anything for you. I would take care of you above myself,” I assured her.

“You already are. I know the danger you are putting yourself in doing this for me.”

“Don’t worry about me. I will be fine. I promise.” Zyaire laid her head on my chest as she had done before. It was as if it was becoming one of the places she felt most safe.

She was still feeling fatigued, but she got up and walked around anyway. It turned out to be good for her. The more she moved around, the better she felt.

Of course, I continued to fuss over her. “Drink some more water, please. I want to make sure you are well hydrated,” I pushed.

“I am fine, stop worrying about me, you saved my life.” She gave me another hug. She had no idea how true that statement really was, but I continued to downplay it.

"It's starting to feel good being a hero," I said. I leaned down and kissed her gently on the forehead, and she smiled and wrapped her arms around my neck even tighter. Then she jumped suddenly, startled by a loud knock at the door.

Boom, boom, boom was the sound that poured through the small cabin without halting. "Get in there," I said, directing her to hide in the tall cabinet that housed the fishing rods.

She slumped off into the cabinet with my help, and I closed the door once she was inside. "Who is it?" I asked, grabbing my hunter's rifle from out of the secret compartment stored by the door. I then put my ear up to the door and asked again, "Who is it?" I strained to hear the response.

"It's Marco, sir."

I flung the door open then pulled Marco inside. "Get in here, what would possess you to come here?" I asked, furious that Marco would take such a risk.

"I am sorry, sir, but I had to come and warn you," Marco said, panting and out of breath.

"Warn me about what?" I put the rifle back in the compartment by the door and walked over by the table. Marco followed.

"When the king discovered what you had done, he was furious, and so was King Abas, who was at the castle at the time," Marco explained.

"Marco, we knew that what I did would be discovered eventually, so why are you here, and how did you find me?" I impatiently asked.

"I didn't find you, sir. King Abas did."

Marco's words left me bewildered. "How is that possible?"

"I don't know, sir, but King Abas has been believed to have spies in North Aphrodan. It is possible you were tracked here before and he figured this is where you might go now."

"Figured? He doesn't know for sure that I am here?"

"He seems confident, but I guess there would be no way of him knowing for sure until he gets here. They plan to raid the cabin, Acaeus."

"When do they plan to raid it?"

"Now, sir, and King Aimilios is with him. I headed them off, but you do not have long."

Marco scanned the room. I knew he was wondering where Zyaire was, so I opened the cabinet door and told her to come out. She had obviously overheard it all, and she was visibly shaken.

"We have to get out of here," I informed her.

"Okay, but where will we go?" Zyaire asked.

"I have a plan."

"Plan B? The more dangerous one?" she asked, worried.

I reached out and grabbed Zyaire's hands. Looking her straight in the eyes, I asked her again, "Do you trust me?"

She searched my eyes curiously, as if she was hoping to see a glimmer of something that would tell her what I had planned next. She sighed in frustration, assumingly never seeing what she was hoping for, but she replied nonetheless. "I trust you completely," she declared.

I turned to Marco, who was standing there watching our heartfelt exchange with a look of adoration on his face. I could tell he had seen that the two of us had grown much closer from our exchange. Because he knew me well, I also knew that he could see without a doubt that I had fallen in love with Zyaire.

"Marco, thanks for coming. I know you put yourself in great risk coming here to warn me, but your job is done. Go now before they discover you were here, and do not go back the way you came. I am sure they will travel the same direct route to the cabin as you did."

"Be safe, sir. Good luck," Marco said, as he rushed out from the cabin and travelled a different path as I had instructed him to. Once Marco was out of sight, I closed the cabin door.

Wasting no time, Zyaire and I quickly filled our packs with supplies. I had no idea how long we had before King Aimilios and King Abas would arrive, so we moved frantically. My mind raced as we prepared to leave the cabin in a panic. I could not believe they had discovered us so quickly. At the very least I thought we would have been able to stay at the cabin for many weeks before being found out. Marco may be right. King Abas might have had spies in North Aphrodan all this time, and it might be how he had discovered where I would go. Then I was reminded that one person did know of my retreats to this cabin, one person that I told enough information about the cabin's whereabouts that they could lead King Abas straight to me, and that person was my best friend, Yanni. I became sick as I thought about the possibility that Yanni might have betrayed me.

"Are you ready?" Zyaire asked, interrupting my thoughts.

"We just need one more thing," I said, and then I walked over to the table and reached for a metal handle that stuck out from the floor beneath it. I tugged at it, opening a small compartment, and pulled out the pocketbook. "We wouldn't want to leave without this."

Chapter 26

The War

(ZYAIRE)

The wind blew as Acaeus and I quickly travelled through the woods.

"Are you okay?" Acaeus asked me.

"I am fine," I assured him, but he was still worried about how our fast pace could be affecting me. I had just been through a horrible ordeal, and he knew I was not back to my full strength. We had a long hike ahead of us to get to where Acaeus had destined as his plan B, and he wanted to make sure I was up to it.

"Here, let me take your pack for now," he offered.

"I got it. If it gets too heavy to carry, I promise to let you know," I said stubbornly.

We continued through the forest, travelling a particular path until we heard the faint sound of barking dogs in the distance.

"They're here," I said, frightened.

"Wait," Acaeus said, stopping abruptly. He took off his pack and pulled out small binoculars, still hearing the faint sound of barking dogs in the distance. He peered through the binoculars.

"What do you see?" I asked.

"It is blurry, but I see what appears to be King Aimilios and King Abas leading both soldiers from the North and the South." Then Acaeus gasped.

"What, what do you see?" I asked impatiently. Then I grabbed the binoculars from him to see for myself. I skimmed over the crowd of people approaching, and then finally I saw what Acaeus had. Standing there amongst those pursuing us was Yanni. My heart sank. It was no longer a question. We knew for sure now that his best friend had in fact betrayed us. Acaeus zipped his pack quickly, not even closing it all the way, before he threw it onto his back.

He grabbed my hand. "Let's go!" was all he said and took off in another direction with me in tow. We hurried our stride now, trying to create more distance between us and the ones hunting after us.

The wind's velocity was unyielding as Acaeus and I scampered through the forest. I tried to keep up but was growing increasingly weak. I was slightly dehydrated still, and the exertion of our hike was taking its toll on me. I stumbled as we stepped over what looked like tiny trunks from trees growing in the ground. Acaeus turned back to look at me.

"Are you all right?" he asked.

"I'm fine, let's keep going, we don't want to lose our distance ahead of them," I reasoned.

Acaeus shook his head. "No, look at you, your face is completely flushed, and your lips are dry. The color in your face is beginning to look sallow. Let's stop for a moment so you can drink some water," Acaeus insisted.

"No, let's keep going, I can drink later," I rebutted.

"No, we are going to stop now, you're not well. I can see it just by looking at you."

I didn't argue any further. I honestly didn't have the strength to be stubborn at that moment.

"Sit here," Acaeus said and directed me to sit on the uneven stump of a tree that had apparently fallen down. He took out a canteen from his pack. "Here, drink it all," he demanded. "But slow, I don't want you to get nauseous, okay?" I nodded my head in agreement and took small sips from the canteen.

Acaeus took out his binoculars once again and looked off into the distance to see how close King Abas and King Aimilios were. We had gained some distance from them, but he admitted that the gap was getting increasingly smaller since we'd stopped. He turned back to see how I was doing with the water, and he caught me gulping it down quickly.

"Hey, I said drink slowly," Acaeus chided me.

I smiled over the bottle then quickly chugged the last bit down.

"You're so stubborn, you know that?" he said.

"Yes, I do, as a matter of fact," I said, putting my nose in the air and then smiling. Acaeus put his pack on his back and carried mine despite my resistance. He looked through his binoculars one more time before we continued. "Now they are jogging," he said. "Let's get back on the move."

While those who hunted us jogged along through the forest, mine and Acaeus's pace had slowed down. I tried hard to keep up with Acaeus's swift movement, but I was still too weak.

"I'm sorry, I am just so tired," I apologized.

"It's okay. You're doing great. We are almost there," Acaeus lovingly assured me.

"Is it just me, or is it getting colder?" I asked, shivering.

"It's not just you. It *is* getting colder. It's getting colder because we are approaching the Black Forest," Acaeus finally revealed to me.

I stopped in my tracks. "What? Why? What are we doing?" I asked.

Acaeus gave me a look that I had definitely seen on him before, and I could almost predict the next words that would come from his mouth.

"Do you trust me?" he asked.

I threw my hands on my hips and shot him a look of defiance, like my grandmother did whenever she was upset about something. "Trust you with what?" I asked.

"With your life," he responded.

I hadn't predicted those words to come out of his mouth. His request for me to put that much confidence in him was immense, but he had in fact saved this life before that he was now asking me to trust him with again.

"Yes, I trust you with my life," I finally said honestly.

The brisk winds swept across my face, and I shivered and rubbed my hands together trying to produce heat.

"Here take this," Acaeus said and took off his black, hooded sweatshirt for me to put on.

"No, then you will be freezing," I protested.

"No, I won't, I'm fine." Acaeus handed me his sweatshirt, and I put it on over the one I was already wearing. I could smell his scent as I pulled it over my head. He smelled like the fresh pinecones that my grandmother bought each week to put in the bowl centered on the table in her den. My grandmother said the smell reminded her of her mother, Lillian, who also used to be partial to the scent of pine. She said my great-grandmother would buy candles fragranced in pine and light them each night in her bedroom. She also said when she was a young girl, each night when Lillian was home, and after she had taken her evening bath, she would climb into her mother's bed, and my great-grandmother would stroke her hair until she fell asleep. She said the smell of the pine and the tender strokes from her mother's hands gliding though her hair was one of the many things she yearned for after she died. She could never again have the comfort of her mother's touch, but the pine served as a lasting memory.

"Let's go, we are almost there," Acaeus said and grabbed my hand. As we travelled on, to my dismay, the forest got colder, and without the prompting of evening hours, it had begun to grow dark. A thick and misty fog started to engulf us. I looked ahead and could barely see the drawbridge that Acaeus had told me about—the one that separated us from the deadly Black Lions.

"What do we do now?" I asked.

"We cross," Acaeus boldly revealed.

"You're a brave young man," a deep voice said from within the fog.

"King Abas," Acaeus said as an intimidating figure stepped forward and stood before him and me.

"Brave, but foolish," the startling man continued. "You would risk your life by going into the Black Forest to save a mortal who has no hope of longevity. You have sealed your fate for a feeble being that is not even promised." King Abas laughed.

Acaeus pulled me to stand behind him. "If she is so feeble, then why kill her?" he asked.

"Because she possesses something that is a threat to our world!" King Abas screamed in fury.

I nervously peered around Acaeus's shoulder, my head partially buried into his back. Then another man stepped forward. His face expression was kind and his eyes were gentle. I knew right away that he was King Aimilios. He stood on the right of King Abas, and then Yanni came and stood at his left. I could see the other men in the near distance. Acaeus stared at Yanni. I looked deep into Yanni's eyes, and they had changed from the day before. Now they were blank and cold even. I remained behind Acaeus. My heart was pounding, and I was gripping the back of his shirt. I didn't know what frightened me the most, the threat standing before us or the threat that lived on the other side of the still-drawn bridge.

"This little game you are playing is over, now hand the girl over, and the pocketbook," King Abas demanded.

"If you want her, you're going to have to get through me to get her," Acaeus hissed.

"As you wish," King Abas replied.

A loud sound suddenly filled the air, and the ground beneath us shook. It was the sound and weight of the drawbridge thumping to the ground. Chaos erupted, and I looked over to see Marco scampering away into the forest. He had obviously let down the drawbridge to facilitate our escape.

King Abas yelled out orders to his men, "Kill him."

Just as Marco was getting away, one of the soldiers from the South, large in stature, with a block-shaped jaw and huge forearms, grabbed him from behind. Marco attempted to get away, but he was no match for the South soldier's strength. King Abas gestured to his soldier, and he nodded his head in agreement just before taking his bare hands and snapping Marco's neck instantly. Marco's body went limp and then lifelessly slumped from the soldier's hands onto the ground.

"Noooo," I screamed out in horror.

Acaeus, without hesitation turned and grabbed me to run, but King Abas grabbed him from behind and threw us both to the ground. Acaeus got up quickly to defend me, his strength exceeded King Abas's. As the two of them struggled, the men from the North instinctively turned on the men from the South. Acaeus was one of them after all, their leader even, and they were not going to let him go down alone as Marco just had. Fighting was going on all around, the dogs were barking loudly at the commotion, and the men were being slain one by one. All I could do was lie there paralyzed with fear.

Through the fog, a hand reached down toward me, and I grabbed it. When the eyes of the man standing before me met mine, he froze. I knew immediately I was right in my assumption about the man who stood to the right of King Abas, and that even now, I was holding the hand of King Aimilios. I also knew that he had just saw what many others had seen in me before… my great-grandmother.

"Lilly?" he asked, confused. Somehow, a moment of calm centered on us, and the commotion was held at bay.

"No, Zyaire, but my name was supposed to be Lilly," I revealed as King Aimilios stood there in disbelief. He was staring into the eyes of the great-granddaughter of the love of his life.

"Watch out!" I screamed as one of the soldiers from the South zeroed in on him. King Aimilios ducked then came back up with his elbow hitting the South's soldier with a devastating blow to his neck. His body limply fell to the ground, and I could see he had just died instantly. Before I had a moment to take in what I had just witnessed, King Aimilios turned back quickly and looked at me with a million questions written on his face.

"Go, please help Acaeus," I pleaded.

King Aimilios ran off to enter the fight. The stakes had now changed for him. He didn't know it yet, but he was no longer fighting solely for North Aphrodan, but also for the life of the great-granddaughter of the woman who probably still had his heart.

The men of the South were no match for the men of the North. I looked on and watched as they systematically destroyed the men of the South in hand-to-hand combat. Oddly enough, the only weapons used were those that the woods supplied—large branches that had fallen from the trees. At one point, a soldier from the South locked eyes with me and began to charge toward me in fury. I was motionless. I could not move to save myself from what was about to happen. As he got closer, I cringed, but at the moment he was only steps from me, I heard Acaeus yell out someone's name, and a soldier from the North holding a large branch turned swiftly and met him with a blow to his head. I could hear the cracking sound his skull made at impact. He blankly stared at me just before his eyes rolled into the back of his head, and his body plummeted face first into the ground. It was like watching a martial arts movie. Beaten bodies lay just steps from me. Before long the remaining men of the South began to give up, and one by one they retreated into the woods. King Abas had gained an upper hand on Acaeus and had ripped the pack containing the pocketbook from off his shoulders. When it hit the ground, the pocketbook came rolling out from inside it. A blue light, great in appearance, commanded everyone's attention. Acaeus and King Abas stood silently as the pocketbook illuminated the forest as it sat on the ground between them. Without warning, they both lunged for it. King Abas arrived first and grabbed it before stumbling backward. Acaeus leaped before him, and King Abas without hesitation pulled a small handgun from his boot, aimed, pulled, and fired.

I screamed in horror watching the scene unfold. Acaeus fell to the ground but sprung right back up and headed toward King Abas with persistence. King Abas, presumably infuriated by his relentlessness, lifted the gun again. This time he pointed it toward Acaeus's heart, but when he went to pull the trigger, he was tackled to the ground and the bullet strayed off and struck the leg of one of the North's soldiers. When King Abas turned to see the face of Acaeus's defender, he met his own son Yanni's eyes.

As Yanni stared into the eyes of his father, a look of remorse fell over his face. He reached down toward his father and extended his hand. When King Abas reached up to grab it, Yanni slapped it away and instead grabbed the pocketbook before tossing it up. Acaeus leaped and caught it in midair.

The sound of chanting turned everyone's attention to the distance where a sea of soldiers dressed as the men had been from South Aphrodan were fast approaching. Acaeus grabbed me by the hand

and ran to the edge of the drawbridge. I looked back and saw King Abas reach for his gun in an effort to stop us, but Yanni knocked it from his hand and seized it. He pointed the gun at his father and held him at bay.

"Traitor," King Abas uttered as he stared into his son's eyes. Yanni ignored his father's words and continued to point the gun at him.

"Go now!" he screamed to Acaeus and me as we stood at the drawbridge looking on. Acaeus looked out in search of his king.

"King Aimilios," he yelled out and looked up to find him standing in all his glory on a rock in the distance.

"No, Acaeus, don't," King Aimilios yelled in protest of what he knew we were set to do.

Just as the South's soldiers ascended on us, Acaeus grabbed me tightly by the hand, and we ran across the drawbridge and into the Black Forest. The soldiers dared not follow. When our feet stepped onto the grounds of the Black Forest, the distant sounds of the lions' loud and angry roars filled our surroundings. I looked back on the other side of the bridge. Frightened, King Abas and his men descended. Only Yanni from the South stayed and helped the men of the North bring the drawbridge back up. It took all six men and Yanni to draw it. As Yanni pulled the bridge to a close, our eyes locked and I mouthed "Thank you" to him.

YANNI

King Aimilios came and stood with me looking down at the gaping hole that once again separated the North of Aphrodan from the Black Forest. He put his hand on my shoulder. Regret and guilt was all that filled his face.

"Are you okay, King?" I asked.

"Yes, Yanni, you did a very brave thing today. Protecting your friend from your father could not have been easy," he said.

"No, it wasn't easy, but it was the right thing to do. It is time for all this fighting to stop. I could not stand by and watch an innocent girl be put to death, just like you could not stand by and watch Queen Lillian be put to death all those years ago."

King Aimilios's expression grew grave at the reality of my words. His face hung with burden. "Yanni, my decision to protect the North's treaty with the South of Aphrodan may have cost me Acaeus, and any hope I would ever have of knowing what happened to Lillian and why she never returned to me. My sister may never forgive me if something bad happens to her son, and I don't know if I could ever forgive myself."

King Aimilios and I both looked on somberly knowing that no matter what happened on the other end of that bridge, both our lives had just changed forever.

Chapter 27

Gone but Not Forgotten

(ACAEUS)

The silence after the bridge was drawn was deafening. All that was left to hear was the weeping in my soul. I collapsed down on to one knee and wept. Zyaire knew right away to whom my tears were owed. She came and wrapped her arms around me from behind.

"I am so sorry, Acaeus, I know Marco was your dearest friend," Zyaire said, consoling me. "I feel like this is all my fault," she said.

I turned around on my knees and looked at her. I took her face into my hands. "Zyaire, don't ever say that again. None of this is your fault. You are innocent in this. This is all King Abas's doing. Marco made a choice to help us, and he made the right choice. He wouldn't be the Marco I knew if he had not made that choice."

Zyaire looked at me with her beautiful eyes. I could see the pain in them. "You were very lucky to have a friend like him, Acaeus," she said and hugged me.

"He was loyal to the very end. He did not deserve to die like that. Now, I must honor him so that his death won't be in vain. The only way to do that is to get you out of here safely," I said.

Zyaire and I reluctantly walked deeper into the Black Forest. She had her arm intertwined with mine, and I could feel her body shaking from the cold. She spoke to me through shivering teeth.

"Don't get me wrong, I am no stranger to being cold. I mean there are times in Massachusetts that the cold is numbing, but this frigid air is paralyzing. I don't understand this cold. I thought lions lived in warm climates," Zyaire remarked.

"Not these lions," I professed. The Lions continued to roar from the distance, and their roars were terrifying. "Are you okay," I asked Zyaire, worried that she was frightened.

"Honestly, I am so over being afraid. I am just so cold, and all I want to do now is get back home." She shook violently as the cold winds swept around us.

"Yes, we have to get you back home. This temperature isn't good for you," I said and pulled the pocketbook out from my pack. To Zyaire's surprise and mine, it no longer illuminated with the great blue light. Zyaire looked to me for answers.

"Why isn't it glowing anymore? Did we wait too long?" she asked.

"I do not know. This is not how it was supposed to happen. You were supposed to have a full twenty-four hours to enter back into your world once the pocketbook illuminated."

"Well, maybe I just need to read the passage to get it to glow again," Zyaire said and held the pocketbook in the air to read the passage underneath. "When the leaves are at their best, and the moon first lights the way, then shall you come, but you cannot stay." She repeated the passage three times, but nothing happened.

"I guess it is not time for us to leave each other yet," I said with a smile, trying to relieve the worry that was now evident on Zyaire's face.

"Don't get me wrong, Acaeus, I don't want to leave you any sooner than I have to, but isn't it dangerous to be in here with the Black Lions?" Zyaire asked, concerned.

"I have a plan. We have to make it there, but I do have a plan," I assured her.

"Make it where?"

"Remember I told you about the top of the cave and how it overlooked the lions' den?"

"Yes, I remember."

"Well, the outside of the cave is irregular, so it can be climbed. A deep ledge is halfway up the outside walls of the cave. If we can make it there, we can camp on the ledge until the pocketbook allows you entrance again."

"Maybe it is safe now for us to enter back into Aphrodan," Zyaire said. "There was a look in King Aimilios's eyes when he helped me off the ground. I don't think he would hurt me. Maybe we don't have to risk going anywhere near those lions."

"I can't take that risk with you, Zyaire. King Abas is out for blood. He will not stop until he kills you and destroys the pocketbook, and besides that, what I did was treason. I do not care if they throw me into jail, but I cannot bear that happening to you. When you are gone, I will go back to Aphrodan and face my punishment, but not until you are safely in travel back to your world."

Zyaire sighed deeply at my words. I had nothing to offer her now but my protection and promises.

Then she grabbed my hands. "Acaeus, I have to tell you something." But her words were halted by a lion's roar. This time, it was more ferocious than before.

"We have to get moving," I said and placed the pocketbook into my pack before putting it on my back. "I'm sorry, can you tell me what you have to say later?"

"Sure, if I live to tell it. Let that be the motivation for you to keep me alive," she said, still keeping true to her humor.

Zyaire and I travelled along the outer parts of the forest. I had studied the lions' behavior for many years and knew they only ventured off from the land just outside the cave to hunt. I also took notice that the five male lions of the pride hunted together only in the break of morning, with Basil, their leader, leading the hunt. The females rarely hunted. They usually stayed behind, keeping guard over the Gate of Passage. Agape is the matriarch of the pride. It was fitting that her name meant love. She often licked the wounds of the males if they returned injured from their hunt. The males always returned with food for the pride. The white deer were their preferred prey, a delicacy believed to have been put in Aphrodan by Zeus himself for the sole purpose of feeding the Black Lions. It was said to be a miracle that they had never gone extinct and to the contrary continued to grow more abundant in numbers, overpopulating Aphrodan, and could often be seen out in the open fields.

As a white deer shot between the trees right in front of us, Zyaire and I both jumped out of our skin.

"Great, I'm screwed," Zyaire declared, looking at me.

"Why do you say that?" I asked.

"Because you're just as afraid as I am, Mr. Jumpy," Zyaire teased.

"And here I thought I was your knight in shining armor," I teased back. Even facing death, she somehow made me smile, and that to me was worth whatever fate lay ahead. Protecting her meant everything to me.

The fog began to clear as we travelled closer to the Gate of Passage. The brisk winds had also calmed, but the temperature was still biting. Zyaire felt bad that she was wearing my sweatshirt and I only had a black short-sleeve T-shirt to keep me warm.

"Please let me give you back your sweatshirt now. The winds have calmed down," she reasoned.

"Not a chance," I said and wrapped my arm around Zyaire, pulling her in close to me as we walked in between the tall trees of the Black Forest. I had a well-thought-out plan up until the point we were about to approach. The problem with climbing the outside wall of the cave was the lions were sure to be right there within steps of it. It was where they lived, rested, and kept guard. As Zyaire and I got closer to our proposed location, the cave began to come into view.

"We have to be very quiet at this point and take light steps," I whispered. "When we get to the cave, we will climb up on the far side of it, furthest away from the lions."

"How high is the climb?" Zyaire asked.

"It's about one hundred feet before we reach the ledge. Let's collect some sticks for a fire before we go any further," I suggested.

We collected as many sticks as we could fit into our packs and then headed quietly toward the cave that once served as an entrance between our worlds. The Black Lions were in plain view as Zyaire and I peeked our heads around a large tree only a few feet away from the cave we were set to climb. Zyaire was in awe. She had never seen such a sight. The Black Lions were real, as I had told her. The males' manes were shining black and long, and the female lions' bodies were beautiful and sleek. Above all, their color was striking to look at, and despite the fear that centered on them, the Black Lions were regal and enchanting. Their mesmerizing eyes were blue like the deep sea.

I did a quick count, and all twelve lions of the pride were there resting in the habitat they were made for. I pointed out the side of the cave we would climb to Zyaire. She looked up and saw the deep ledge I spoke of. She told me on one of our night talks that she had gone rock climbing many times with her adventurous father. Judging on the climbs she described, the cave that was before us now was not the easiest she would climb, or the hardest, but the stakes were much higher, and the possibility of a deadly outcome more probable. As we stared at the lions' land, Zyaire got her first glimpse of the enchantment I spoke about. A small pond was being fed by a waterfall suspended in midair. There was no source of the waterfall, yet its crystal clear water flowed from nothing and into the pond below it.

We quietly looked on as Agape, the matriarch of the tribe, walked over and drank from the pond. Basil got up shortly after and joined her. After quenching their thirst, they stretched out alongside the pond together. Agape cuddled up very close to Basil, and as they lay there on their sides, Basil threw his paw over Agape. It was a beautiful sight, and for a moment, I could see by the expression on Zyaire's face that she had forgotten the danger these magnificent predators posed to her.

"Let's go," I whispered, seeing this as the best opportunity to attempt our climb.

For no reason other than the fear of the outcome we were about to face, I thought back to the moment she and I were at the lake with the goldies. I remembered that the elegant birds would not eat from her hand but practically gorged from mine. I wondered if it was an omen of her fate—that she would not survive this tremendous feat we were about to undertake. The thought was chilling, but it was too late to turn back now. Furthermore, I was determined to see her make it home safely without so much as a scratch upon her.

Inching along the outer parts of the forest leading to the cave, Zyaire practically held her breath, afraid to even breathe too loudly and alert the large beasts that rested only a few feet away from us. When we reached the foot of the cave, I gestured for Zyaire to climb first. I wanted to put her before myself in case the lions attacked before we could get to the ledge. That way it would be me they got to first, and not her. The climb was more difficult than it looked from the distance, and the fact that we were attempting it with no harness and rope to protect us from a potential fall was almost as nail-biting as the risk of the lions that lay beneath us.

So far, we were climbing the wall without incident, but frequently struggling to find areas safe enough to grip or plant our feet. I looked down at the land below us, and eyed Basil and Agape along with the other lions still resting peacefully, but with a closer look, I noticed there were only eleven lions now in sight instead of the usual twelve. I looked over the whole of the area, and there was no sight of the missing lion. I continued without alarming Zyaire. I hoped the lion had wandered off into the forest to look for food.

Zyaire took her steps carefully but as quickly as possible. We were still close to the ground, and the higher we could get, the safer we would both feel. Distracted for a moment, Zyaire looked down at me to find me climbing diligently beneath her. She then looked back up and reached for the area she had targeted to grip before looking down, but when she gripped the rocky surface, she hit a loose medium-sized rock situated on the edge next to it. The rock balanced itself there for a moment before finally spilling toward the ground. Its fall seemed to be in slow motion, and I leaned to the left, avoiding its path. When it struck the ground, the lion missing from the pride ascended on us without warning. Its ferocious roar shook the cave that we now clung desperately to.

"Go!" I yelled, motioning Zyaire to climb more swiftly than before. The lion swiped at my legs, just missing me as I scurried up the wall of the cave. The commotion alerted the other lions and they all swarmed around. Basil leaped through the crowd, and with his mouth wide open he clamped down on my foot, but he only got his teeth into the sole of my boot and pulled it off, leaving me with only a sock. Zyaire had stopped for a moment to look down and see what was going on with me. I had screamed out when Basil had taken hold of my boot. Fearing the worst, she bolted out my name in agony, "Acaeus, no!"

"Keep going!" I yelled up to her and came up behind her swiftly. The lions continued to jump and roar after us, but we were no longer within reach.

When Zyaire and I finally reached the deep ledge of the cave, we were exhausted. We hugged each other for a moment, amazed that we had actually made it. We looked down on the lions' land. All the others had given up on their prey and returned to resting, but Basil remained at the foot of the cave. As we looked down on him, he stared into my soul as he had before. I stood there locked in place, and unable to break our gaze, until Zyaire put her arms around my waist and hugged me again.

"I was so afraid that you were being eaten. You have no idea how terrified I was of losing you," she admitted.

I looked down at her and kissed the top of her head. "Luckily the only thing we lost is my shoe," I said, staring down and watching as Basil carried the shoe in his mouth back to his place near the pond.

"What do we do now?" she asked.

"We wait, and hopefully the pocketbook won't make us wait long."

"Let's start the fire," Zyaire suggested, feeling the cold once again now that her adrenaline rush had begun to wear off. I gathered some loose rocks and placed them in a circle on the ground, and then I took some of the sticks we had collected and placed them in the center of the gathered rocks. Then I grabbed a few matches out from my bag and lit the fire. When the fire was lit, Zyaire and I snuggled up next to it.

"What do you think will happen to you when you go back home?" Zyaire asked.

"I'm not sure. It all depends on whether I have the support of my uncle, but do not worry about me. I will be fine. I am more worried about you. You have been away from home for weeks now."

"I know my parents and grandparents are worried, but when I get back home, everything will be fine. I wish it could be like that for you too."

"It may very well be. King Aimilios has a good heart despite all of this."

"You and your uncle seem pretty close. You talk about him more than you talk about your parents," Zyaire pointed out.

"There is a lot about me that you still don't know, that no one knows," I said, staring up at the sky that had now grown dark.

"Well, tell me. I want to know everything about you." Zyaire sat up and looked at me, letting me know I had her full attention.

I sighed. "Well then, for one thing, I am not the king's real nephew."

"What do you mean? Your mother is his sister, right?"

"The woman you met is not my mother—well, not my real mother at least. I was adopted after I was abandoned as a baby on the castle's grounds."

"Oh no, I am so sorry," Zyaire said with empathy.

I smiled. "Don't be. It was a long time ago. My real mother had no choice. She did the only thing she could do."

"Have you ever met her?"

"Only in my dreams," I said somberly.

The stars were perfectly aligned. "I wonder if my family and friends are under this same sky, Zyaire said.

"Maybe they are, and even if they're not, whatever sky they are under right now, I am sure they are under it thinking of you," I assured her.

"I have something to tell you too, Acaeus," she finally said. I had remembered that she began to tell me something earlier, but I did not want to bring it up until she was ready.

I now looked at her and gave my full attention.

"I ended up in Aphrodan because I found a box, and inside it was that pocketbook. It was given to my mother by my great-grandmother. Her name was Lillian Grace Varella." Zyaire then waited for the shock to come over my face, but it never did.

"I knew who you were," I admitted.

"What? How did you know?"

"How could I not? Look at you. You look just like her, your eyes, your smile. Her picture still hangs in the king's study. For years her photo was covered by a red velvet cloth because it was just too painful for him to look at."

"The picture, the one that was missing from the Great Hall, was that also a picture of my great-grandmother?" Zyaire asked. "Yes, it was," I confirmed.

"Why didn't you say anything?"

"Because I figured you would when you were ready to tell me."

Zyaire got up and grabbed the pack she carried. She pulled out a book and handed it to me. "This is her diary," she proclaimed.

"Where did you get this?" I asked finally, shocked. "There was a legend of the queen's diary, but until now, it was just that, a legend."

"It was underneath her bed in the Gold Room."

"No, it could not have been somewhere that simple."

"Yes, it really was," Zyaire assured me.

I flipped through the diary and turned right to a specific date, May 22, 1993. It was the last entry in the diary. "You won't believe this, but my earliest memory is of her. I was not even two years old yet. She spent the whole day with me, and we made a sweater for my favorite teddy bear. I still have it." I smiled as I reminisced about Queen Lilly. "My earliest memory is also the last day she was in Aphrodan, May 22, 1993. I read Queen Lilly's words aloud:

> *Today was a beautiful day. I got to spend it with my favorite little boy, Acaeus. He is such a precocious child. I would swear he has been here before. Not even two years old and he already talks well, and can even write his name. My mother's sewing lessons came in handy today. We made his teddy*

the cutest sweater, and he loved it. He rewarded me with a huge hug. Oh, he gives the best hugs. I cannot wait to hug little Lilly when she arrives. Geri is perfectly miserable with this pregnancy, having morning sickness every day when I left to return to Aphrodan, but I know she will forget all that very soon when she holds her beautiful daughter in her arms. I hope one day that I can bring them here. I told Acaeus that one day he and my great-granddaughter will be good friends. I only hope that will come true. There is so much I need to reveal to my family and Aimilios. I am ashamed that I have waited so long.

"The entry ended there and was simply signed, Lilly."

A smile was all that Zyaire and I could muster up after hearing Queen Lilly's words. In fact, we had become good friends just as she had hoped, and so much more.

"It sounds like my great-grandmother was keeping some sort of secret," Zyaire said.

"Yes, it appears so," I said, wondering what Queen Lilly could have been hiding.

"How did the king feel about my great-grandmother having a daughter?" Zyaire asked.

"Well, it was well known that Lillian had given birth to a daughter before she ever met the king, and that her husband was killed before that daughter could be born. Apparently, the queen was quite embarrassed about the situation, and fearful of what the king might feel about her having a child. It was a few years before she admitted to the existence of her. Of course we never got a chance to meet her, since she was never brought here, but I have been told Queen Lilly talked about her all the time, and that the king was understanding and sympathetic about that situation."

"Wait," Zyaire said, grabbing the diary from me and staring at the entry I had just read. "How did she get here in May? I thought the pocketbook only allowed entry during autumn's first full moon."

"Well, the king speaks of it like it was a miracle, I was told. He told my mother that one morning in May, Lilly awoke to find the pocketbook glowing with the great light, and she came to him. It turned out to be the last visit she ever made to Aphrodan."

"What do you think she was keeping secret?" Zyaire asked.

"I don't know, but that was her last entry, so I guess you will have to ask her when you get back home."

Zyaire's face went pale suddenly. "Oh my gosh! I never imagined that you did not know," she said.

"That I did not know what?" I asked.

"I can't ask her. She's not there anymore," she revealed.

"Where did she go?" I asked, now confused. Zyaire's eyes grew saddened, then she reached out to grab my hands.

"She died, Acaeus. I never even met her. She died a month before I was born."

I was dumbfounded. We had never entertained the idea that Queen Lilly never returned to Aphrodan because she was no longer alive. I was obviously spoiled by the long life span so prevalent here in Aphrodan that I never even imagined this unthinkable outcome.

"What happened to her?" I asked, still in shock.

"From what I was told, it was very sudden. She got very sick and was diagnosed with cancer. Months later, she was gone."

Concern filled my mind then. "Poor King Aimilios, he has no idea she is deceased. He thinks that she didn't return because of an ongoing dispute they were having over her staying in Aphrodan for a year. Queen Lilly wanted to stay, but King Aimilios would not allow it."

"Why wouldn't he want her to stay?" Zyaire questioned.

"He didn't want her to stay because of the penalty. If a mortal stays beyond the time the pocketbook intended, then they would have to wait until the next full moon in autumn the following year to leave again."

"What's so bad about that? It sounds like that is what she wanted, right?"

"Yes, but there is more. If a mortal remains after the pocketbook's intended time of return, then ten years will be taken from their life span. King Aimilios would not risk that. As a mortal, her life span was already short-lived compared to his, and he could not bear ending hers any sooner than was intended. Queen Lilly, on the other hand, did not see it that way. She thought the risk was worth it. Your great-grandmother was willing to trade ten years of her life just to wake up next to him every day for a year."

My own words shot through my heart, and I could imagine the unwavering love that was shared between Zyaire's great-grandmother and my king. I now looked into Zyaire's eyes and knew I would trade anything to be with her. I had already traded so much just to be with her for a few more hours.

This time Zyaire came close to me. We shared a gentle kiss and then continued to snuggle there next to the fire. More and more, it seemed that fate had brought us together, and as Zyaire dozed off in my arms, I looked down at her adoringly, and wondered what I could do to make sure this was not the last time I would see her.

Chapter 28

The Time Has Come

(ACAEUS)

The sound of a lion's roar within inches of me was deafening, and I turned around swiftly to find Basil standing on the ledge before me, his long black mane blowing in the wind. Our eyes met again as they had before, and Basil stared deep into my soul. I could feel my secrets and all my inner thoughts being unveiled. I was trapped there under the power of the Black Lion's gaze, and before I could break it, Basil lunged at me in all his fury. I sat up quickly, sweating profusely. I sighed with relief, realizing I was only dreaming. It was still dark, and Zyaire was fast asleep, her head lying peacefully on my lap. I ran my fingers gently through her hair, grateful that I had not startled her. I leaned forward to look down at the pride of lions below us. They were all resting peacefully, except Basil, who was pacing back and forth.

I looked up at the sky and noticed that the moon was now in view and full. It was so large and bright I felt as if I could reach up and touch it. I then noticed a light peering from behind me, and I turned around to find the pocketbook in full glow. Its blue light illuminated the area around it. I put my arms around Zyaire savoring what I now knew would be my final moments with her. There was so much that I wanted to say to her that time had not allowed, so I reached for one of our packs and grabbed a notepad and pen out from it. I began to write without effort. The words flowed from my pen like water and dripped down the margins of the two pages I filled with many confessions. When I was finished, I folded it neatly and stuck it into the pocket of my sweatshirt that Zyaire still wore.

I eyed Basil as he continued to pace up and down on the ground below. I knew our presence was unwanted. Not taking for granted the real possibility that this magnificent creature, with enough time, could figure out how to get to us, I decided to wake Zyaire and send her home now. I kissed her forehead, and then her lips, and she stirred. I kissed her lips one more time before she finally opened her eyes and looked up at me smiling. She leaned up, kissed me back, and snuggled her face into my chest.

"It's time," I said.

Zyaire turned around and looked to find the pocketbook illuminating in all its glory. She sat up and looked at me with sadness. "I wish you could come with me," she said, tears filling her eyes. Then she leaned forward abruptly. "You *should* come with me," she blurted out desperately. "Who knows what will happen to you if you stay here. You have broken laws. They could throw you in jail or worse." Zyaire's voiced cracked.

"I'm not the only one who helped save you, Zyaire. Yanni did too. I cannot just desert him. I have to make sure he is safe, and Marco—" I paused. "I need to be there to bury my dear friend."

I pulled her into me, trying to erase all her fears with the comfort of my embrace.

"We will see each other again one day," I remarked, more a hope instead of a promise.

"I don't have to leave right now. I have twenty-four hours, right?" she remembered.

"No, you need to leave right now. I do not want to risk anything else happening. It is time. The pocketbook knows it, and so do I."

Zyaire hugged me for a long while, inhaling deeply as if she was putting my scent to memory. I squeezed her tightly, imprinting in my thoughts the soft feel of her frame close to mine. When she finally pulled away, she repeated the words that she now knew by heart: "When the leaves are at their best, and the moon first lights the way, then shall you come, but you cannot stay." With that utterance, the blue light grew brighter and burst into the sky. The pocketbook began to shake furiously. It screamed with an alarming sound as it opened in size, and then it was silent. Zyaire turned and hugged me one more time, grabbed the bag with her clothes, and dropped her great-grandmother's diary back inside it. She reluctantly walked toward the pocketbook. It was taking everything in me not to stop her from going. She moved slowly, pausing at moments, as if she was searching for a reason to turn back and look at me, or for a reason to stay a little longer. When she finally found one, she turned briskly.

"Wait, do you want your sweatshirt back?" she asked.

"No, you keep it. It will be something to remind you that this all really happened." I smiled.

Zyaire smiled back at me. "Well, this is it," she said, taking in the last memory of me, and I her. She now stood only a few inches from the pocketbook. I stood further back, watching her. Yet I could still feel the force of its pull. Her hair and garments were helpless as they unwillingly gravitated toward it.

"I love you," I finally screamed out with her back to me. She turned to look at me, her blue eyes wide and blazing, but before she could say a word, she was sucked away from me posthaste. Just like that, she was gone from Aphrodan, and I was left to wonder if she loved me back.

Chapter 29

Home Sweet Home

(ZYAIRE)

My return was nothing like my departure. "Thank God," I thought to myself. In the blink of an eye, it was all over. My eyes remained closed. I slowly opened them to find myself back in my bedroom by the window. I squinted as the sun was brightly shining. Unlike where I had just left, it was daytime in Massachusetts. I looked on the floor beside me, and there was the box my great-grandmother had made. I opened it, and wouldn't you know it, there situated neatly inside was the pocketbook and my great-grandmother's letter. "How bizarre," I thought. I hadn't travelled with the box or the letter, yet there they were, back in the box like nothing had ever happened. I didn't ponder on it for long. After what I had just gone through, nothing would surprise me ever again. I realized I was still holding the bag I had in my hand before leaving Aphrodan. "So you can bring things back," I said, wishing I had brought Acaeus back. I looked inside, and there was my dress from the last night I was home, my shoes, and my great-grandmother's diary and brush. I took out the diary and put it into the nightstand's drawer next to my bed. Then I braced myself to go downstairs and finally face my parents. I had no idea what I would tell them.

As I walked down the steps, I noticed the house was quiet. I walked into the kitchen and it was empty. A note was propped on the table. I opened it and found out that it was from Mary Josie:

> *Mrs. Ryan, I have gone home to meet the plumber as we discussed. I will be back after you return, but in time to make dinner. Call me if you need me sooner. I hope you had luck finding Zyaire today. Mary Josie.*

I put the letter back on the table and reached for the phone to call my parents. I listened to the heavy sound of the dial tone until it turned to a buzzing busy signal. I put the phone back on its receiver. I decided to wait on that call. I needed this time to adjust and decide what I would tell them. I returned to my room and stretched across the bed. My mind was racing, and I had already begun to miss Acaeus. I remembered his words before I left. "I love you" rang in my thoughts like sweet music, love songs from my favorite artist. I looked down at his sweatshirt that I was still wearing. I pulled it close to my nose. I inhaled deep, taking in the scent. It still smelled like him. "It was all real," I murmured to myself, still hardly able to believe all that had happened. I reached down and took my great-grandmother's diary out from the nightstand, and held it close to my chest. It also would serve as memory of all that I had gone through.

Holding my great-grandmother's diary reminded me of a gift that my Vovó had given to me. I jumped up and grabbed a chair, pulled it into the closet, and retrieved a small box from the top shelf. I opened the dusty box that was first put there two Christmases ago, and inside was a diary. I had never written in it before because there was not anything I felt compelled to tell, but now all that had changed. I took a pen from the nightstand drawer and opened the diary to the first page. There I found a spot to place my name. I neatly wrote "Zyaire Ryan" on the line following the words "This diary belongs to," and just underneath, on the blank canvass I wrote "My Pocketbook Diary." I turned to the first page and filled in the top right hand corner with the day's date, October 12, 2009. Then carrying on the tradition my great-grandmother began decades before, I started writing my first entry about my miraculous encounter with the enchanted pocketbook. Pen to paper, and my mind steadily on the woman who had intrigued me for so many years, I began:

> *It's funny how we teenagers go through life thinking we know everything, thinking we have the whole world figured out, then something incredible happens, something out of this world, and we realize we actually never knew anything at all.*

Epilogue
(ACAEUS)

When I turned away from the empty space that the pocketbook and Zyaire once stood in, I was met with another great light descending from the sky. This one was even greater than the one coming from the pocketbook. The light was white, and inside it was the sculpted figure of a woman. In her hand glowed a golden scepter.

"Acaeus, look at you, so strong and handsome," the angelic yet sultry voice said. "I have dreamed of this day. A day where I could stand face-to-face with you. However, you took a great risk today, and could have possibly revealed your identity. Even worse, you used your powers, something you know puts you and myself at risk."

"Mother, I can't believe it is you." I reached up, trying to touch the beauty that stood before me. "Wait." I paused. "Why have you come to me like this? I have only known you in my dreams before. Is this safe for you, Mother?"

"I am only here in spirit, Acaeus, not in body. It is a risk, but it is one I am willing to take for the safety of my son whom I love."

"I am safe, Mother. I am sorry I used my powers, but I could not let Zyaire die."

"Because you love her?" she asked.

"Yes, I do love her," I admitted.

"Then maybe you have done a good thing to save her, but remember you have been chosen for a purpose. Now you must leave the mortal unbothered in her own world. She is safe now. You have a responsibility to your people that you must fulfill. I have come to warn you that the revelation of your responsibilities is nigh. Are you ready, my son?"

I took a deep gulp of air, forcing myself to digest my mother's words concerning Zyaire. Then I hardened my chest and prepared myself for the answer I knew someday I would have to give. "Yes Mother, I am ready."

About the Author

A former resident of Massachusetts, L.C. Rogers was inspired by her time there to create the narrative for the compelling Pocketbook Diaries series. These days she lives in Maryland where she grew up listening to the spontaneous stories of her father on long car rides with her mother and three siblings. She now carries on the tradition with her three children, while also working full time in her career as a Regional Sales Manager. When asked how she finds time to write, Rogers said, "I spend most nights checking homework, cooking dinner, watching movies, dancing to music with the kids, refereeing fights, and squeezing in attention for my husband—all before jumping on the computer and letting my imagination and passion for writing run wild."

So far her passion for writing has birthed *A Lesson in Listening*, a children's book that was published in 2012. She has since went on to add two more publications to the popular TJ's Lessons series: *Justin the Incredible* and *If I've Told You Once I've Told You Twice It Pays to be Good It Pays to be Nice*. Rogers says she feels fortunate to have been able to present the series she created in the likeness of her son TJ to thousands of children in multiple schools across the east coast. The series quickly became popular, even being awarded along the way by the mayor of Baltimore, Maryland, for its contribution to the community. It also garnered Rogers a nomination for an "Inspire" award by *Slantress Magazine*, where she went on to be named one of the "100 Influential Woman of the Year" in their year-ending 2013 publication. These days Rogers is lost in the world of Aphrodan alongside Zyaire and her magical pocketbook. She says she is looking forward to having readers join her in this new adventure.

CPSIA information can be obtained
at www.ICGtesting.com
Printed in the USA
BVOW04s1915230517
484969BV00001B/60/P

9 781683 480969